# SOUL
## ENCHILADA

# SOUL ENCHILADA

## DAVID MACINNIS GILL

GREENWILLOW BOOKS
*An Imprint of* HarperCollins*Publishers*

Soul Enchilada
Copyright © 2009 by David Macinnis Gill
All rights reserved. No part of this book may be used or reproduced in any manner whatsoever without written permission except in the case of brief quotations embodied in critical articles and reviews. Printed in the United States of America. For information address HarperCollins Children's Books, a division of HarperCollins Publishers, 1350 Avenue of the Americas, New York, NY 10019.
www.harperteen.com

The text of this book is set in 11-point Ehrhardt.
Book design by Paul Zakris

Library of Congress Cataloging-in-Publication Data

Gill, David Macinnis, (date).
Soul enchilada / by David Macinnis Gill.
 p. cm.
"Greenwillow Books."
Summary: When, after a demon appears to repossess her car, she discovers that both the car and her soul were given as collateral in a deal made with the Devil by her irascible grandfather, eighteen-year-old Bug Smoot, given two-days' grace, tries to find ways to outsmart the Devil and his minions.
ISBN 978-0-06-167301-6 (trade bdg.) — ISBN 978-0-06-167302-3 (lib. bdg.)
[1. Devil—Fiction. 2. Grandfathers—Fiction. 3. Conduct of life—Fiction.
4. Racially mixed people—Fiction.] I. Title.
PZ7.G39854So 2009     [Fic]—dc22     2008019486

First Edition 10 9 8 7 6 5 4 3 2 1

 Greenwillow Books

To Ted Hipple,
who taught us all to be well

# CHAPTER 1

# The Rent Man Cometh

Most folks don't know the exact minute that life's going to be over. I wasn't any different. I had no idea the end was coming, so I didn't realize when the landlord woke me up by beating on the front door of my apartment—a two-hundred-square-foot roach motel with a half bath, no phone, no cable, and no air conditioner—I only had sixty-one hours and forty-four minutes before my soul was taken away.

"Wake up if you know what's good for you," the landlord hollered in a thick peckerwood accent, repeatedly ringing the doorbell. "Rent's due!"

"Mr. Payne?" I groaned, and rolled off the couch, which I'd collapsed into at three A.M.

I stumbled across the apartment, shaking my dreads out and wishing to hell I hadn't slept in my work clothes, which were now more wrinkled than my Auntie Pearl's rear end.

I opened the door a crack. Light flooded into my eyes, half-blinding me, and I blinked at Mr. Payne like a groggy Gila monster. "You know what time it is?"

"Yes ma'am, Miss Smoot, I sure do. It's rent time." He stuck a yellowed, liver-spotted hand inside and started groping around. "You're five days late, Eunice, for the third month in a row. Ow!"

"Sorry," I said, because I'd leaned on the door, pinching his wrist in the crack. But I didn't give an inch.

Mr. Payne had pipe-cleaner wrists, a head shaped like a sapote fruit, and a long shank of hair he swirled over his bald spot like a hairy soft-serve ice cream. He was always getting in the tenants' business, especially mine.

Speaking of business, it was time to go to work. I had just an hour till I was supposed to clock in.

"Rent!" Mr. Payne said, trying to yank his hand free.

"Uh." Did he think bullying me was going to make a stack of Benjamins magically pop into my wallet?

"Uh. Uh. Uh," he said, mocking me. "Cat got your tongue, young'un? Cat got your rent? You sure ain't got it, I can tell that much."

If I had the rent, I would've already paid him and gone back to bed. "Like I done told you—"

"Talk is cheap."

So was he. "Like I done told you," I repeated, "my boss, Vinnie, he don't pay us but every two weeks, so I'll get you the money tomorrow, a'ight?"

"Tomorrow, tomorrow, tomorrow. That's what you people always say."

No, he didn't. He did not just go there. "You people? You people? Now listen here, Mr. Payne."

Then he said something about me being so cranky all the time and why couldn't girls like me learn to go along to get along. Girls like what? I wanted to ask him. Poor girls who wear dreads and secondhand Baby Phats from the Goodwill? Mixed-race girls with hazel eyes and good hair, a pinch over five feet, with double-pierced lobes, who want something more out of life than somebody's prejudice or pity? All my life, folks had been looking at me sideways, especially when I was with my mama. The Tejanos didn't accept me because I was black. Black folks didn't accept me because I was a Tejana. There was a nasty name both groups called girls like me—coyote. They could all kiss my ass because I didn't need them to tell me who I was.

"Mr. Payne," I said, "you best move your bony hand before you have to 'go along' without it."

He yanked his arm out of the crack, and I took the chance to slam the door with all my weight—one hundred and two pounds sopping wet.

"Rent, Eunice. By five P.M. today. Or I'm starting eviction."

Eviction? That sent a shiver down my spine. I couldn't lose this apartment. It was the only thing between me and a cardboard box beneath an overpass on the Trans-Mountain Highway.

"What. Ever," I said through the door, which was as thin as Mr. P's comb-over.

"Tell that to the sheriff's deputy," he yelled, "after he chucks your belongings out on the street." His slippers made a shuffling sound on the stoop, and I let out a nervous breath, thankful he was gone.

I lived in mortal fear of landlords. Before Papa C died, me and him moved to a different place every six months, each worse than the one before. This apartment was the crappiest place I had ever lived, but I had promised myself when I moved in, there wouldn't be no eviction notices nailed to my door. Which gave me less than six hours to get the man his money.

I pinched my bottom lip. Other than selling my body, which ain't ever going to happen, there was no way I'd ever come up with that much cash so fast.

*Bam! Bam!*

4

I jumped back from the door, a hand over my thumping heart. He wasn't serving me notice already, was he? Bug, girl, I told myself, you been way too jumpy lately. Best calm down. All he wants is the rent money, and you're getting paid, right?

"What you want now?" I said through the door.

"Get that junker of yours cleaned up pronto before I call a tow truck to haul it off as a public nuisance."

My car? My classic 1958 Cadillac Biarritz? Wasn't no tow truck ever touching it. Over my dead body. "What happened to my ride? And don't you be calling it no junker."

I swung the door open, slipped past Mr. Payne, and jogged around the corner of the building. My studio apartment was the last unit on a long row house. The building was yellow-brown brick with a flat roof and sagging awnings over the concrete stoops. There were little patches of dirt yards in front, and a crumbling sidewalk. My unit had a long driveway with a carport awning, which is where I had parked my ride last night at three A.M., right next to the NO PARKING sign.

I stopped mid-step, and my mouth dropped open. Somebody, some asshole, had egged my car.

# CHAPTER 2
# Dude, Who Egged My Car?

Papa C had actually been Charles Smoot II, the father of my deadbeat daddy. He lived with his sister, Auntie Pearl. She took care of both of us like we were her own children. She taught me Southern cooking, blues music, church going, and how to be a good Christian sister. Papa C being an unreliable man who lived with the bottle, she also taught me how to scold a grown man while putting his drunk ass into bed.

Auntie wasn't my Mita, but she was the closest thing I had to a mother for a couple of years. Then the worst happened. One Wednesday night at church, when she was hollering and carrying on during the service, the Holy Spirit taking over like always, she started babbling in voices, then grabbed her chest.

With one fat hand waving in the air, she sunk to her knees and fell over dead. I cried for three days. Papa C cried for a week.

At the ripe old age of eleven, I became an orphan twice over and had to take care of my granddaddy, too. He wouldn't never pay his bills, but the man loved me, I know that, because he quit the liquor, cleaned himself up, and got work. He couldn't never hold down a job for more than a couple of weeks at a time, so we kept moving around El Paso, like checkers jumping around a checkerboard. The only thing he ever owned was his car, a 1958 Biarritz that we both loved—him because it made him feel like a man and me because it gave me freedom. He taught me to drive when I was thirteen, so I could go anyplace I wanted, as fast as I wanted. No more walking everywhere like me and Mita had to do. No more bus riding like Auntie Pearl, neither. We could travel to any dot on the map, no matter how far away it was—the beach at Corpus Christi or the salt dunes at White Sands—as long as there was gas money.

Last year, when Papa C made me an orphan for the third time, that car was the only property he owned, the only thing he could pass down to me. Now it was the only thing I had that felt like family.

And some asshole had messed it up.

"Who done this?" I hollered at Mr. Payne. He didn't answer, and when I turned around, he was long gone.

There were dried-up egg whites all over the hood, the rag-top, the trunk, and even the grille. Damned neighborhood kids, you'd think they'd have the decency to hold off pranking until Halloween. But no, they had to hit my house ahead of schedule. My eyes started burning, then got all blurry. I pressed my fingertips against my lips, holding in my breath to keep from crying.

"When I find out—and I will find out—" I yelled down the empty street, "which one of you punk-ass fools egged my Cadillac, you'll be getting a slap upside your stupid head."

I was biting my fist, holding in a scream, when a coyote jogged out from around the back of the car. It sniffed the chrome molding all along the door and then the front tires before it saw me. I recognized it as the same mangy coyote that had got into our garbage cans two nights in a row last week. It was undersized, with an almost black coat, a white belly, and a white tip on its tail, and in its mouth was a half-eaten meatball sub. What a waste of food. How could anybody put a perfectly good sandwich like that in the garbage can?

I picked up a pebble and bounced it off the head of the coyote, which huffed twice at me. Then a deep growl came from the back of its throat. Its lips parted enough to show its long fangs clenched around the sub sandwich. My ass froze right there. I knew for sure I was about to get bit.

"Sorry, dog. Nothing personal, a'ight?"

Then the coyote changed its mind. It swallowed the sub, barked twice at the car, hiked its leg, and let out a long stream of piss on the whitewall. Damn, I had just bleached those tires yesterday, and now all I had to show for my trouble was a big yellow stain. You know you're having a bad day when somebody punks your car and a wild animal takes a piss on it.

I owed the perpetrator a beatdown. Except I didn't have the time. I had to get to my job. I had to get Mr. Payne his rent. Only I couldn't leave a vintage car messed up like that, not all egged and pissed on. But my boss, Vinnie, he didn't play when it came to being late.

What was a girl to do?

# CHAPTER 3
# Girls Just Wanna Have Suds

Fifteen minutes later, I was driving through El Paso with the top down, watching flakes of egg white fly off the car hood, which was weird because the more stuff that blew off, the more there seemed to be. Since when did egg white make that big a mess?

At a red light, I looked over and saw a bunch of brothers playing some ball. The sun had warmed up the weather, so they wore shirts and shorts. The court was asphalt, the rim a rust-caked bent circle fringed with a tatter of metal netting, and the players looked tough enough to bite phone books in half. Dog, I wanted so much to step in on the game, my mouth was watering. I hadn't touched a basketball since my last game at school, and my fingers ached at the thought of palming that leather again.

Then I spotted her, this sister with funky eyes, muscling her way into the lane, wearing a lime green tank top, neon orange shorts, and dirty white Starbury high-tops. She didn't stand as tall as the men, but she was a double-wide load in the hips, and her thighs could break concrete. In school we called her Tangle-eye, and her ugly face was one I'd hoped to never lay eyes on again. On her finger was a gold ring, big as a walnut, a ring that reminded me of why I didn't play basketball no more. That's right, I thought, you got the jewelry but you're still stuck in El Paso, just like me.

The light turned green, and I hit the gas.

Back to the question at hand: What *was* a girl to do when she's late for work but her ride's a mess? Get her car washed, that's what. So I called in to my job, explaining to Vinnie how I was having the worst day since my high school team got knocked out of the state basketball playoffs and how I was going to be "a couple minutes late on account of some asshole egging my car last night. That's okay if I'm late, right, Vin?"

Vinnie was the owner of El Paso Pizza and an import from New Jersey. Me and him was straight. Well, as straight as an EP homegirl like me could ever be with a transplanted Yankee like him.

"So, Bug, let me get this right, if you don't mind?" His voice barked out of my cell phone as I was pulling into traffic. "So, for the second time in five days, you're going to be late for the lunch shift. Is that what you are telling me? Wait. Don't answer that. It's what you call a rhetorical question."

Like I didn't know what a rhetorical question was. "Something like that," I said.

"So," Vinnie said. "Are you, or are you not, coming in to work on time?"

I held on to the phone with my teeth as I used both hands to turn left onto the Trans-Mountain Highway, the loop that cut across the Franklin Mountains and connected one side of El Paso with the other.

When I didn't answer straightaway, Vinnie whistled into the phone. "That was not a rhetorical question, in case you had not noticed."

Why did the man always have to yell at me? "Yeah."

"Yeah, as in, you're coming in on time?"

"No, as in, yeah, I know that ain't no freaking rhetorical question. And yeah, as in no, I said I'm going to the car wash before the sun fries my mint-condition paint job like—like—um."

"An egg."

"No, like *frijoles*." I hated when somebody else finished my similes.

"So, I'm a good guy, right?" Vinnie said. "So when you take

12

advantage of my good nature, it's offensive. So, I deal with your mouth and your attitude because I've got sympathy for a girl trying to get off the government dole, y'know?"

Government dole, my ass. He knew I didn't take no welfare or food stamps. "Uh-huh."

"That offends me, too."

"Uh-huh."

"Lookit, Bug, your attitude is rubbing off on the other employees, and this, I cannot have. I'm drawing a line in the sand, *capiche*? Either show up on time or keep driving straight to the unemployment office."

"Why you always hating on me, Vinnie? Ain't I your best delivery person?"

"Either. Or."

Freaking Jersey boy. Who did he think he was, threatening me? Nobody told me what I could and could not do, even my boss. No, especially my boss. I was a grown woman taking care of herself. If I had to make my own rent, then I was making decisions of my own free will. My teachers at El Paso High used to preach that "with freedom comes responsibility." I got stuck with responsibility early in life. Now I wanted the freedom that went with it.

"Be there when I get there," I said, and punched the button to hang up on him.

I smacked the wheel. Why did he have to be so hard-assed all the time? If Vinnie had just listened to me, I could've explained the whole drama to him. Then he would've understood what was stressing me out. On second thought, after he accused me of living off the government, he could just kiss my ass. I didn't need him putting me down. I didn't need nobody but myself. And maybe, a lucky break once in a while.

Besides, Vinnie was a businessman. I made money for him and this "silent business partner" (who I ain't never met), so no matter how he ran his mouth, there wasn't no way he'd fire me. Once I got to work, I'd sweet-talk him a little bit, and everything would be fine.

Just fine.

## CHAPTER 4

# The Devil Is in the Details— and the Front Seat, Too

The Rainbow Auto Wash and Coffee Shop was famous for two things—fine-looking rag boys and the best *huevos rancheros* in the EP. I hadn't eaten any Mexican food since my mama, Mita, died so I'd lost my taste for it, but there was this one boy, Pesto, who ran the car wash. He was worth the trip all by himself.

The Rainbow didn't look famous from the outside. It was a high-roofed steel building with two lanes for detailing and another lane that led to the Rainbow Sparkle conveyor belt. You could stay in your car for the wash. Or if you were hungry, you went inside the coffee shop. It had two plate-glass windows looking onto the conveyor line, so you could enjoy some *rancheros* or a plate of *carne picada* while you watched your ride roll by, which was Papa C's favorite part. Since I couldn't afford to eat out, I always stayed inside the car to enjoy the show.

When I got to the Rainbow, I swung out wide to the left and pulled into the third lane. I was the third one in line, which wasn't bad considering it had rained just this morning, and there were mud puddles everywhere. Folks in the EP ain't used to rain, so when a little precipitation falls, they do one of two things—get their cars washed or get in pileups on I-10.

The sun had come out, baking the mud, egg, and coyote piss onto the car. I hated mud. Hated sand, too, along with scorpions, rattlesnakes, and cactuses, all of which were poisonous. Whoever said living in the desert was good for your health never lived in the EP.

I was kicked back, listening to "All My Love's in Vain" by Robert Johnson, who was one of Papa C's favorites, when the manager, Pesto, came up to my window. He was wearing baggy shorts, Teva sandals, and a black T-shirt with "Talk Nerdy to Me" stenciled on it.

In high school, he was a year ahead of me. I always thought he was pretty cute then. He hung with the artsy kids, though. Me, I hung with the other sisters who played ball. We had one class together, ever, which was drivers ed.

"'S'up," I said, not wanting him to think he was all that, even if he was.

16

"*Buenos días*, dude," he said, smiling with a mouthful of white teeth. The boy must've had either a good dentist or some damn good DNA, because his teeth were almost perfect.

"Speak English," I said, sounding more surly than I meant to. "*Yo no comprendo español.*"

"Dude, me neither," he said, still smiling. "Speaking a language is nothing like truly understanding it. Nice dreads, by the way."

"Uh." Think of something to say, Bug. Something not stupid. "Nice tattoos you got, too."

He kind of winced and stuffed his hands in both pockets. "They're birthmarks."

"Oh." Did you not hear me, girl? I said to myself. What part of *not stupid* do you not understand?

Pesto started filling out an order slip. "That's a good look for you, the dreads. You had cornrows before, right?"

"Maybe." Damn, he remembered how I wore my hair two years ago? He never acted like he even knew I was anything but a ballplayer. "Maybe not."

That's when he noticed the flaking egg white covering the Cadillac like dried snakeskin. "Dude, what did you do, drive through a *casa de gallinas*?"

A chicken house. "Ha-ha." I snatched the ticket out of his hand and circled the box for a double rinse hot wax with a hand dry to go. I handed over the money I'd been planning to use for lunch. My stomach growled. "Did anybody ever tell you that you're funny?"

He smiled. "Yeah, lots of times."

"They lied."

He winced again. "Dude, that's harsh."

"Well, life's harsh," I said, and knew that was way too cranky even for me, especially considering how fine he looked. My Auntie Pearl always said I had a gift for chasing boys away. It wasn't a gift I especially liked. "Wait! I'm sorry, Pesto, my boss is busting my ass about being late, and I got to get this egg off, so I'm crazy stressed. Know what I'm saying?"

"*No hay problema*," he said, and stepped back from the car. "We'll take it from here."

"You mad, ain't you?"

"Are you staying in the car, like always?"

Like always? I nodded but didn't answer. When I pulled into the car wash lane, my hands were shaking a little bit, feeling a little cold. A fine-looking young man interested in me? Whoa. And how was it that boy could be noticing me without me noticing him doing the noticing? Bug, I told myself, you'd best start paying attention.

When the green light flashed, I rolled onto the conveyor belt. The Rainbow Sparkle Wash felt like being alone in the middle of a cocoon. Hot water sprayed from all angles, and I leaned back in the seat, cut off from the rest of the world and its stresses, chilling to the sound of water dancing on the roof of the car. Outside the windows, a fine mist from the washing jets caught the sun and formed a faint rainbow across the hood, which was about the coolest damn thing I'd ever seen. Life didn't get any better than this.

Until the car filled up with the stink of sulfur, like somebody had let a sour egg fart. I sat up, coughing and pinching my nose.

"Excuse me, miss," said a man in a high-pitched British accent. "Might I have a word with you?"

My heart stopped—somebody else was in the car.

I checked the mirror. He was hiding. In the backseat. Probably waiting to carjack me. We'd see about that. Quick as a scorpion, I whipped around and screamed like Jackie Chan, trying to scare him out of his mind.

"Nobody's there," I said out loud.

"That depends," someone said, "on what your definition of *nobody* is."

## CHAPTER 5

# Time Is Not on My Side

Bug, girl, I told myself, you're hearing things. See what happens when you got too much on your mind? Then I turned around and looked straight into the face of a carjacker. That was my first thought, that he was stealing my car, except he didn't move a muscle. Not a twitch.

"How did you get in here?" I yelled, scrambling back against the door to open some distance between us.

"From somewhere over the rainbow, of course." He pushed a pair of horn-rimmed glasses up on the bridge of his nose and smiled this freaky smile, not showing his teeth.

"Get out of my car before—" I tried to sound hard and tough, but my voice cracked. When I tried to talk, a sound like a coffee grinder came out of my mouth, and I couldn't breathe.

Out! Out! I told myself and grabbed the handle, but the door locks slammed down. I popped the lock up, and it snapped down again. Pop, lock, pop, lock. I kept trying, and it kept locking. I was trapped inside my own car.

"This is your vehicle?" the man said, deadpan, which made my skin crawl. "You claim ownership?"

The day after I buried Papa C—next to Auntie Pearl, so she could keep an eye on him for eternity—I went down to the courthouse to change the title of the car into my name. The clerk wouldn't do it without a death certificate, even though I had a notarized copy of Papa C's will in my hand. It took six weeks for the certificate to come in the mail, the longest six weeks of my life. When I finally got the title in hand, it was powerful. I finally owned something.

"Damned right, I claim ownership," I said, still yanking on the door handle. "Of this car. Of this seat. Of that seat, which you're sitting in without permission. How'd you sneak into my car, anyhow?"

He turned in the seat and stuck out a plain business card. It read, BEALS: REPOSSESSION AGENT. "Mr. Beals at your service," he said. But that didn't explain nothing about invading my car.

"Service? Who said I needed service from you?"

Instead of answering, he pulled out a clipboard full of

yellow legal papers and put it in my face. "Sign here."

"I ain't signing nothing," I said. "Let me out of this car before I hurt you."

He sighed and tapped the clipboard, impatient. "This vehicle is one 1958 Cadillac, exterior maroon, interior white. VIN 897766-60032. Texas license plate XBR-343. Former owner was one Charles Arthur Smoot, 11 Guadalupe Drive, El Paso, Texas."

So he knew Papa C's real name and the address of the last place we lived, a subsidized apartment for terminal indigents. At least it had been air-conditioned, which is more than I could say for Mr. Payne's roach motel. Dang, I had to hurry up and get to work, so I could get my check cashed in time to pay that asshole.

"Yeah," I said. "Any fool could get that same info from the tax record office; I learned that in civics class."

He laughed and told me he had access to data that I'd never dreamed existed, and if necessary, he'd use it all to settle the contract. "Miss Smoot, your grandfather purchased the vehicle with financing from my employer."

"Possession is nine-tenths of the law," I said, "and I possess the car now."

"And I, Miss Smoot, am here to repossess it. By any means necessary, up to and including"—he licked his lips with a thin, snakelike tongue—"your death."

22

"My death?" I said, and called him all sorts of four-lettered names. "Lay one finger on me, asshole, and I'll rip it off at the knuckle."

He chuckled. Not laughed, chuckled.

I grabbed my cell phone, punched in 911—keeping an eye on the man in case he pulled a gun or knife—and waited for the operator. Though I had no love for cops, didn't nobody threaten my life and get away with it.

The phone beeped: *No service.*

Two seconds later, the drying blowers kicked in. Warm wind beat against the windows, rocking the car back and forth. I grabbed the wheel, getting ready to escape the first chance I got. This asshole thought he was going to threaten my life *and* repo my freaking car? Uh-uh. That'd be a cold day in hell. The last person to cheat me out of something was that girl Tangle-eye, and I swore then that nobody would ever cheat me again.

"Pity," Mr. Beals said. "Your rescue by the cavalry will have to wait, I fear. However, I have no intention of harming you . . . at the moment. Nor do I have a weapon."

He opened his blazer to prove it. Then he pulled out a summons and dropped it on my lap. I took my hands off the wheel to open it. The paper was red and folded in thirds. There was a funky-looking seal on the outside and some kind of foreign writing on it.

"The seal is written in Akkadian," he said, and then added, "You might know it as Babylonian."

"Babylonian? What the hell? I don't even speak Spanish, much less some biblical language." I wished Auntie Pearl was here, because she knew her Bible inside and out. She was always talking about Hittites and pharaohs. "Do I look Babylonian to you?"

"You look like many things to me, Miss Smoot. None of them pleasant. Open the document before I lose patience."

There was an edge in his voice that made me obey. Even if he said he wasn't going to hurt me, I was still watchful. Inside, the language was English, all right, but since it was written by some lawyer, there wasn't no chance in hell I was ever going to figure it out.

"Your signature is at the bottom of the contract, Miss Smoot. I believe you signed it on the date of your thirteenth birthday, which makes you the legal cosigner. Your thirteenth birthday. Does that ring any bells?"

It sure did. It was the date that, by some miracle, Papa C got the Cadillac financed, and he took me to the mall for a new outfit and some sneaks. Then me and him drove the freeway all the way up to Santa Fe, where I bought my first and only cowboy hat, a white Stetson. It was one of the happiest days of my life. Maybe the last happy day.

"I ain't admitting nothing," I said. "This here is all legal mumbo-jumbo. I'm a working girl, not a freaking law firm."

He sighed, a sound that put my teeth on edge. "Then let me put it to you simply, Miss Smoot. According to the terms of the contract, your grandfather was to pay the loan in full following his death. However, Charles Arthur Smoot has chosen to act in such a way so as to defeat the terms of this agreement. Thus, I am repossessing the first part of the collateral, which happens to be this vehicle. My employer will himself foreclose on the second part of the collateral seventy-two hours from midnight last night—unless you can produce your grandfather before the deadline."

"You're talking crazy. I can't produce my grandfather. He's dead. D-e-a-d. Dead." Wasn't going to be no repossession, neither. Not of my car. "I know my rights; I'm getting me a lawyer."

"Feel free, if you can afford it on your—ahem—limited income," he said. "It is fair to warn you, however, that no attorney will take your case. My employer keeps them all on retainer."

I laughed, because I thought he was being funny. He wasn't. "So what's this second part of the collateral?"

"It's for me to know and—well, you know the rest. Of course, if you would like me to cease repossession, you only have to reveal the location of your grandfather."

That was easy. "He's in the graveyard, stupid. The National Cemetery. Where they buried his body?"

"Ah, there's the rub." He clucked his tongue. "Mr. Smoot's decomposed corpse is of no interest to my employer. Present your grandfather or suffer consequences, painful as they may be. Do you like pain, Miss Smoot?"

"You best stop threatening me." I got up in his grill, even though it freaked me out to be so close. There was a faint smell, like rotting garbage, drifting off him. "If you got a problem with something my Papa C signed, then you are out of luck, because he is dead and gone to meet his maker, like I said. I don't know what kind of freak you are, but as soon as this wash is over, I'm kicking your ass to the curb."

Beals smiled at me, showing teeth that looked like needles of bone. The thin tongue flicked out, a snake tasting the air. "Careful not to dawdle, Miss Smoot. The repossession clock is ticking."

"Ain't nobody"—the Cadillac was my only way to work, my only way to take long drives to escape my stresses in the desert, my only tie to Papa C and the life we had, my only hope of making a mark in this life—"touching this car."

"Ticktock. Ticktock."

# CHAPTER 6
# A Hunk of Burning Snot

The second the car wash ended, I hit the gas. I pulled into a side lane, where the rag boys armed with towels started wiping down the car to get rid of water spots. None of them paid any attention to me or to the man beside me, either, even after I put the top down.

"Best get your ass out my car right now," I said, shaking my cell phone in his face. "I'm hitting 911." Which I did, twice, because I still couldn't get a dial tone.

"Alas," Mr. Beals said, yawning. "The best laid plans of mice and men and all that."

Then a realization dawned on me—he was responsible for the phone not working. "What did you do to my freaking cell?"

He winked at me, and I wanted to scratch his eyes out. Then an alarm bell on the side of the building started clanging. One of the rag boys looked up from polishing my hood. He dropped his towel and took off running to the other side of the parking lot, toward Pesto's office.

"Hold up, rag boy!" I hollered after him, but he was long gone. What was that alarm ringing for? What the hell was going on?

I forced a smile at my passenger. "Things could get ugly if I have to call the police. I'm just saying."

"Miss Smoot," Mr. Beals said, "I am as bound to this vehicle as a galley slave is chained to his oar, so I could not leave if I wanted to. As for contacting the police, I have every legal right to repossess this vehicle, and we both know about your feelings for the boys in blue. I believe you carry an ancient grudge against them?"

My heart sank. How did he know that about me? That I'd hated cops since I was six years old, since the day I let my Mita die.

The fire had started in the kitchen, where Mita was frying tortillas. A stove burner shorted out and burnt a hole straight through the skillet. Mita screamed, and I ran in from the bathroom in time to see flames bubbling everywhere. The fire burnt straight into her dress, which was polyester, and it melted the fabric to her legs. She started slapping at the flames, which only fanned them. The kitchen caught on fire, too, and Mita hollered for me to help her. I was too scared to move . . . all that smoke . . . her screaming . . . so loud.

Then I ran for help. But the front door was locked with a keyed deadbolt, and I couldn't open it. An El Paso cop kicked out a window and threw his jacket over the pieces of glass to crawl through—I remember that clear as a bell. Light poured in, smoke poured out, and that's when I realized Mita had quit screaming. The cop pushed me back outside, me fighting and biting and scratching to get to my mama. It took two other cops to hold me down on the dirt yard. The only thing they said to me was, "How did this happen?"

"Indeed," Mr. Beals said to me, like he'd been reading my mind the whole time. He licked his lips like they were covered in melted ice cream. "How *did* the fire happen? Did you play a part in it?"

"Shut up," I screamed, just as the rag boy showed up, along with Pesto, who had a worried look on his face. "Before I rip your tongue out."

"My, so defensive."

"Bug?" Pesto said, and shooed the rag boys away. He met my eye, and I could tell from the way he was making his voice all calm, he thought I was crazy. "Who're you yelling at?"

"This, this, this. This asshole." I thumbed at the passenger's seat. "He's trying to repossess my car."

Pesto rubbed his forehead with a damp towel. "Um. Bug? There's nobody else in the car."

"He's sitting right here! In the passenger seat. Can't you see him? A skinny-ass little man with Tweety Bird eyes and glasses? Striped suit? Says he came over the rainbow."

Pesto's voice got real high. "Rainbow? Is that what you said?" He patted his chest, feeling around for something. "Dude, don't go anywhere, okay? I'll be right back. I left my mirror in the office."

"Your what?" What did a mirror have to do with anything?

"Just—just don't go anywhere, okay? This is serious stuff."

"Hurry up," I said, watching him bounce around like a jumping bean and then sprint for the office. He had good moves for an artsy kid.

"Miss Smoot," the man interrupted my thoughts, "you have the most delicious emotions."

"Damn it!" I hopped out of the car because I had every intention of going around to the passenger side and dragging him out onto the pavement. Then my cell phone rang.

Ha! It was working. I grabbed it. But I saw the name "Payne" on caller ID and hit the reject button.

"Your straits," Mr. Beals said, "are becoming more dire with each passing moment."

"Shut up." The phone rang again—from Vinnie this time. I rejected his call, too. "I'm due at work right now, you nosey-ass fool, which means you're getting out of this car, even if I have to knock your ass out."

I ran around to the other door and yanked on the handle. It wouldn't budge. "Unlock this damn door."

"It is not locked."

Sure enough, the knob was still raised. I pulled on the handle again, and it still didn't open. So I pounded on the window with the side of my fist.

"You rang?" he said, rolling the window down.

Lips clenched, I snatched at his head, meaning to pull him out by the hair. Then I got the shock of my life—my hand went through him like he wasn't even there. It smacked on the back of the seat, and when I pulled away, my skin was covered in egg white, the same stuff I'd found on my car this morning.

He chuckled, and I called him the worst four-lettered names I could think of, because I realized—"You're not just some repo asshole, you're the asshole who egged my car. This is a classic. The paint job is in mint condition, and you throw egg on it? You owe me a car wash, and I owe you an ass kicking, which starts right now." So I smacked him with the other hand. Same result, same slimy stuff. What the f—

"I assure you, Miss Smoot, that while I admit to performing

the deed, the substance in question is not egg. It is a caustic binding agent that my employer placed on the vehicle. The binder is now coating your skin. I suggest you remove it."

The egg white had crinkled up, leaving my arms covered in wisps of dried something. "What the hell is this?"

He smiled that ironic way again. "How apropos. You should really clean those appendages as quickly as possible."

"I'll decide when to wash my own damn hands." I stuck them in my pockets, and they felt all puffy and swollen. The veins started throbbing.

"Do not complain, then," he said, "when the binder dissolves the flesh from your bones."

"You serious?"

"Eternally." His tongue flicked out, wrapping around my wrist and stinging my skin. "It is not wise to make physical contact with a repossession agent, Miss Smoot."

Then my arm started burning like a mouthful of habanero pepper seeds. There's nothing like pain to make you forget your fears, so I ran back over to the car wash bays, looking for a water hose, anything to wash with.

Pesto ran out of his office holding a funky necklace. "Bug! Whoa!" he said when he saw my hand.

He grabbed a rinse bucket and plunged my arm into it.

The pain hit like the sting of a thousand jellyfish. Eleven seconds of loud, long, throat-tearing screams later, the hurt stopped. The water steamed and then turned black.

"Thanks," was all I could think to say.

When Pesto took the bucket away, he held it out like radioactive waste. "Let me take care of this. Be right back." He carried the bucket straight to one of the drains and started pouring it out slowly, careful not to spill it anywhere.

What the hell was going on? Egg whites that melt flesh? A ghost in my car? I had to get out of there now, before I lost my mind. Maybe I already had lost my mind.

"Bug, wait," Pesto hollered after me as I stumbled back to my car. "I need to use my mirror. This situation *es muy peligrosa*, very dangerous."

Thing is, poor folks get used to being in danger. In danger of going hungry. In danger of not making rent. In danger of getting jacked for your food stamps walking to the store. In danger of getting sick and not being able to pay the doctor. I waved Pesto off and slid into the driver's seat.

"Ticktock, Miss Smoot."

"I got to go," I hollered back at Pesto.

"Stop," he called. "You are in serious trouble."

Like I didn't know that already.

# CHAPTER 7

## Vinnie and the Wretch

After Papa C died, I had to move out of the apartment we shared. Him being so sick, we got to stay in this place called Elderly Village, which was quiet and air-conditioned, a big improvement from the place we'd stayed before. Officially, he was the only one who got to live there. We pretended I was his live-in nurse, which I really was after his strokes, and the apartment manager let it slide.

Once I was on my own, I had to make rent, which meant I had to find a job. During summers, I'd worked part-time at a couple of hamburger places, a grocery store, and a kennel, where I learned to hate everything about pets, especially dogs. What I wanted was a job where you got tips without having to actually wait on folks. The only job that fit all my needs was pizza delivery.

I applied to every pizza restaurant in a five-mile radius, but me having no insurance was a problem at most places. One day, I came out of the SuperStore and found a flyer for Vinnie's Pizzeria on my windshield. At the bottom, below the coupons, was a notice that they were hiring drivers. Funny thing was, mine was the only car with a flyer on it. I took it as a lucky sign, so I drove over to the store, and Vinnie hired me on the spot.

At first, he wasn't such an asshole, but over time, especially the last couple months, he got louder and harsher, like I couldn't do nothing right. He was always mad at me for something. Most of the time, I didn't know why. But I needed the cash, so I put up with his disrespecting me.

Auntie Pearl used to say the three most important words in business are location, location, location. Obviously, she never told Vinnie, because he had the worst business location anybody could possibly imagine. His pizza store was off the Trans-Mountain Loop, hidden in a rickety old strip mall in a neighborhood behind the SuperStore. Vinnie's Pizzeria was too small to be called a hole in the wall. It was more like a rat hole, especially with Vinnie around. There was a yellow rectangular sign over the door with PIZZERIA VESUVIA written on it (he was too cheap to remove the previous owner's sign), and a walk-up window for folks who did the carryout thing or wanted to bring their pies out to a broke-down picnic table in front of the store. No customers ever got inside the door if Vinnie could help it, though. He said it was for sanitation reasons, but I thought it was to hide his health inspection score, which was always barely high enough to keep the pizzeria open.

Truth be told, it was a depressing place, and I only worked for Vinnie because I needed the job *and* I knew all the shortcuts and back roads, so I could score some damn fine tips from the rich folks who lived down in the canyons, *and* driving like hell over the Trans-Mountain Loop was the only way to keep Vinnie's "New York Minute" guarantee, *and* like hell was the way I loved to drive.

In the daytime, the Trans-Mountain Loop was this serpentine strip of blistering asphalt that cut through the mountains and canyons from one side of the EP to the other, with a military base and state park in between. There were cacti and yucca, big spiders, and lizards with tails as long as a bull whip, and most dangerous, the rattlesnakes with bodies the size of a double *gordo burrito*.

At night, though, the road transformed into something different. The hot winds blew cold, snow fell in the high elevations, and you could see the whole Borderlands. On a clear night, the city lights of the Paso and Juarez burned like your own personal Milky Way.

Driving on nights like that? I wouldn't trade my job for nothing. Nothing in this world. Sometimes, when I was behind the wheel, it felt as if I was gliding through the air again. Like back in the day, when I was still the starting point guard at El Paso High. Coming down the floor, directing traffic, looking to pass, then taking the ball myself and flying through the lane, me and the ball floating together as it rolled off my fingertips and into the basket.

Today, when I finally got to work, I knew Vinnie would be waiting to jump me. All along the way, Beals had sat quietly with his hands folded on his lap, staring ahead at the road, not even blinking.

I parked in the front of the store, told Beals not to mess with the radio, and ran inside to clock in, hoping Vinnie was taking a nap in his office. Maybe if I got lucky, Beals would be gone when I got off work.

The pizzeria was hopping. With lunch rush full on, the ovens were loaded with pies, and the steamy-hot kitchen was filled with that fresh-baked bread smell. My empty belly howled.

In the mad crazy press of workers in neon orange shirts taking phone orders and making pies, I ducked into the back of the store, which was empty. Yes! I'd given Vinnie the slip. I thought I was home free until I saw that somebody, some asshole, had pulled my time card.

"Hey!" I hollered into the kitchen. "Any of y'all seen my time card?"

All the other drivers acted like I had head lice and they were afraid to come close to me. The boys that cooked the pizzas were acting scared, too. Something sure had come over them since I helped close the store last night. I bet I knew what.

"Yo, Vinnie," I said when I found him in his office, which was a big closet with walls covered in four different styles of paneling. "Whazzup?"

"Whazzup with youse?" he said.

Bug, I told myself, try sweet-talking the man. Remember what Auntie Pearl always said about catching more flies with honey. Be a honeybee. Be a honeybee.

"Hey, Vin. You know what? My time card's missing. You think maybe some assh—somebody might've misplaced it or something?"

Vinnie yawned and put his feet up on the desk. The pizzeria's Six Meat Pie wasn't the only thing famous for being meaty around here. Vinnie was a big man. He rode this big motorcycle, too, which was so wide, it had a freaking luggage rack. Vinnie was always trying to zip up his extra luggage inside a leather jacket. He wore bikers' boots, too, with big square buckles, and jeans so tight he could sing soprano.

"I did," he said.

"You?"

"Me."

"You, what?"

"The asshole who pulled your card. It's me, *capiche*?" He sniffed so hard his nostrils closed. Then cracked his neck without touching it. "You don't seem so worried about time, except wasting it. So, here's your check, okay? You're fired."

Fired? The hell I was. "Vinnie, come on," I said, trying to be a honeybee. "You threaten to fire me at least once a week. I'm the best driver you got. Who's going to deliver your pizzas in a New York minute?"

He yawned. "Plenty of schmucks out there can drive. All they need is a license or a reasonable facsimile."

"But nobody can handle the Loop like your girl Bug. You know that."

"So this is a thing somebody should aspire to?" He sniffed. "To drive like a frigging maniac?"

There he went, disrespecting me again. My fake smile fell. "I been late before, Vin, and you never said much about it. What's the difference this time?"

He cracked his neck again. "The difference is the camel's back is broken and you're the straw. So maybe Vincent Capezza doesn't need big mouths like Bug Smoot working here."

"No, you didn't."

"Didn't what?"

"You didn't just go third person on me." Which meant he was taking himself, as well as this firing thing, way too seriously. So I decided honesty was the best policy. "You and me, Vinnie, we're straight, so I'll tell the truth about why I'm late."

Vinnie had a doughy face with a double chin and a zipper-shaped scar that formed a U the length of his jowls. "Don't do me any favors, okay?"

I leaned close, smelling pepperoni and beer on his breath, and whispered, "My Cadillac got repossessed."

"Liar. Your car is sitting in the parking lot." He waved his beefy arms around. "Here's a little tip for youse, okay? When I lived in Jersey, I did some work for a repo business. So I got firsthand knowledge. When the repo men do a job, they actually take the frigging car."

"Not this repo man, he's just riding around with me until his boss gets into town."

Vinnie made a sucking sound with his face. "There's another lie, okay? I saw you pull up. There wasn't nobody else in the car."

"That's the thing. This ain't no regular repo man." Vinnie was going to think I was crazy, but I didn't see no other choice but to tell the truth about Beals. Then I checked to make sure none of the other workers could hear us. "He's invisible."

"Invisible?"

"Only I can see him."

"And that's possible how?"

"It's so funny." I forced out one of those TV anchorwoman laughs. "He's invisible 'cause he's a ghost."

"So your car is not repossessed." He snorted. "Instead, it's being haunted by a ghost?"

"I'm the only one that can see him. If I slap him like he deserves, I'll get scalding egg white all over me. Like I said, he's just here to preserve the collateral, or until I can turn over my Papa C, which I can't do because he's dead and I wouldn't do that to my own granddaddy anyhow. So I'm stuck with Mr. Beals until his boss comes to close the deal on Hallow—Yo, Vin, what's wrong with your lip? It's all jumpy."

Vinnie mouthed the word *Beals* without saying it out loud. His left eye twitched. Then he pinched his lip to hold it still while sliding my paycheck across the desk. "I got two pieces of advice. First, stay off the weed. It's turned your pea brain into a peanut. Second, get out of my office, okay? Before I call the cops to carry you down to the psycho ward."

Get off the weed? Like I'd do drugs. And calling me a psycho? I didn't care if I had to live on the street or that cardboard box under the overpass, I wasn't letting this man disrespect me no more. All the tip money in the world can't buy your dignity back.

"I'm a grown woman, Vinnie, and I do not appreciate you treating me like a child." I snatched up the check and stuffed it into my pants pocket. "When your rich customers down in the valley start hollering about the New York minute taking an hour, you're going to be sorry you ever fired me."

"I'm already sorry."

"See?"

"Sorry I ever hired you. Get out of here, you're wasting my time."

"I'm gone," I said, though I didn't budge.

He stood up, his arms flung out all wide. "Gone? You're still standing there."

"That's 'cause I wanted you to see."

"See what?"

"See my ass for the last time as I am walking out of this sorry dump." I turned heel and stalked away, trying to look all hard, but inside, I was asking myself a hard question.

Bug, girl, how you going to make a living now?

After giving the employees of Vinnie's Pizzeria a one-fingered wave good-bye and taking a bag of breadsticks as severance pay, I slammed out the front door. My stomach growled like a caged feral cat, and I realized my mouth was as dry as the Chihuahuan Desert. I wished that before my grand exit, I'd grabbed a soda, too.

I wasn't stupid. I knew that by not taking welfare, I was giving myself a heavy load. My life would be easier if I gave up and went on public assistance. I could get ahead, stand on my own. But to my way of thinking, if I took the help, it meant I'd already failed. Maybe I was shooting myself in the foot. Maybe I thought I was a good enough dancer to sidestep the bullets. Maybe I was wrong. At least I had the paycheck. My next stop was the bank to cash out.

But when I opened the car door, there was the asshole, still sitting straight as if a board was stuffed down his shirt. He had a look on his face like there was a little turd under his nose.

"Don't even start with me," I warned him, and to my surprise he didn't. I bit off a chunk of breadstick and threw the bag into the backseat.

"Ow!"

What now, another repo man? "You brought your boys along?" I asked Mr. Beals. "One girl's too much for you to handle, huh?"

"Ahem," he said sharply, looking like he'd taken another big whiff of lip turd. "We appear to have collected a hitchhiker, Miss Smoot."

In the rearview I saw my boy Pesto staring back at me. "Dog," I said, "where'd you come from?"

"I followed you from the car wash." He opened the bag I'd tossed in the back. "A car the size of Amarillo is easy to tail."

"What are you doing sitting in my car?"

Taking a bite of a breadstick, he said, "Dude, you just can't wash binding agent off and pour it down the drain. It's like motor oil. It'll ruin the environment. Kill all the fish in the Rio Grande and stuff."

Yeah, right. Like the big industrial plants, the *maquiladoras*, in Juarez hadn't already turned the Rio into an oil slick. They were also responsible for the polluted stink cloud that covered downtown El Paso most days. "That means what to me? And quit eating my lunch." Which was also my breakfast.

"Dude, when you were at the car wash, my sensors registered a huge amount of negative energy coming out of that bucket of black water. So I check the gauges, right? I see that an unclassified djinn has come through a portal without authorization from the ranking Waste and Disposal Officer, namely me, so I have to investigate."

"Investigate? Boy, I think you been out in the sun too long." I turned around to face him. "I ain't ever heard of no djinn. What're you trying to be, the Psychic Friends Border Patrol?"

"A djinn is an entity made of smokeless fire, aka a spirit with free will." He shook a breadstick at me. "Yes, really, it's my job. And no, it's not the Psychic Friends whatever. It's ISIS, the International Supernatural Immigration Service. I work in the Waste and Disposal division."

"Say again?" I snatched his breadstick and ate it.

"Dude, when you were at the car wash, I sensed—"

This boy needed to take the same advice Vinnie gave me— get off the weed. I made a time-out sign. "Do not repeat that. I heard it the first time. ISIS? Please. Quit trying to punk me, Pesto. You're a car wash manager, not some Waste and Disposal whatever."

"Do you or do you not have a passenger that only you can see?"

Damn, this boy was full of surprises. "A'ight. You got me. He's sitting right here, about to bust a seam."

Pesto pulled a can of hair spray out of a plastic bag. Before I could ask, what's that for? he leaned over the seat, aimed the nozzle toward Beals, and in one quick motion sprayed him in the face.

"Got you, djinn!" Pesto hollered. "I so got you!"

While Pesto was celebrating, I watched in shock as hair spray filled the air with a cloud of misty glue. The cloud drifted down, settling on my leather seats, the dash that I just polished, and the glass on the window that I cleaned every week with rubbing alcohol and newspaper. Some of it blew right into Beals's face, which I didn't mind. He must've felt as surprised as me, because his expression froze, his mouth half-open and his eyes widening like an elf owl with a flashlight shining in its face.

I didn't know whether to laugh or to smack Pesto upside the head.

I picked *B*.

"Ow! Dude, what was that for?"

I shook my stinging hand. "For messing up my car. What kind of punk fool empties a can of hair spray in a vintage automobile?"

"But," he said, looking all hurt, like a kindergartener when you say bad things about his lump-of-clay pencil holder, "I affixed a djinn. Do you know how totally righteous that is?"

I had no idea what he was talking about, so I decided to smack him again. Then I noticed that Beals still hadn't budged. I pretended to smack him, too, and he didn't even flinch. "Dog, he's frozen like a Popsicle."

"Righteous!" Pesto pumped his fist. "I've captured my first Illegal. Mamá is going to be so psyched."

Whoa. His mama was going to be proud? "She knows you're a Psychic Friends Disposal whatever?"

"Dude," he said, practically bouncing in the rear seat. "She's a witch."

46

# CHAPTER 8

# In Your Face, Beals

Couldn't nobody call me prejudiced. Growing up half-Tejana and half-African American, with a mama who was half-Anglo herself, I learned real quick that folks were going to put you down because of the color you were, no matter what color they were. Because of that, I always tried to look past what a person looked like or dressed like or sounded like and judge them on how they treated other folks, especially when they thought nobody else was looking. That's why I was ashamed of myself for doing a double take when Pesto blurted out that his mama was a witch.

My Auntie Pearl was a good Christian woman, but she had her weak spots, and one of the weakest had to do with witches.

She was raised fundamentalist, which meant she took the Bible at its word, including Exodus verse 22, chapter 18, "Thou shalt not suffer a witch to live." Which to her meant that she couldn't suffer a witch to live in her neighborhood. Growing up, I couldn't have jack to do with witchcraft. Not vampires, werewolves, or ghosts. Not Jason, not Freddy, nobody in a hockey mask. Not even ballerinas in pink tutus. On Halloween, our house was dark. No candy for the kiddies in the 'hood. When I first came to live there, it about killed me not to go trick-or-treating, because Halloween was big in the EP on account of the Día de los Muertos celebrations in the *barrios*.

As I got older and smarter, I learned to spend the night with one of my girls, and we'd sneak out trick-or-treating without Auntie knowing it. Not once, though, did I dress up as a witch. Auntie burned that lesson into me because she was always freaking out about this one neighbor we had for a couple months. She was some kind of fortune-teller or healer or something. The sign on her house—she ran a business out of her living room—was a red-orange butterfly with its wings spread, labeled MARIPOSA, SPIRITUAL ADVISOR. All her customers called her La Bruja.

One day, one of the customers came to our door looking for Mariposa. The man asked if La Bruja lived there. When Auntie Pearl asked what that meant in English, he said, "The witch."

He got the door slammed in his face, and Auntie Pearl got so worked up, she almost foamed at the mouth. She spent the next two days on the phone, rallying her church ladies into action, and they set up a picket line in front of La Bruja's house. KDBC-TV even came out to film the protests, and Auntie got herself interviewed. In less than a day, our neighbor was evicted by her landlord. Auntie swore La Bruja put a curse on her 'cause she caught a bad cold right after that. Personally, I wouldn't have blamed the witch one bit if she had.

So that's why I decided not to say nothing to Pesto about his mama being a witch. If he was straight with it, that was his business, and considering that I had a repo djinn in my front seat, who was I to judge? And I had to admit it *was* pretty righteous that Pesto had frozen Beals. If I'd known that was all it took to shut him up, I would've sprayed his ghostly ass from head to toe with some of that Super Hold Auntie Pearl used to buy. It made her wig so hard, you could use it as a football helmet.

"How long's he going to stay stuck?" I asked, meaning Beals.

"I'm not totally sure. This is my first try at affixing."

Just my luck. He was a rookie. "Then you best hurry and do whatever needs doing. When Mr. Beals comes unstuck, he ain't going to be happy."

Pesto about choked. "Mr. Beals? Did you say Beals?"

"Yeah, Beals. You know him?"

Pesto tossed the breadstick out the window and then pulled out a small mirror, which he wore on a chain around his neck. He held it up so that it caught Beals's reflection.

"*Mierda,*" he said. All the color drained out of his face. He made this little gasping noise, and his body bucked like he was about to puke.

"Not in my Cadillac," I hollered, but he was already bailing out of the backseat.

He backpedaled away from the car. He caught his breath and didn't puke, but there was this wild, panicked look on his face.

I was right on his heels. The parking lot was empty, except for a flock of rock doves pecking up trash from the asphalt and deciding if it was food. The wind was whipping around, and even though the sun was bright, my arms and face were chilled. I didn't like being cold, and I wasn't happy about having to chase after Pesto.

"A'ight," I said, after he stopped near an abandoned shack that used to be a drive-thru cigarette store, "what the hell did you see?"

"Beals is definitely no ordinary djinn."

We were about a hundred yards away from the Cadillac, and I turned so that I could keep an eye on it. El Paso was the grand theft auto capital of Texas, and I didn't want nobody walking off with my ride.

50

Pesto pulled out a package of squished Twix candy. He unwrapped the melting bars and then held them out, crossed, like he was fighting off Count Chocula. "This will protect us."

"Candy?" What grade was he in?

"It's a chocolate crucifix."

"Ain't."

"Is."

"Where's the chocolate Jesus? It ain't a crucifix unless Jesus is on it."

"I had to improvise."

Uh-huh. Definitely, somebody was in serious need of getting off the weed. I threw my hands up and turned back for the car.

"Wait," he said. "At least tell me why Beals is in your car."

"A'ight then, you asked for it." I broke down the story about the repossession contract. The whole time, his eyes got wider and wider, and his hands started shaking. He grabbed my wrist but let go when I cut him an acid look.

"Dude, you're totally unaware of what you're dealing with, aren't you?"

"How am I supposed to know what I'm dealing with?" I threw my hands in the air and turned my back on him. "I ain't the one working for the Psychic Friends."

He put a hand on my shoulder. "Please, trust me. I can help.

I've got connections in the network. Take the business card in my back pocket."

Pesto had a cute butt and all, but I wasn't that kind of girl. "Get it your damn self."

"I'll ruin the fabric. The chocolate's melted on my fingers."

"And?"

"These are my best pants. Work with me."

So I dug the card out, kind of slowly.

"E. Figg, Attorney at Law?" I read from the card. "What kind of bull job is this?"

"Call her. You need a professional. She's part of our network, and she's got experience with unique cases."

"Does she take food stamps?"

"You're in danger, dude. You have to take this seriously."

"I am serious," I said, trying to emphasize my point. "My boss Vinnie just fired my ass. I ain't got the cash to hire no lawyer. So excuse me, Mr. Ghostbuster, for not taking stories about smokeless spirits seriously."

"I'm not a ghostbuster. That's Hollywood. This is the real thing." He tried a smile on me. This time, it didn't work. I'd built up immunity.

"No disrespect, but ain't you young to be an immigration agent? You're eighteen years old."

"Nineteen."

"My bad." Like a year made that big a difference.

He leaned against the cigarette shack, his shoulder resting against the wood, and folded his arms. The muscles in his forearms rippled, and his chest flexed under his black T-shirt. I shook the image out of my mind and tried to concentrate.

"While I admit that nineteen may sound young," he said, "this is my seventh year on the job. You know the age of consent in the spiritual world is thirteen, right? That's the age you start training to be an immigration agent. But yeah, if you look at it a certain way, I'm unusual for an agent. That's because I'm totally special."

He sure was. Not that I was about to tell him so. "Uh-huh. All the brothers use that line."

Pesto blushed a little. "These mean," he said, showing me the birthmarks on his wrists, "that I'm attuned better than most agents. I can't see demons directly unless they reveal themselves. But give me a double mirror, and I can see them in their natural form. Totally disgusting. Rancid. Putrid. Pustulized."

"ShutyourmouthrightnowbeforeIpuke!" A pustulized Beals was not a sight I wanted to see.

"When I was six," Pesto continued, "I saw my first demon. *Era muy feo*. He was crawling out of the bathtub drain behind me. I was playing with a shaving mirror and the mirror on the medicine cabinet to look at the back of my head. And there he was, stuck on a hair clog."

"Do what?" I said. "You mean every time I take a bath, one of those djinn is in the tub? Looking up at me?"

Pesto busted up laughing, then bit his lip. "That's right, dude," he said. "Immigrants from the Underworld access Earth via the plumbing system. But only under certain conditions: one, a valid visa or two, the creation of a doubled teleportic prism effect, aka a supernumerary rainbow, which is used only for nonstandard transportation."

"A rainbow? You're freaking kidding me."

"Nope. Except what I'm talking about isn't your ordinary rainbow. The supernumerary rainbow has several arcs, and instead of the regular color spectrum, its colors are pastel."

"You're making this up."

"Seriously, dude, I'm not. They were first documented in the early 1800s by a Brit named Thomas Young."

Dang, my boy had smarts. "If Beals came over a super-whatever rainbow," I said, "then why I ain't ever seen one?"

"You must have," he said, nodding, his bangs falling into his face, "when Beals appeared in the car wash with you."

Then an idea dawned on me. "Wait. You busted Beals. You're going to deport him, right?"

Pesto looked away, staring at his shoes, which were a pair of beat-up Vans and not worth looking at.

"Right?" I repeated.

"It," he said, swallowing hard like a cow pie was stuck in his throat, "it's not that easy, dude. Immigration rules don't apply to high-level djinn like Beals. Also? That hair spray definitely isn't going to affix him for long. He's maybe already free."

I glanced over at my car. "And probably outrageously pissed. You get to attack him, but I'm the one who's stuck riding with him."

"You don't have to be," he said. "Based on what you told me, Beals is attached to the car. You could just abandon it here. Take the city bus or something."

"Like Hell. That Cadillac is mine, and I ain't about to leave it for some thief to strip and dump down by the border." Plus, my Papa C didn't leave me a Sun Metro bus as his last will and testament. There wasn't any bus that rides into the Chihuahuan Desert at one hundred and twenty miles an hour, the cold night wind in your face and the light of the moon so bright you can read a newspaper in the dark.

Pesto had another idea. "Here's a compromise. Park the car at your house. You'll know it's safe, and you can still keep away from Beals. He has a reputation for messing with peoples' heads. He can poison your mood. Suck the hope right out of you. Make you suicidal."

"A'ight!" I held up a hand like a stop sign. "I get what you're saying. I'm okay with parking the car for a couple days, but ain't no way I'm abandoning it." How could I explain that the car meant everything to me? It wasn't just transportation from point A to point B.

The wind shifted. A dirt devil started spinning a few yards away. The rock doves scattered as the baby twister picked up paper cups, pieces of old newspapers, and other garbage and then lifted them thirty feet in the air. My mind was full of garbage, too, all twisting around and putting me in a bad mood. I didn't need to take it out on Pesto, though.

"Dude, I'm just trying to help," he said. "Look, I've got to get back to work."

"You're deserting me, huh?" I tried to hand him the lawyer's business card back. "You can take this back then. Beals says all lawyers work for his boss anyhow."

"Not this one. But if you're worried, call me later, and I'll go to see E. Figg with you. My cell number's on the back of the card." He checked his watch. "I'll start the wheels turning on my end—a couple of guys at ISIS have experience with Beals. Promise me you'll drive straight home."

"Okay," I said but didn't mean it. "Ain't none of this real, anyhow." I reached out and snapped off half a melted Twix bar. "Fanks fo da socklit."

"It's cool being in denial, dude," he hollered after me as I walked to the Cadillac. "It takes everybody time to adjust to the reality of the supernatural."

Ha. I lived my whole life in denial. I lived paycheck to paycheck, and if everything went perfect, I had a couple dollars at the end of the month to see a movie or buy some clothes at the thrift store. But it seemed like nothing ever went perfect. The electric bill was higher than I expected, the price of gas went up fifty cents a gallon overnight, I got sick and had to see the doctor. Being without health insurance was the worst. You lived in constant fear of something simple like the flu taking you out. Folks who were insured, they paid fifteen dollars to go to the doctor and got their medicines for ten. Even at the health center, they used a sliding scale, so my visit was fifty dollars and the same prescription that cost others ten bucks was a hundred dollars out of my pocket. There had been times in my life when I had been able to imagine the future months, even years ahead. Now, I took it one day at a time not worrying about the next problem until I had the one on my plate taken care of. If the supernatural wanted my attention, it had to get in line.

Beals was still frozen, and I was sorry it wouldn't last. I started the Cadillac and headed for the strip mall exit. The traffic light was red, and I waited to make a left turn.

A couple minutes later, Beals yawned and stretched, and I waggled my chocolate-stained fingers under his nose.

"Wanna lick?" I said.

Beals squeaked like a baby javelina. "No chocolate in the vehicle!"

"What you got against chocolate?" I licked my fingers, and he turned green.

He actually drew back like the Wicked Witch of the North—or West. Whatever—getting dunked with a bucket of water. You'd think I offered him liquid Drano.

"Disgusting," he said, curling his lip.

"You should talk. You made my boy Pesto almost puke, you're so nasty. You must be one ugly djinn because your face was so foul, he had to hose it down."

"Hose it down?" he said, sounding confused. Then he touched his face and hair where the spray had landed. "He attempted to affix me!"

"Damn right." I tried to sound all cocky because I wanted to grind his nerves the way he'd been grinding mine. An alarm bell was going off in my head, though, because Beals suddenly wasn't acting his usual prissy self. His voice had got deeper, sounding like it'd been amped through a sound mixer.

"Meddlesome brat," he said, his voice ringing. "Mark this, Miss Smoot, when you and I have settled this affair, your boy, as you call him, will feel my wrath."

I stuck a finger in his face. "Don't you dare be threatening him with no wrath. Go messing with Pesto, and you'll be messing with me."

He laughed deep and harsh as he took off his glasses. Shivers ran down my spine all the way to the tailbone. He kept his eyes closed, but I thought I saw a red light around the lids. As I leaned closer for a good look, he opened his eyes. They were the compound eyes of a fly. Inside, red hot coals burned, like charcoal on a grill. White dots appeared in the red coals. They grew longer and thicker until they started wiggling. They dropped out of his eyes onto his face, and I realized they were maggots. Dozens then hundreds then thousands poured out, covering his face, his shirt, the seat, and me. I beat at them to chase them away, but they turned into flames and blanketed me.

I screamed, and I was not in the car anymore, I was in the kitchen frying tortillas, and the walls and stove and floor were covered in flames, and my whole body was sizzling and popping like burnt bacon. Then I looked down and saw myself as a little girl. I was crying and running toward myself, slapping at the flames, trying to put them out, until the fire spread to the child me, too. We both were burning, burning like a pair of candles.

I really screamed then. I mean, *screamed*. Slobber came out of my mouth, and I almost climbed through the door to get out. "Son of a bitch! Son of a bitch! You son of a bitch!" How dare he use my grief against me.

Beals laughed, bringing me back to reality. "That is just a taste, Miss Smoot, of what the future holds for your young man. And you as well, if you dare affix me again."

Beals put his glasses on. His eyes shrank back to normal, and the maggots disappeared. He tugged the lapels on his suit, then sat straight up in the seat. I collapsed over the steering wheel.

My breath came in deep gulps. I was drinking the air. My skin felt burned, like I'd been held over a pot of steaming water.

"Oh my God," I said after I got hold of myself. "What kind of monster are you?"

"I believe the vulgar term for those in my profession is *demon*. Such an inadequate word. It simply does no justice to the myriad—"

"Demon," I whispered to myself.

Oh hell. What kind of trouble had Papa C got me into? Pesto was right. I had to dump the car ASAP. Bug Smoot was not about to end up floating above a bed and puking pea soup.

The light changed. The fool behind me laid on his horn, and I stomped the gas pedal to the floor. The Cadillac roared down the highway, headed for the Loop.

"What is the rush?" Mr. Beals said. "Have a hot date?"

"I'm doing exactly what I promised Pesto. Dumping this car."

"As in, abandon the vehicle?" he hissed. Then the hiss

turned into a cackle. "I assure you, that is an empty, impossible threat. Simply returning the vehicle will not satisfy the terms of the deal. There is far more at stake here—"

"Shut up! Ain't nobody making me abandon nothing. I *own* this freaking car. I'm just driving home to park it."

"A waste of time."

"And then I'm calling my lawyer."

"Also a waste of your precious time, Miss Smoot. Did I not inform you that all attorneys are on retainer with my employer?"

"I got one that ain't. E. Figg, Esquire."

He started coughing, and for once, he didn't say nothing smart back. From the look on his face, I could tell he didn't like the idea of me seeing E. Figg, which convinced me to make an appointment. Even if it took every penny I had, even if I didn't make rent, even if I had to beg money on the street, I was going to find a way out of the contract.

# CHAPTER 9
# Power of Attorney

Since he was a young man, Papa C had wanted a Cadillac. Not just any pimped-up land boat, but a 1958 special edition Eldorado Biarritz. He craved one more than a palm tree craves water. So it wasn't no shock when one day me and him was riding on the Sun Metro bus, past the car lots on the Boulevard, and Papa C hopped up like he'd been stuck with a straight pin.

Papa C was out the door before the bus stopped rolling. It left us there, standing in front of a used car lot. There was a string of red and blue triangle flags hanging overhead, flapping in the wind. All the cars had prices marked with white shoe polish on the windows. In the middle of the lot was a little-ass metal building with a sign over it: CASH AND CARRY PRE-OWNED AUTOS.

"You're wasting our time, Papa C," I said.

*"Silencio,"* Papa C told me, which was one of three sayings he knew in Spanish. The others were *muchas gracias, amigos,* and *el inodoro se derramó,* which meant "The toilet is overflowing."

"Look at that, Bug, look at that beautiful lady."

The beautiful lady was an Eldorado Biarritz, maroon exterior with cream interior. Papa C had showed me pictures of one lots of times, but I hadn't ever seen one in the flesh. It was one fine-looking car, all right. Not that we could afford it. We had to pinch pennies so hard, we squeezed boogers out of Abe Lincoln's nose.

"Good afternoon, sir." The salesman, Stan, swooped down on us. He was a slick brother with a double-breasted Italian suit and shoes so shiny, you could see the cloudy sky reflected in them. "You got that look in your eye, sir," he said, shaking Papa C's hand.

"What look?" I said.

"The look of love," he said, and winked. "Cadillac love, if I'm not mistaken. Isn't that right, Mr. Smoot?"

"That's right," Papa C said, like he'd swallowed Mad Dog 20-20 love potion. "I been searching for her all my life."

"How'd you know his name?" I said, being born suspicious.

"A little black magic." Then he stage-whispered, "It's written on his pocket."

Duh. Papa C still had on his olive green work shirt. On one pocket it said, "Tri-state Custodial Services." On the other, it said, "Smoot."

Stan jingled a key ring. It sounded like bells ringing. "Care to take her for a spin?"

Papa C snatched the keys. Stan took shotgun, and I slid into the backseat. The leather on those seats was money. Not a tear, not a scratch, just leather that wrapped around you like a hug.

Papa C started the motor. The Cadillac turned over and hummed. "How much for this baby?"

Then Stan leaned and whispered a number in Papa C's ear. In the rearview, I saw his eyes bug out.

"That's more than I bring home in a year, Stan."

"Me, too," Stan said, "but she *is* a classic, a one-of-a-kind dream car."

I crossed my arms. "With a one-of-a-kind price, Papa C. Our rent is—"

"We offer easy financing," Stan said, cutting me off. "Sign and drive, Mr. Smoot."

"I, uh, my credit ain't—"

"We specialize in 'credit ain't,' Mr. Smoot. If you want this car, we'll move heaven and earth to make it happen."

Papa C had tried to buy a car before and nobody, I mean nobody, would finance him. My Auntie Pearl always told him, that's what comes of not paying bills until the repo man was at the door. Turned out, I was right, too.

They went into Stan's office shack to do the paperwork. But after seven banks turned us down, Papa C looked like somebody had emptied a can of whup-ass on him.

I led us out the door while Stan was busy on the phone, holding Papa C's hand like he was the child and I was a grown woman. We were standing at the bus stop when Stan popped out of the doorway. He ran all the way up to the flags and stopped short, like a dog that had reached the end of its chain.

"Don't run off," he yelled. "There's one more lender we can try, a private lender. He's never turned anyone down. Come on now, don't let that little girl pull you away from the one thing keeping you from dying a happy man."

Papa C's shoulders drooped. He said softly, "Some men wasn't meant to die happy."

We got on the bus, and I breathed a sigh of relief because I thought the whole business was done with. But once Papa C had got a taste of his dream car, he could no more stop thinking about it than a wino could stop thinking about his next malt liquor.

The whole day after that, Papa C walked around like a zombie. The second day after, he got out of bed in the same clothes he'd wore the day before. For breakfast, he wouldn't eat nothing, and when it was time to catch the bus for work, he didn't move a muscle.

"Be that way," I said, opening the door on my way to school and running face-first into a big belly. The big belly had a big man behind it. He smelled like fried fish, and he was wearing a brown blazer, a bright red shirt, and a gold medallion the size of personal pan pizza.

"Jesus," I said.

"Not hardly."

"I meant, Jesus, you got one big gut. Whatever you're selling, we ain't wanting, so how 'bout stepping off so a girl can get to school."

"The name's Ferry, Luke Ferry. Here's my card. I'm looking for a Mr. Smoot."

I read the card: "Luke Ferry, Carns's Loan and Lending. Financial Officer. We Make Wishes Come True."

He pushed by me, bumping me into the wall, and headed for the kitchen where Papa C was still sitting in his stanky clothes, staring at a bowl of cold grits.

"Ah, Mr. Smoot. Good to see you, sir. I am here to arrange financing on your Cadillac."

Papa C perked right up. "That's the one all right. That's my girl."

I marched over to Mr. Ferry and shoved the torn-up business card into his lardy hands. "Every finance company in town turned him down. Ain't nobody going to help him buy that car, so why don't you take a walk before I have to go ghetto on your ass."

"*Ma chère*, I believe you've already gone ghetto." Ferry laughed. "What I wish to offer your grandfather is a one-of-a-kind guaranteed financing contract. No one who agrees to our contract terms has ever been turned down."

"Nobody?" Papa C said.

"No one."

"Where do I sign?" Papa C said.

One look, and I knew it wasn't no use arguing. The Cadillac fever had got hold of him, and even though I knew that fancy-assed Mr. Ferry was going to break his promise and Papa C's heart, I'd had about enough.

"I'm gone, then," I said, and walked out the door.

That night after ball practice, Papa C met me at the door. He wore his church suit, and he twirled a houndstooth hat on his finger. Papa C was a tall brother with broad shoulders but real skinny so that his arms dangled loose like they'd been attached to his shoulders with metal brads. He had silver hair, which stuck up straight, like a Q-Tip.

The table was set, and I could smell the special meat loaf and black-eyed peas from MeMo's restaurant.

"You got a hot date or what?" I said.

"Happy Birthday!" he said. "Ain't every day a girl turns thirteen, now is it?"

I gasped because I thought he'd forgot, like he done the past three years. "Aw, Papa C. I don' know what to say."

"I got something for you to sign," he said.

Next to my place was a stack of papers three inches thick. "That's the contract for the car. Mr. Luke Ferry's word is as good as gold. All you got to do is sign it, and that Cadillac is all mine."

"Huh?" I said, all confused. "I thought this was my birthday party."

"That it is, that it is," he said. "After supper, we is going over to the mall to buy you them new clothes you been wanting. Some music, too." He pulled a wad of Benjamins out of his pocket. "They was a rebate offer on the Cadillac. One thousand dollars cash back. It's all ours, child, as soon as you sign the contract."

I knew something wasn't right. Maybe I was only thirteen, but even I knew poor folks like us didn't get that kind of cash 'less we stole it or sold something for it. I wanted to tell Papa C to give it back.

Then I looked into his face, and he had this expression like a child getting ready to open Christmas presents. This man had quit drinking for me. He had tried to give me a home. He wasn't a very good provider, and he was the daddy of a man I despised, but he was all I had left. This was his last chance at a dream, and if I could do anything to help that dream come true, I knew I had to step up to the line.

Before I could spit, I was signing my name on the contract.

"This is it, Bug," Papa C said, "what I been wanting my whole life. Now I can die a happy man."

Too bad it wasn't true.

Papa C had died a very unhappy man—just owning the finest car in the world ain't going to make nobody happy—and now he had stuck me with his problems. Problems so bad, it was going to take a lawyer that I couldn't afford to get me out of them. Problems so terrible that I couldn't even wrap my mind around them, even though I kept trying to break it down for myself as I drove to the bank to cash my check.

The bank was slammed for a weekend afternoon, and almost twenty minutes passed before it was my turn. By the time I got to the teller window, I was feeling all witchy. Except for a handful of change in a dish by the sink, this was all the money I had in the world, and I was about to hand it all over to Mr. Payne.

I signed the back of the paycheck and slid it across the counter with my ID. The teller punched a couple buttons, frowned, and punched some more.

"I'm sorry, hon. This check's no good."

"What?" I said too loud. All the other customers turned to stare at me. "You saying there's no money in Vinnie's account?"

"No," she said with a fake smile. "This account's been closed, miss. There's no money because there's no account. This check's not worth the paper it's written on."

"That asshole."

She wrinkled up her nose. "There's no need for that kind of language, young lady. I'm sorry you—"

"You ain't sorry at all. You're just saying that to make yourself feel better. Lady, the only hope I had was that check, and if it's worth nothing, then nothing's all I got."

I pinched the bridge of my nose and squeezed my eyes tight.

"Well," she said, patting the counter, "would you like to see a bank officer about a loan?"

"A loan." I laughed out loud. "Lady, you and me live in different El Pasos."

I stuck the check back in my pocket and slammed through the door. Outside, I let out a growl and kicked the sand. Damn Vinnie to hell.

"Lost in thought, Miss Smoot?" Beals said as I pulled into the carport next to my apartment building. I hadn't said a word since leaving the bank. "Or is that whirring sound the fan belt?" Then he winked at me.

I didn't answer him. I parked the Cadillac under the carport and hoped that he was telling the truth about being chained to the seat by the binding agent. Turned out, he was. Once I got out of the car, he stayed put. So Beals got stuck in baking heat with the top up and the windows shut tight. I figured a demon wouldn't mind a little heat, since he spent most of his time in the fiery pit. I could still hear him talking, though, and the last thing I heard was a reminder that I had less than sixty hours remaining.

The clock was ticking.

"What. Ever," I yelled through the glass and walked off like I was all that.

Once I got inside the apartment, though, I started to worry about that wink. What was up with that? Was he just messing with me? Or was something else going on?

Before I could even get myself a drink of water out of the tap, there was a knock at the door. "Rent's due!"

"Mr. Payne," I said, swinging the door open after I had filled up my plastic glass. "Chill out. I heard you knock the first t—"

Payne snarled at me, raising his liver-spotted lip. "You'd best watch that attitude with me, Eunice. I don't appreciate disrespect from young'uns, even from tenants that pay on time. Where's my gall-darn rent?"

Beside Mr. Payne stood a sheriff's deputy, which is who I

was listening to. He had a red eviction letter in his hand.

"Miss," he said, nodding. "I'm here to serve this unless you can pay your landlord in full right now."

I pulled Vinnie's bad check out of my pocket and crossed my fingers behind my back. "I got it right here. All I have to do is cash it."

Mr. Payne spat a stream of tobacco on my stoop. "Why ain't you cashed it yet?"

I stamped on the tobacco. Juice squirted from under my shoes and splattered the cuffs of his pants. "Because I been busy, and you give me to five P.M." Like it was any of his business. If he found out the check was bad, he'd lose his freaking mind. Which might be fun to watch. I thought, Maybe I ought to take him around to the carport to meet Beals. Those boys could kick it for a while while I called Pesto to set up an appointment with the lawyer.

The deputy stuck the red notice into his ticket book. "I'll hold this for now, miss. But don't be late, or I'll be back later." He held up a Taser. It buzzed like an overcharged bug zapper. "Ready for action."

He shook hands with Mr. Payne—but not me—before walking across the road to his cruiser.

"Why you got to call the cops on me?" I yelled at Mr. Payne. "I said I'd pay—"

"Why? Because the power company turned off your juice . . ." He reached inside and flicked the switch on and off to prove it. "And I figured you'd run out on me. You'd better fetch my rent money, Eunice, or you'll find a red eviction letter nailed to this here—"

*Slam!*

"—door!"

He let out a string of four-letter words so full of bile, they would've melted wax. Hearing him cuss was almost as much fun as slamming the door in his face.

When I was sure he was gone, I leaned my back against the door, then slid down to the floor. A tear rolled down my nose, and I swatted it. I swung too hard and smacked my head. My nose started streaming snot, and I couldn't help thinking that Bug Smoot was her own worst enemy.

# CHAPTER 10
# Attorney of Power

After checking the lights, I did some cussing of my own. I called the power company to complain about cutting me off early, which did no good. They said I was due for disconnection today, which meant my payment was due yesterday, which meant yes, I was screwed.

I dug some old birthday candles out of a drawer and set them by the door. When I got back, it might be dark, and I didn't want to be stumbling around with no light. The power company wanted the whole bill paid, plus a reconnect fee and extra added to my deposit. That made no sense to me. If a girl couldn't pay her bill in the first place, how was she going to raise enough cash to pay twice that in fees? It was times like this that I understood why folks broke the law. Didn't seem to be much sense in playing the money game when the banker was always kicking you in the ass.

Later, when Pesto picked me up, there wasn't much I wanted to say. My mind wandered off, thinking about Mita and Papa C, until Pesto parked the Jeep on the street a couple blocks from the law office.

"Okay to walk?" he asked me, and offered his hand, like the Beast asking Belle to dance.

"Huh?" I said.

Nobody had ever treated me like that. Then I realized he thought I was just stupid or not listening because he practically had to shout to get my attention.

"Dude, we're here," he said.

"Sorry, this whole contract thing's on my mind. I got to find a way out of it or something," I said as I locked the car door. I checked my shirt and my hair in a store window. I saw our reflection and thought we'd make a cute couple. We looked good together, both of us fit and light skinned, with a different kind of style.

Pesto smiled. He had perfect white teeth and the kind of full lips you'd want to kiss. "E. Figg will help, dude. Cross my heart."

How could a person who worked with demons stay so positive all the time? It seemed like the boy didn't even need a cloud to find a silver lining. We strolled down the sidewalk, staying under the shade of the red metal awning that covered an open-air flea market, the Grande Mercado. The air was full of the scent of chiles, hot oil, new plastic, and car exhaust. The smell of *rellenos* cooking somewhere in the back made my stomach hurt. I still hadn't eaten nothing but half a Twix bar and some breadsticks.

You could about buy anything in the market—canned drinks, underwear, tropical fish, fish sticks, power tools, hot-from-the-grease chile *rellenos*, and *piñatas* shaped like any animal you wanted. It was a *barrio* version of the SuperStore without the smiley-faced stickers. I remembered when me and Mita used to window-shop at *mercados* like this, trying on clothes or testing out perfumes. We never bought nothing, but sometimes the folks working the booths would give me a piece of candy because I was so damn cute.

E. Figg, Esq., shared an office with a neighborhood restaurant next to the *mercado*. The building had a phony mission facade with "Restaurant" written in red Old West letters, and an aqua-marine corrugated plastic awning held up by 4x4 posts bolted to the sidewalk. The menu was written in orange, black, green, or blue letters on the sun-bleached walls. MENÚ DIARIO: GORDITAS DE MAÍZ, ALMUERZO ESPECIAL, all for $1.99, which looked tempting, but the flies buzzing on the window didn't.

The law office was around the back. If Pesto hadn't been with me, I would never have found it. Even if I had, I never would've gone in by myself.

"Come on," he said, holding open the office door for me. "They don't bite."

There was a thin plaster wall between the office and the restaurant's kitchen, so we could smell frying corn tortillas, mixed with the sweet scent of red wine. Not a bad smell for an office.

E. Figg's secretary showed us to the inside office. The room wasn't nothing like I expected. No thick carpet, no modern furniture, no fancy desk. Well, she did have an oak desk, but it looked like it had been carved out of a tree trunk with chainsaws. The floor was covered with rice mats, and there were plants everywhere, including vines crawling down the bookshelves. It felt like we'd walked into a garden.

The lawyer herself was a short blonde with chin-length hair and rectangular Gucci glasses. I couldn't figure out her age—not young but not old, either.

Pesto handled the introductions and most of the talking. He explained about Beals and the contract Papa C had signed. I noticed he left out the part about hosing Beals down with hair spray.

E. Figg asked me if there was anything else I wanted her to know.

"My boy Pesto about covered it," I said. I gave her the contract to study and asked why Beals could try to repossess my car when Papa C didn't own it anymore. "The title's in my name now."

She held a finger to her lips. "Give me a few minutes to look this over."

"A'ight," I said. She started reading. I could see her lips moving as she went line by line down the page. I started tapping my heels. Fiddling with my dreads. Bobbing my head to the rhythm of a song playing in my mind.

"Miss Smoot," E. Figg said, looking up from the contract. "Please."

"Please what?"

"The fidgeting?"

"Oh yeah. Sorry." Embarrassed, I slunk back in my chair and waited until she was ready.

"The idea of title to property," she said, clearing her throat, "is a singularly human concept. The contract is still in force, so the demon is unable to collect on part of the original collateral," E. Figg said, holding the contract under a big magnifying glass, "i.e., your grandfather's soul."

"His soul?" I wanted to make sure I'd heard her right.

She nodded yes. "Mr. Smoot offered both the Cadillac and his soul as collateral for the loan. Instead of fulfilling terms of the contract when he died, however, he ducked the collection agent."

"Are you crazy?" I stood up and leaned over the desk. "How stupid do you think I am?" In school we'd read stories about men who had sold their souls to the devil. They were just stories, though, not something that happened in the real world. But a little voice in my head pointed out that demons didn't exist in the real world, either.

E. Figg didn't back down. "Sit, please." She got up and pulled a book off the shelves. From the way she caught its weight in both hands, it had some heft to it. The outside cover was thick with dust, the pages torn and flaking like the skin of an onion left out in the sun. After dropping it on the top of a table, she clicked on a reading light and cracked the book open.

"Come take a look," she said, and waved us to the table.

When she opened the pages, I got a shock. I was expecting all this fancy handwriting with big flourishes and pictures like in the Bible in my Auntie Pearl's house. The pages, though, were all blank. Not a single thing written on them. Then E. flipped to the middle of the book and pulled an iPod out of a space that had been sliced out with a razor blade.

"We're not exactly cutting edge in terms of technology," she said, seeing the surprise on my face, "but even we know print is dead."

She started thumbing through a list of files. I watched over her shoulder as a text doc popped up.

"The Testament of Solomon?" I said.

E. Figg thumbed down through the document. "It's an Old Testament pseudepigraph, supposedly by King Solomon."

"Pseudepi-what?"

"A pseudepigraph is a work that somebody writes and then claims a famous person wrote it. It was a good way to keep your neck intact when somebody didn't like what you wrote."

"So Solomon ain't the author of his own Testament?"

She shook her head. "Not a chance, even if there really had been a King Solomon. The Testament was a self-help manual for ancient ISIS agents who were fighting demonic activity. The story is that King Solomon used a ring to capture a demon that was sucking the life out of a mason. Solomon made the demon use the ring to capture some other demons to help build a temple in Jerusalem. The last demon seized was the most powerful, the Great Deceiver, the guardian of Hell. Wait, here's what I was looking for, the dirt on Beals."

"Uh, this ain't about him, it's about somebody named Bellyzebub."

"It's pronounced Beelzebub."

"Oh," I said, and the wind went out of me because I'd heard the name Beelzebub in church when the reverend preached about the fall of Lucifer from heaven, and at the same time in another part of my brain, I figured out that "Beals" was shortened from Beelzebub, which meant that a fallen angel had been riding shotgun in my front seat.

The thought was enough to make a girl's knees buckle, and that's what happened. My ass swooned. Just like the white ladies do in the old movies back in the day when they heard somebody cuss.

Lucky for me, Pesto was quick because he caught my elbow in time to keep me from hitting the floor.

"Why didn't nobody tell me this?" I said once my voice had come back.

Pesto chewed his thumbnail. "Dude, I thought you knew. The name. The maggots."

The maggots? "Those nasty bugs are some kind of clue?"

"Could be." E. Figg showed me a graphic on the iPod of a big fly with giant pincers and an abdomen that looked like it was made of armor. "In Hebrew, his name means 'Lord of the Flies.'"

I read that book in ninth grade. The teacher never asked nothing about Beelzebub on her multiple-choice test. All I remembered was a bunch of English boys chasing each other with sticks and blowing on a seashell. "That book wasn't about him. Didn't none of them boys sell their souls to the devil."

"I think," Pesto said, "it's more about the devil inside all of us."

"Speak for yourself," I said, crossing my arms. "Ain't no devil inside of me."

E. Figg cleared her throat. "Getting back to the Testament, this is the part where Beelzebub tells Solomon how to banish him: 'By the holy and precious name of the Almighty God, called by the Hebrews by a row of numbers, of which the sum is 644, and among the Greeks it is Emmanuel. And if one of the Romans adjure me by the great name of the power Eleéth, I disappear at once.' "

I read the passage three times while Pesto read it out loud. "What's that supposed to mean? You saying I can kick Beals to the curb by saying God's name? Dog, even I can do that. Watch this. *God!*"

I winced, half-expecting the heavens to open up and thunder to roll. Nothing happened, not a single sound, except the noise of my empty stomach rumbling.

"It doesn't work that way," E. Figg said in answer to the questioning look that must've been on my face. "It's not as if you can say 'God' and the demon disappears, because God is a title, not a true name."

"Oh." I plucked my lip in thought. "This Testament of Solomon is a waste of time then."

A blush of color rose up her neck and into her cheeks. The muscles in her jawbone started working, letting me know that I'd hit a nerve. I felt bad about it and expected her to start hollering at me. Instead, she rubbed her eyebrows with her fingertips and shut down the iPod.

She handed it to Pesto, who handed it to me.

"Hang on to this," he said. "It might be useful later, maybe?" He patted my shoulder to make me feel better. It didn't help.

"I'm sorry, Miss Smoot," E. Figg began.

"Call me Bug."

"If that's what you'd like." She motioned for me to sit back down. "Bug, you only gave me time to do a cursory review. There are sections written in hieroglyphics, and I'm not well-schooled in Egyptology. I'll need to consult with a colleague before I can give you any definitive answers. In contracts like these, the devil is in the details. Forgive the pun."

"What're you trying to say?" I cocked my head, trying to act like I had an attitude so nobody could tell what I was thinking.

"I am saying, once again,"—she got that tone, which meant she was running out of patience—"that at this point, I'm only sure of one thing: your grandfather purchased the Cadillac in exchange for his soul upon death. There may be more to this contract—"

I held up a hand to hush her. "I'm sorry. I keep asking the

same question because I can't get my mind around this. He sold his soul for a freaking car? I mean, come on, a Cadillac Biarritz is the bomb, but how could he think it was worth his eternal soul? Ain't no car on Earth worth that."

E. Figg perked up. "I once had a client who sold his soul for tickets to the seventh game of the World Series."

"Did his team win?" Pesto said.

"It was a rainout."

"Dude, that's harsh."

"You two ain't helping," I said.

"Please forgive my gallows humor," E. Figg said, sounding kind of embarrassed. "There is nothing funny, I realize, about someone being desperate enough to sign away his soul. Most people don't worry about the cost because they're already doomed to damnation."

"Is that true?" The pastor at Auntie Pearl's church always preached that folks didn't know if they were getting into heaven or not. That's why you always had to walk the straight and narrow. "Is everybody really doomed?"

"All humans are born with the ability to choose their paths in life. It's called free will, and it's the essence of our humanity." E. Figg sighed. "If it's any consolation, it's unheard of for a lost soul to evade capture. Your grandfather must be a very bright man—"

"He's not smart," I said. "Just real good at ducking the bill collector."

E. Figg smiled like it pained her. "It's a valuable skill in certain situations."

I snorted. Easy for her to say, with her two-hundred-dollar hairdo and thousand-dollar Prada outfit. Wonder what her rent was every month.

"Is there a family member you can rely on?" E. Figg said. "Someone who can help with the fee?"

"I got nobody," I said, shaking my head. "Papa C is dead, and Auntie Pearl is, too. My Mita died when I was six. That's the only family I have."

"Then have you considered simply walking away from the car?" she said.

"No, I have not."

"Why not?"

"Because you can't deliver pizzas on a Sun Metro bus, that's why." I caught Pesto's eye, and I knew he was thinking that I'd lost my pizza job. "I like to keep my options open. Besides, Beals said something about me walking away from the contract was an empty, impossible threat."

She nodded like she understood. "I'll ask around, see if there's a strategy we can pursue. In the meantime, stay away from Mr. Beals as much as possible. The more time you spend in his presence, the stronger his hold on you will become. He may be working for someone else, but Beals always has something up his sleeve."

Stay away from Beals. Easy for her to say. I stood up and offered my hand. "So you're agreeing to represent me?"

E. Figg straightened her blazer. "Miss Smoot, my initial consultation is free of charge. However, if I spend billable hours on the rest of the contract or act on your behalf, there will be a fee incurred."

"A'ight." What could I do? Let Beals take my car? "I'll pay you what I can, when I can. What else I got to lose?"

"There is always something to lose, Miss Smoot." She shook my offered hand. "Never forget that."

When we left E. Figg's office, Pesto took my hand. We walked together down the sidewalk past the stores we'd seen on the way in. An older *señora* was frying *empanadas*, and Pesto bought us some, along with a drink. I stuffed one in my mouth, not caring how greedy I looked.

The *señora* winked at us. "What a cute couple," she said, smiling through a sun-wrinkled face. "You must be very happy."

I jumped like a bee had stung me. "But—but," I sputtered, because we weren't a couple at all, and I was a long way from being happy.

Still, things could be worse. Much worse. So I decided right then, with my mouth full of *empanada*, that this girl wasn't taking it anymore.

I squeezed Pesto's hand. "If E. Figg's right, Papa C is out there somewhere. I've got to talk to him, straighten this whole thing out. You got connections. Know anybody who can hook me up?"

He let go of me and started bouncing on his toes like a boxer. "Dude, I am so on it. I know a psychic who'd be perfecto."

"You heard E. Figg say I got to ditch Beals, too, right? So I was thinking you could also hook me up with these folks from the Psychic Friends whatever."

"I like the way you're thinking." He clapped his hands and danced sideways down the sidewalk. "But I keep telling you, it's ISIS. We can go there now, if you want."

I gave him some dap. "A'ight then. I'm tired of playing defense. It's time Bug Smoot started running the fast break again."

"Dude, did you just go third person on me?"

I pumped my fist. "Damn right, I went third person, just like I was the first highlight of the night on SportsCenter. Bug Smoot is back in the house."

# CHAPTER 11

# Third Floor, the Abyss

El Paso was a city with its own beauty; a high-desert, rust-brown landscape where plants grow far apart from one another so they won't have to share the tiny amount of rain that falls. Plants growing in the desert have to be tough to survive blinding heat, unrelenting sun, and weeks without rain. They also have to be patient, saving their energy, then blooming in a blink to take advantage of the summertime monsoons.

El Pasoans were the same way. A lot of folks in town were elderly people who liked the warm winters and lack of humidity, which was good for arthritis and bad for traffic. They learned to get out early, like the birds, before the sun turned the ground into a city-sized kiln. It was hard for young people to make a living in the EP. Most of the work was service jobs for the retired folks or for the base at Fort Sill, so you didn't get ahead without a college education.

So when Pesto parked the Jeep in the slot reserved for the manager, I felt a little tug of pride for my boy. He was still a young man, and even if being a car wash boss was a front for his real job, it meant he had accomplished something in life already. It made me feel ashamed of myself, too, because I could've been doing more with my own life.

We walked around back. He unlocked the outside door and led me down the hallway to his office. There, he flicked on a light and spread his arms wide. "*Ta-da!* My work station. You like?"

The whole room was about the size of my car's trunk. There were three beat-up file cabinets against one wall and a gray metal desk on another. The desk had three legs and a stack of cinder blocks holding it up, and there was a rickety cane-back chair to sit in. The top of the desk was piled a foot high with office papers—blue invoices, pink order sheets, packing labels, bills of lading—grease-stained McDonald's bags, empty drink cups, candy bar wrappers, and an opened package of yellow Peeps bunnies with all the ears bitten off. The room smelled like mildewed carpet, even though the floor was linoleum, and the fluorescent lights kept flickering overhead, giving it this weird, disco-ball glow.

"Uh. Yeah. It's interesting." I was having trouble thinking of something nice to say. "Who, um, does your filing?"

He laughed. "That junk's camouflage, dude." He walked over to the filing cabinets, knocked once on the top and then gave the bottom middle drawer a swift kick. The wall started humming. "This is where I work for real."

The front of the cabinets lifted up like a garage door, revealing a set of metal stairs that led down to an elevator on the next floor.

"Da-yum." My boy was something else.

"After you," he said.

We ducked under the filing cabinets and came out of the other side. Pesto pressed a red button on the wall, and the door closed behind us.

"What do you think of it now?"

His grin was so big, he looked like a Little Leaguer who just hit a home run.

"It doesn't suck," I said.

The humming stopped, and Pesto pointed at the elevator. "That's for us."

The elevator was something straight out of a black-and-white movie. It looked about as old, too. Pesto slid aside a white metal outer door, which opened on an inner accordion door made of two-inch thick bronze slats. It smelled of dirty grease and moldy towels. Even though it looked clean, it had a creepy feel, like it should've been covered with cobwebs and dust.

We stepped inside—after he nudged me in the back a couple times—and he reached for the button marked "The Abyss."

"The what?" I said at the same time Pesto pressed the button.

The bottom dropped out.

For a second we hung in midair. Long enough for me to make a small gasping sound, and then I was falling straight down a ten-foot-wide pipe. My butt hit first, then my back, and I was hurtling at breakneck speed down the wall of the pipe. The light died, and the only sound other than the scrape of my pants on metal was Pesto behind me, laughing.

"Dude!" he yelled. "Isn't this majorly righteous?"

"No!" I screamed as the tube curled tighter, and the speed increased.

We whipped around and around in a huge corkscrew until I got dizzy and my stomach twisted. As I was about to puke, a patch of light appeared ahead, and Pesto called, "Watch your head!"

Bright light flooded the pipe, and I laid back to keep my head down, just as the top of the pipe opened up, and we hit a bump. For a second, I went airborne, then landed smack-dab in a pile of dusty, worn-out throw pillows.

"Majorly righteous, yeah?" Pesto said, climbing out of the pillow pile.

He offered me a hand. I smacked it away. I could get up my damn self. "You could've said something. You ain't right, letting a girl fall like that."

"Sorry, dude," he said, but I could tell he wasn't. "It's kind of an initiation. Same thing happened to me."

"Uh-huh." I rubbed my sore butt and took a look around. "So you work here? This is the Abyss?"

"Part of it," he said. "The best part."

We stood at one end of a long corridor full of closed doors. Maybe hundreds of doors. This section of the Abyss was dirty, neglected, littered with junked furniture, rolled-up carpets, and random empty cans of hair spray in all sizes and brands.

"Hair spray?" I said.

"We do target practice sometimes."

"Ever thought of cleaning up? Get a Shop-Vac up in here or something?" The air was clogged with dust, and I sneezed three times.

Pesto spat on the ground, jumped into the air, and crossed himself. "Sneezing three times is how demons steal your soul," he said when I asked him what the hell he was doing.

"That's just superstition," I said. "Be serious."

"I am." Pesto picked a door marked "D.C." He knocked

three times, then three times again before entering. The door opened into a long, narrow room. The floor was downright nasty, two inches thick with dust and cracking tiles underneath. The walls were made of plaster. Layers of old paint and wall-paper were peeling off, not like they'd been stripped, but more like the paint and paper just got tired and fell off.

"What's this," I said, "the slums?"

"It's where I'll work."

"Here?"

"Once I'm promoted."

The ceiling was even more bare, with just a few globs of old wallpaper glue here and there. The chain of an old chandelier hung down from the center of the room. The chandelier itself was gone, and underneath on the floor stood a wooden chair. Its red paint was peeling, too, showing naked wood underneath, and there was a line of footprints leading from it right back to where we stood.

Pesto sat down on the chair and patted his lap. "Sit."

"If you're thinking romance, boy, you better think again."

"You can trust me."

He looked at me with those puppy brown eyes, and I couldn't help but believe him.

"Keep your hands to yourself," I said, taking a seat.

Whoosh! The center of the floor dropped away, and we were

in free fall again. This time, I couldn't even get a scream out, the air got sucked out of my lungs so fast.

A few seconds later, we hit bottom. The landing was a little hard, and I fell off Pesto's lap and onto the floor. I hopped up and punched him in the stomach again.

"I said to warn me next time."

"Oops," he said, "I forgot."

"Forgot, my ass."

He put an open palm on a touch screen, and the wall opened like a camera shutter. "This is going to blow your mind."

Like my mind hadn't been blown a thousand times already. One look inside, though, and I said, "Now that's what I'm talking about. This is what a place called *The Abyss* should look like."

The room was like something out of *The Matrix*—dark, moody, bathed in green light, with computer screens everywhere, a police scanner with at least two hundred LEDs, and two men in black stocking caps with pentalphas on the brim. They wore *Terminator* sunglasses and Hawaiian shirts with pink and orange flowers, cargo shorts, and Birkenstock sandals. They looked more like Juarez tourists than secret demon catchers. Both men sat at a half-moon–shaped console made of a solid sheet of black glass, leaning back in funky chairs at the control panels, all caught up in their work.

They were playing *Halo*.

"Stop tea-bagging my body," said the first guy, who had long, stringy blond hair and a head shaped like the center branch of a saguaro cactus.

"I so owned you. In fact, I pwned you." The second guy had a gut like a pregnant woman and a black, lower-lip beard.

"You are such a noob. Noob. Nub. Nublet."

I cocked an eyebrow at Pesto, like what the hell? He nodded silently, like he was saying, yeah, they don't look like much, but it's all good. Uh-huh. Girl, I thought, if two middle-aged, badly dressed gamers is all ISIS can throw against Beals, your ass is in bigger trouble than you thought.

"Castor, Pollux," Pesto called. "Knock, knock."

Castor, the blond one, and Pollux dropped their headsets. Pollux eyed me as if I was a shoplifter, but Castor hopped out of his command chair like we was family.

"Pesto!" he said. "Whazzup? This is the girl you've been telling us about? Bug, isn't it? Gotta say, *hombre,* you got a good eye. Hey, there, I'm Castor, the handsome one, and that's Pollux, the smelly one. We're brothers by different mothers, not that you could tell by looking at us. So welcome. *Mi casa es su casa, sí?*"

"I don't speak Spanish," I said.

"Really? My mistake, my mistake. Please, Bug, take a load off. So. Pesto, what's this advice you asked for over the phone? Clue us in. We're dying to hear this. You said it was juicy, correct?"

Now I know why they played video games. Castor looked like a grown man, but he acted like a middle-school boy. Or a puppy. I ain't sure which.

"They're always like this?" I whispered to Pesto.

"Sometimes worse." Pesto pulled up two stools for us. "But when they're on a call, it's all business. Trust me."

After we got settled, Pollux spun around in his chair to face us. He took a deep sniff of air and wrinkled up his lip. "She stinks of djinn, or is that her perfume? Does she have clearance to be in the command center?"

Stink? I'll show you some stink, I thought, and was rising off the stool when Pesto stuck out an arm to block me. He screwed up his face like, don't go there, and I screwed up my face like, I'm going to kick his ass. And his face was like, please don't. I was like, then tell that fool I don't play that.

"If anyone stinks," Castor said, spotting me and Pesto making faces, "it's you, noob."

"Tea-bagger."

"Noober, noober, nub."

I checked Pesto's watch. Time was flying, and this little boy thing was getting old. "About this problem we got. There's a demon we need to get rid of."

"Wait, wait," Castor said. "Where are my manners? You haven't had the grand tour of the command center."

"No tour." Pollux turned off all of the computer screens, and the green glow died. The room was almost pitch-dark. "She doesn't have security clearance."

Castor turned the screens back on. "Clearance, smearance. Let's share our knowledge."

"A little bit of knowledge is dangerous thing, Cas. You've heard that expression?"

"Then let's show her everything, Poll."

He pushed Pollux's rolling chair out of the way. On the screens, Castor pointed out how they track djinn who've got visas. Each djinn is a dot of light—a green dot for djinn with valid visas, yellow for visas that're expiring soon, and red for expired visas.

"Once the visas expire," Castor said, "we send in the cleaning team."

"What happens if the red one gets away?"

Castor grinned. "That's where the extraction team comes in. That's us."

"The jerks upstairs," Pesto told me, "call them the plumbers."

"But not to our faces," Castor said.

Pollux narrowed his eyes at Pesto. "And not if they are currently exiled in Waste and Disposal but have aspirations of joining the NADs."

"The what?" I said, barely holding in a laugh.

"NADs," Pollux repeated.

Castor cut in, "Don't call us NADs. How many times must I tell you? Bug, N-A-D is short for Necromancer Abstraction Division."

Pesto cleared his throat and tapped his watch. "Castor. Pollux. Bug's time is almost up. We need answers to our questions. Now."

They snapped to attention and put their headsets on.

"Name of entity?" Castor said.

"Mr. Beals," I said.

"Aha, the Great Deceiver is back in town." Pollux rolled back to his station and typed in the name. A dozen screens popped up. "Nephilim Class. Diplomatic immunity. Rank is indeterminate and classified. Standard containment protocols ineffective. Immigration status: Visa not required for entry or exit, meaning he is not only a nephilim, he's a free radical, second in power only to Scratch himself. Untraceable."

Castor pulled off his headphones. "You sure know how to pick 'em, kiddos. Beals is a nasty one, and he's completely above ISIS control. Our hands are tied. We can't do anything to him or about him. If he's got his hooks into you, you're in for one helluva ride."

"Tell me something I don't already know," I said.

Pesto asked them about the Testament of Solomon that E. Figg had given us on the iPod. "What about it, Castor? Will it work?"

"Let's distinguish between *contain* and *banish*," Castor said. "I may know of a home brew that can pull off the containment but not the banishing. *Amigos*, I don't think the Testament is going to do the job for you."

"It never has," Pollux said, sounding superior.

"That we know of," Castor pulled Pesto to a corner of the room. "Let's concentrate on my home brew idea."

While they talked, I strained my ears to listen. Castor said something about flour and water, which made me wonder if they were trading recipes.

"So you are the young lady with the repo issue," Pollux said to me.

Damn, now I couldn't eavesdrop. "Yeah."

"Pesto referred you to an outside attorney. E. Figg, of course."

"Yeah."

"She's adequate. For minor issues. Repos. Cases such as that. We handle the heavy lifting, so to speak. Level Thirteen and above. We never, ever touch nephilim, though. Strictly hands off. ISIS policy."

"Y'all just let demons go about their evil business, huh?"

"It's part of the job."

"So you got nothing in all these computers about Beals?"

He shrugged. "Eh. They don't call him the Great Deceiver because he's good at selling Girl Scout cookies."

I wasn't feeling the love for NADs that Pesto did. The jerks that called them plumbers had the right idea.

"He does have one idiosyncrasy that should be interesting to an attractive young woman such as yourself."

Attractive young woman, my ass. "What's that?"

"Beals has a Svengali complex."

"A what?"

"He likes to discover a female to groom, then teach her how to achieve great power and wealth. Unlike Svengali, Beals enjoys undermining them and watching their fall from grace. Think Eve and other queens in the past—Medea, Cleopatra, Marie Antoinette. Who knows? You might be next on his list."

"Shut your mouth." The thought of it made my spine itch, and that ended our conversation. Over in the corner, Castor and Pesto had finished conversating.

"*Muchas gracias,*" Pesto said. Him and Castor shook hands, then he checked his watch. "Bug, we should go."

"Thanks for y'all's help," I said as Castor let us out. Not that it was any help whatsoever: Pollux was a waste of breath.

"Anytime," Castor said. "Y'all come back now."

"Or not," Pollux called.

"Those two," I said as we walked back to the red chair, "are a trip. NADs. What fools name themselves NADs?" Then I noticed Pesto was whistling. "Why you all happy, dog? The whole trip was a waste. We got nothing to help us with Beals."

He held up a scrap sheet of paper, which was full of his scribbled handwriting. "Dude, you're so wrong. The answer to your prayers is written right here."

# CHAPTER 12

# Misfortune Cookies

By the time Pesto dropped me off at my apartment, it was past dinnertime. Since we were both hungry, he volunteered to grab some takeout, plus he wanted to run by the grocery to pick up some stuff. The home brew Castor at ISIS had given him was a "little surprise" for Beals. I hoped it was a good surprise, and that it truly was the answer to my prayers.

Before I went into the apartment, I checked the car. Beals was still sitting inside. His eyes were closed, like he was sleeping. Did demons sleep? I was curious, but not enough to check. Once inside, I flicked on a light switch and cussed, remembering that the power was disconnected.

After lighting most of the candles I'd left by the door, I

washed my face in the kitchen sink and dried with a handful of Vinnie's Pizzeria napkins. The apartment was a mess, so I ran around picking up clothes, throwing out pizza boxes and empties, and spraying a can of old Pledge for air freshener. It didn't help much. The worn green carpet gave off the faint odor of dirty diapers, and the sink stank like burped-up sulfur water. Nobody had ever visited me here, and now that Pesto was about to stop by, I saw the apartment with new eyes. It was dark, small, and putrid, and I was ashamed to let anybody see it.

I opened Mrs. Furtado's newspaper to the classifieds, reading by candlelight. There were hundreds of jobs listed under Help Wanted, including some for pizza delivery, which would've been perfect, except they wanted a clean driving record, and I collected speeding tickets like old stamps.

Quit being picky, I told myself. Grab the first job, any job you can, girl. What's the point of finding work, said a negative voice in my head. You know you're doomed to end up on welfare no matter what.

"Shut up," I said. "You're starting to think like Beals." So beginning with the first ad, I took a deep breath and started dialing.

Thirty minutes later, I had about lost all hope. Most of the places said the manager was out, to call back tomorrow. The one store where the manager was in, El Mundo's Taco

Takeout House, they said they needed to check my references before I even came in for an interview. I gave them Vinnie's number and hoped that the asshole wouldn't keep me from getting another job.

The same time that I hung up, Pesto knocked on the door. He had bags in each hand.

From the first bag he unloaded sesame chicken and egg rolls from the Golden Chinese House of Yum-Yum. From the second, a ten-pound bag of flour, two pounds of real butter, three cartons of kosher salt, and two king-sized Hershey's bars.

"Dude, candles?" he said, checking the place out. "Very romantic."

"What's up with this stuff?" I said, ignoring him as we unloaded it onto the table. I held up the kosher salt. "I didn't know you were Jewish."

"It's for Beals." Then he winked, and I almost dropped the salt.

"Thanks for supper," I said. "How much I owe you for my half?"

He slipped past me into the kitchen. "Did you know there's a coyote outside?" he said, washing his hands. "It's marking its territory. You've been adopted."

I peeked out of the side window. "Is that stupid dog pissing on my whitewalls again?"

Pesto leaned around the corner of the kitchen. "Chill out, dude. It's marking the trees along the sidewalk, not your car. Coyotes are good to have around, if you keep your garbage covered. They control rats and keep rabbits out of the garden, plus did you know they can run more than forty miles an hour and jump a five-foot fence? The Navajo say that coyotes are guardian spirits. Besides, you'd totally want it to pee on the carport, too. Demons hate the smell of coyote urine."

While he cooked the butter and flour into a roux sauce on the gas stove, he sang a few songs in Spanish. The boy had a nice voice, buttery. He also said that he'd asked his mama, and she was going to set up a séance to contact Papa C tomorrow.

"Thanks," I told him. "You work fast."

He carried the still-steaming pot outside to the carport, and I followed him with the container of kosher salt. Pesto explained, as he spooned the roux onto the ground, that it was a technique for binding a demon to a certain spot.

I tasted the salt, then spit it out. "Think this is going to work?"

"It's Old Law magic," he said, being careful not to spill the roux. "Very simple but powerful. Here, spit in the pot."

"You want me to spit?"

"In the pot. The more, the better."

"If my Auntie Pearl ever caught me doing this." I hocked up

spitballs until my mouth felt like ashed-over mesquite coals. "Why am I doing this again?"

"See," Pesto said, "the stuff you called egg white is actually a binder. Put there by Beals's boss to bind him to the Cadillac. It keeps *you* from taking the car and keeps *him* from escaping. If the roux works, then *voilà!* We'll strip the binder off the car, and Beals will be bound to this spot."

"Why this spot?" I said. "I ain't trying to complain, but ain't there some other place to deposit him besides my carport?"

Pesto said, "No, Castor told me that it had to be the same place where the binder first appeared. It was the carport, right?"

"Riiiight," I said, defeated. It seemed like a month since I first found the egg-white mess. I wished it'd just been some punks egging my car.

Pesto drizzled the roux out bit by bit until it made a circle around the car. "At least he's near the garbage cans."

If Beals knew what was going on, he didn't let on. I watched his face in the moonlight, careful not to get inside the circle of roux, and he never batted a maggoty eyelash. The weather was on the warm side, but for some reason, my hands were shaking.

Pesto took the salt container from me. He made a second circle by pouring the salt about six inches outside the roux line. When he was finished, he poured the leftover salt into my hands and told me to throw it into the air. It fell on the top of the car like tiny hailstones.

"That's to make sure only you can enter the circle," Pesto said to explain the salt.

"Hands up!" Mr. Payne hollered as he jumped around the corner of the row house. He held something, pointing it like a gun, but it looked more like a broom to me. "What's that mess you'uns spread on my property? Eunice, where's my gall-darn rent? Five P.M.'s long gone. Your time is up."

I wanted to answer, but Pesto hushed me. Mr. Payne started fussing when we wouldn't talk, which I didn't understand myself until I followed Pesto's eyes to a shadow behind one of the yellow-leafed cottonwoods along the road. Most of the animal making the shadow was hard to see, but the pointy ears and shining eyes belonged to the neighborhood coyote. It slipped away from the tree, crouched like it was stalking prey, and went straight for Mr. Payne.

His ass would've been chewed if the coyote hadn't let a growl out. He saw it at the last second, which gave him time to swing the broom around. The coyote ducked the swing, and Mr. Payne was off and running. He moved damn good for a bow-legged old fart in cowboy boots.

The coyote padded after him for a few yards, then slunk back into the shadows.

After me and Pesto stopped laughing, he gave me the instructions for finishing the roux line. The circles had to stay in place from midnight till an hour past dawn. In the morning, I was to drive the car outside the circle. If everything worked right, I would finally be able to drive in peace.

I could hear my cell start ringing inside. I ran back in just in time. The manager from El Mundo's was calling back about my references. I listened to her for a few seconds until she got around to the subject to Vinnie.

"He said I had what kind of attitude?" I yelled into the phone. "What you mean, you're not going to interview me? Because of something one fat-assed, foul-mouthed Jersey boy said about me?"

Pesto tried to take the phone away. Until I cut him a look that could slice bread.

"Listen here, sister, ain't nobody saying I'm *muy loca*, 'cause I ain't the one who's crazy. Hello? Hello? She hung up on me."

"Can you blame her?" Pesto said. "Quit being so naïve, dude. Vinnie is not going to give you a good reference. What did you expect?"

"I expected some common decency, that's what. It ain't like I deserved to be fired after I worked so hard delivering his damned pizzas."

"Hating him is not worth it," Pesto said, closing my opened

phone and steering me to the table. "All that negative energy makes the evil forces around you grow stronger. Your aura is all purple and yellow, like a bruise."

My aura was bruised? "How do you bruise something that doesn't exist?"

"Seriously, dude, auras are real. Mamá is a spiritual healer, and she teaches these outrageous exercises for auras. You start by breathing through your left eyelid."

Breathing through your eyelid. "And they call me *loca*."

"Come on, try it. There's more in El Paso, Horatio, than your philosophy allows."

"All I'm saying is," I said, cutting him off, "next time I see Vinnie, there's going to be hell to pay. Bruised aura be damned."

"Dude, why are you opening yourself up to this treatment? It's so unnecessary."

"It's necessary to me. I thought you'd understand why." I opened the box of sesame chicken. "My belly's growling. Let's eat."

He piled my only two plates with lo mein, fried rice, and the chicken. I saw that he'd served me four more pieces of meat. When I tried to give them back, he refused.

"No thanks, I'm watching my weight."

He wasn't the only one. I liked watching his weight, too. "So how many folks end up like Papa C?" I slurped down a forkful of noodles loaded with hot sauce.

"Six hundred forty-three," he said.

"That many people sold their souls? Are you talking the whole world or just America?"

"You're thinking too big, dude," Pesto said. "Six hundred and forty-three souls in this town alone. One soul like yours or mine is just a snack to El Diablo, like an enchilada, y'know? You have to eat a bunch of them before you're satisfied."

"So you're saying I'd be a soul enchilada?"

"Something like that."

"Damn."

Pesto slurped the straw in his drink. "Damned, you mean. This whole business is huge. The marketplace is unlimited. Through-out history, people have been trading their immortal souls for the things they want the most. Some want money, some fame, some beauty. Most of them want something small and insignificant—"

"Like a car."

"—that seems a silly thing to waste something so valuable on—"

"Or a state championship."

"—but there is no accounting for the things people dream about." Pesto got this funny look in his eye. "What about you, Bug? What do you dream about?"

If I'd answer him truthfully, I'd say that I dream about me in some boy's arms, feeling his skin on mine. I dream about him brushing my lips with the back of his fingertips, about his breath on my neck.

I flipped a sticky bun at Pesto. It hit his chest and rolled down into his lap.

"So not cool," he said, popping it into his mouth.

"Don't be asking a girl what she dreams of, dog. It ain't right." Sharing my dreams with him would break down a lot of walls that I didn't want broken down.

My cell was ringing. The caller ID showed the number of a store I had called about a job. I crossed my fingers and answered. If this one went bad, I didn't know what I was going to do for money.

"This is Miss Smoot," I said.

A receptionist transferred me to the boss. He asked me a couple of easy questions about my hours and how hard I worked, and then he said to come the next morning. We'd do the paperwork when I got there, which told me that job was as good as mine.

"A'ight," I said and hung up. "I got a job! A j-o-b."

Pesto acted happier than me. "Righteous, dude. So, where's it going to be? Another delivery place?"

"Naw, not even close."

I showed him the ad I'd circled in the classifieds. It was the last business I'd called, and it was the last place I wanted to work. But a girl's got to work where a girl's got to work.

Pesto laughed. "Pets' Palace? That place sells gourmet dog food that costs more than steak. How are you going to work with people who treat their pets like babies?"

"A country girl can survive."

"Dude, you're about as country as Alicia Keys."

"What, you're busting on me about my skin now?" I said, trying to tease but once again, sounding harsher than I wanted to.

He started apologizing. "No, no, my father was an Anglo. Dude, I get it."

"Why you keep calling me 'dude,' Pesto? I'm a girl, if you ain't noticed."

"'Dude' is a universally accepted asexual reference," he said, smiling, trying to backpedal. "And yeah, I have noticed that you're a girl. Many times."

My face got all hot, so I fanned myself with the newspaper. Many times? Was he sending out a signal I wasn't getting? Girl, you better get yourself a pair of antennae if he is, because you sure don't want to miss that broadcast. I never was good at this girl-boy dating hookup thing, so maybe I was just getting my wires crossed. Maybe the signal I thought I was receiving wasn't the signal he was sending. Damn. Why did everything have to be so complicated?

"Hey. Uh. You ain't read your fortune," I said, pointing at the brown bag he'd set on the table. The thing was bulging. "You bought a whole bag of cookies?"

"The restaurant made a mistake," he said. "But I didn't notice it until I got here and it was too late to return them. You know, my cousin Joaquin used to make some extra cash writing fortunes for cookies in San Francisco. Dude, they paid him by the fortune, so he used to pull out quotes from all the great philosophers: Confucius, Plato, Kant, José Gaos, James Brown."

"James Brown?"

"But after a while, he got bored and began making up his own. Weird stuff, like *Fish in one ear, fowl out the other*. Or *If you love something, set it free before you have to pay child support*. He gave up writing, though, and went into sales. I think now he peddles prosthetic limbs."

"You got some crazy-ass relatives," I said, remembering that his mama was a witch. How could you get any more crazy-assed than that?

"Let me tell you about Uncle Leon."

I popped him on the head. "Just open the damned fortune cookie, a'ight?"

"Dude, if it's that important to you," he said, breaking the cookie open, "I'll read it."

It was that important to me. A feeling like an itch that I couldn't scratch came over me, and I wanted to know what that fortune said. "So?" I said.

"So what?" he said.

"So, what's it say?"

"Ahem." He made a big production out of it. "'If you love something, set it free before you have to pay child support.'"

I snatched it out of his hand and read it in the dim light. "'*You have a collect call from the afterlife; will you accept?*' Aw, dog, your lame-ass cousin did write this after all."

He opened my fortune cookie. "'*You have a collect call from the afterlife; will you accept?*'"

Like two cookies could have the same fortune. "Quit messing with me."

"Dude, that's what it says. Read it yourself."

"Straight up?"

"Totally."

I snatched it out of his hand. Damned if it didn't say the same thing. So did the next cookie I opened. And the next. And the next. I dumped out the whole bag, and we opened them all, leaving us with a pile of crumbs, cellophane wrappers, and dozens of slips of paper reading *You have a collect call from the afterlife; will you accept?*

"These here are some defective cookies."

"You think this is coincidence?"

The air in the room felt colder. "I think that Yum-Yum got suckered on some blue-light special fortune cookies, that's what I'm thinking. All of them say the same damn thing."

But Pesto wasn't buying it. "Dude, what if somebody's sending you a message? Like. Like. I don't know what it's like, but there are forces at work here you don't fully comprehend."

I swept the crumbs and wrappers into the paper bag. "I don't fully comprehend your ass, much less some greater forces."

"Like, what if somebody's using our network to send you a message?" He stood up, started waving his arms around while I cleaned up. "Trying to give you a hint on how to get out of your contract."

I threw the trash into a garbage can and wiped my hands on my pants. "Like who?"

"The dead, maybe? There might be a spirit who's trying to reach out to you."

The wind picked up outside. It blew dust and sand against the windows and whistled through the cracks around the door. Some of the candles blew out, and the light in the room was so dim I could barely make out Pesto's face.

A cold shiver arced through me. It made my teeth itch. "Like who?"

"Like maybe," he said, "your Papa C."

# CHAPTER 13

# Roux, Roux, Roux Your Boat

Across from my apartment, there was a little park with a few picnic tables next to a dry streambed. When it rained, the streambed filled up quick; in the desert, storm water ran off like a cup of Kool-Aid dumped on the kitchen table. It almost never rained in El Paso, but when it did, the skies opened up. Raindrops so big they hurt. Afterward, I liked to check out the stuff floating down the wash. Also, I liked the frogs.

El Paso was home to these weird-ass little marsh frogs, no bigger than your thumbnail. They dug down into the mud when it was wet and went dormant or something during the dry times. As soon as it rained, though, *boom!* They came up by the thousands. For a few days, the whole park would be jumping with them, and their croaking made a lot of noise, too, especially at night.

That night, sometime before dawn, I woke up to the sound of frogs singing. I crawled out of the hide-a-bed and pulled the curtains on the front window aside. It was raining outside, the water coming down in sheets and making huge-ass puddles in the street that looked like they were moving, and the air was full of the sound of frogs singing. The sound was getting louder, too.

Having more curiosity than sense, I opened the door to take a closer look. Damn, I thought and covered my ears. Their stupid croaking was so loud, I could hardly stand it outside. But stay I did because of what I saw. It was so unfreakingbelievable, I couldn't do nothing but stare.

It was raining frogs.

At first, I was thinking the streets and sidewalks were covered in them, like maybe they'd come from the sewers or something, when something landed in my hair. I felt the movement, then pulled a frog out. It jumped out of my hand and down to the stoop. While my palm was opened, three more frogs landed in it, and I did what any self-respecting homegirl would do—I screamed bloody murder and ran back inside, slamming and locking the door behind me.

117

After the alarm went off, I got dressed for work in my cleanest clothes. My belly rumbled. Too bad for it. Last night's dinner had to keep me for a while. Stuffing my paycheck in a pocket, I went outside to check for frogs. The stoop was clear. Nothing on the sidewalks or the street. I was expecting hundreds of little dead frogs squished on the pavement, but no, not a one.

Girl, you done finally cracked from the stress.

Speaking of which. I went to check the roux line. I was afraid the rains last night had washed it away, but the awning over the carport had kept it safe. I bent down to touch the line and realized that it was spongy, like the cap of a mushroom.

I eased into the front seat, with Beals sitting straight up in the seat next to me. I put the transmission in neutral and let the car roll forward. Beals never twitched, never moved a muscle, even as his body sunk into the front seat and then slid into the back floorboards.

I pumped a fist and looked into the rearview in time to see him disappear into the trunk. His eyes were wide and wild, an owl surprised to see the sun.

The Cadillac purred to life. Fingers crossed, I put her in drive, released the brake, and let her roll out from under the carport. As I pulled forward, crossing the circles Pesto had poured last night, I gunned the engine and watched as Beals plopped out onto the ground like a horse apple, right in the middle of the circle.

"Boo-ya!" I parked the car and jumped out.

Beals got to his feet. He cleaned the dust off his glasses with a handkerchief. There was a look on his face that my eleventh-grade English teacher would've called "bemused." Once again, he had killed my buzz. I'd expected him to be as pissed as I was happy—I was ready to get down with some excessive celebration. Instead, he stood inside the roux circle, holding a broken chain that looked like it'd been attached to a pocket watch. The left edge of his mouth was curled up, and he gave the chain a little twirl. I felt a surge of happiness from him, like the first time I felt freedom behind the wheel of a car.

"A roux line," he said. "How clever. A gift from the impudent Immigration Agent, I take it." Beals pinched his nose like he had sinus pain. "Do you ever wonder, Miss Smoot, if it is all worth it?"

"It what?"

"Existence."

"Ain't following you."

"The struggle to exist. The constant uphill push of the boulder to the pinnacle, only to witness its inevitable return to the bottom. What drives us except ambition? A blind ambition to become something greater than ourselves?"

"Shut it up," I said, thinking he was messing with my mind again, trying to make me turn over the car without a fight. But there was something in his voice that made me wonder if he wasn't questioning it himself. My mouth opened automatically so I could keep arguing with him, because that's what I did in situations like this. Then I told myself, Girl, it ain't no use in throwing down with this fool. You won, he lost. Let him deal with it.

And that's what I did.

"Enjoy your alone time," I shouted as I drove away, the top down, the wind in my face, and the blissful sound of the road.

A half hour later, I was in the Pets' Palace manager's office filling out my I-9 and getting my red Pets' Palace smock. I was expecting to start work, but they had to run my social and all that before I was officially hired.

"Be here tomorrow at eight sharp," the manager told me, "ready to work."

Damn right, I will. I shook his hand, saying, "Yes, sir, I will," and thinking, Up yours, Vinnie. You ain't keeping Bug Smoot down no more.

Afterward, the first thing I did was call Pesto at the Rainbow to pass on the news that the home brew had worked. He hooted in my ear and told me to meet him at the car wash right away. His mama had set up the séance. That sounded fine with me, so

I turned around in a parking lot and headed back the other direction on the highway.

My plan was working, but time wasn't on my side, that's for damn sure.

Ticktock. Ticktock.

The only time I ever messed around with a séance was when me and Papa C were staying in this falling-down rental house in Chihuahuita, and these skanky girls next door said they could do voodoo. There wasn't nothing in the Bible about suffering voodoo, so I snuck out at night to a shed in the back of their house.

They brought a candle, a Monopoly set, and a parakeet. The candle was for light so spirits could find their way, and the Monopoly board was our Ouija board because their mama wouldn't let them buy one at the SuperStore. They had a para-keet because you needed a chicken's foot to do voodoo, and they didn't have a chicken. The parakeet was their mama's, and she'd get mad if its foot went missing, so they brought the whole bird, chirping and pecking them whenever it could. I was glad they didn't chop off the foot because I didn't like the idea of hurting a living thing, even to do voodoo.

When I told Pesto that story, as he was driving us over to the séance to contact Papa C, he said, "So what happened next?"

"Before we got started, the parakeet got loose. The girls knocked over the candle, which caught the shed on fire. They ran outside screaming, the bird flew away, and I went back to bed."

"What happened to the shed?" He was still pumped about the roux line working, and his good mood was rubbing off on me. It made me realize how depressed I'd been feeling.

"I put out the fire with the water hose."

He looked impressed. "What happened to the girls?"

"Their mama wore their asses out good."

"What happened to you?"

"Dog, I done told you, I went and got back in the bed. My Papa C never even knew I was gone. Hey, you didn't say we were seeing a priest."

Pesto parked his car in front of a church. Some kids in Bowie High art department T-shirts were scrambling up and down a metal scaffold, painting this big mural on the gym wall—pictures of nuns, priests, Aztecs being saved, and boys in pro wrestler masks. In the middle was a cross and the face of the Virgin Mary. Behind her head was a five-sided star. It was beautiful.

"A priest?" Pesto said. "No, no, this is the Sacred Heart Church gym. The séance will be down on the next block."

We got out, and Pesto hollered in Spanish at the painters.

He complimented their work, which really was fine, and they treated him with respect, which I didn't expect because Bowie and El Paso folks ain't straight at all. But Pesto didn't seem to notice stuff like that. Like the fact that we were in the Segundo Barrio, which I didn't normally go into. With Pesto, though, I thought it was all right.

I noticed murals being painted on other buildings, too, and signs about a festival. "What's up with that?" I asked Pesto, pointing at the signs, after he said *adios* to his boys.

"It's the Resistance, dude. The city wants to tear down the *barrio* and put in a SuperStore. They call it progress. We call it selling out."

He turned the corner and waved to a group of his homies playing ball in a parking lot. Their basket goal was nailed to the side of a building, and the rim was lopsided. One of the boys was trying to drive the lane when his dribble got kicked. The ball rolled out to us. I stopped it with a toe and picked it up. My hand itched to dribble, and I saw me taking the rock to the hole, right past those boys. Then I reminded myself that I didn't play ball no more and rolled it back to them.

Pesto said, "So how's the basketball career going? Rumor around school was that you had scholarship offers from at least four different colleges."

"Rumors was all they were."

We stopped in front of Las Cruces Grocery. It was a two-story, tan stucco building with a wrought-iron veranda on the second floor. The front of the store was painted aquamarine, and the front door and windows were covered in bars of the same wrought iron. "Las Cruces Grocery" was painted on the corner, right above a little mural of two roads crossing each other.

"This is our store," he said, and led me around to a side door.

There was a wooden sign beside the door, and when I saw it, I stopped in my tracks. On the sign was a red-orange butterfly, its wings spread, and below it, written in gold letters, MARIPOSA, SPIRITUAL ADVISOR. Auntie Pearl would've called it a cruel twist of fate. Like fate wasn't already twisted enough.

We stepped inside, into an apartment separated from the rest of the store, and a bell rang. The air was cool, and the room smelled of fried tortillas and something else familiar. I was trying to figure out what it was when his mother burst in from the store.

Oh, my Lord. It was the same woman, La Bruja. My face flushed, embarrassed, and I turned back for the door. No way could I meet her. And Pesto, how could I tell my boy it was my aunt that had run his mama and him out of the neighborhood?

Before I could cut and run, Pesto caught my arm.

"Mamá, this is Bug, the girl I was telling you about."

At first, Pesto's mama didn't look much like him. He was tall, she was short. He was thin and cut, and she had round hips and chubby cheeks. But when she looked at me, I knew they were family. Her eyes lit up like sparklers, and her face practically busted open with a smile. Her dress, which was full of bright reds and golds in the shapes of birds, swirled around her.

"Bug!" She wrapped me in a hug. "Pesto has told me so much about you. You poor girl, you have been through too much. Come. Sit at the table. Have something to eat. Do you like *carne deshebrada*? You cannot attend a séance on an empty stomach."

Whoa. Talk about getting swept off your feet. Mrs. Valencia was treating me like I was one of the family. I'd forgot what it felt like.

She steered me to the back of the room where there was a little triangle table with three chairs. She had hands like steel tongs, and before I knew it, she'd stuffed my ass into a chair and dropped two steaming burritos onto a brightly colored plate in front of me.

"Thanks," I said, inhaling the steam. It smelled of beef and chiles, which was the familiar smell—Mita used to cook burritos the same way. My mouth started watering so bad, I had to wipe it on my sleeve.

"*De nada*. Eat. Look how thin you are. Like Pesto, too

skinny." If she recognized me, she wasn't letting on.

The bell on the front door clanked, and she swept out to answer it.

"They don't call her La Ciclóna for nothing," Pesto said, laughing at the expression on my face. "She's a force of nature, *mi mamá*."

"You sound proud," I said, before taking the first bite of the burrito. Dog, the way it tasted!

"Yeah," Pesto said, "I guess I am."

It was cute the way Pesto admired his mama. You could tell he'd grown up coming home to a table loaded with food and a house full of love. I thought about Mita again, and my throat felt like it was closing, so I kept eating.

"This is the best thing I ever put in my mouth!" I said, then got embarrassed. Trying to play it off, I added, "Y'all got something to drink?"

"Mamá?" Pesto said. *"Por favor—"*

Right on cue, Mrs. Valencia whisked in with two tall glasses of tan milk.

"I'm lactose intolerant," I said, which was pretty much true. One glass of milk, and I'd be farting like Louis Armstrong blowing "When the Saints Go Marching In" on his trumpet.

*"No hay problema,"* she said, setting a glass next to my plate. "It is *horchata*. Made from rice. Nondairy."

"Thank you," I said.

"*De nada.*" Then she was gone. La Ciclóna was right.

"*Horchata,*" I said, holding the glass up to the light. "What's this floating in it?"

"Almonds and bits of orange. She makes her own. Best in the *barrio.*"

I sniffed. Damn, it smelled good. Tasted even better, like soy milk, but with a bigger kick.

"You like?" he said.

Yeah, I liked. The food, the drink, the company. A girl could get used to this. "You talk just like her."

"Who?"

"Your mama. When you're out of the *barrio,* it's like, 'dude' this, 'righteous' that. Here, you talk all clipped off."

He rubbed his nose, thinking. "So that's a bad thing?"

"Naw, ain't what I meant. We all come from somewhere or somebody, right? I'm just saying, it's cool seeing where you fit in. Eat your burrito, dog. It's getting cold."

Instead, Pesto excused himself and followed his mama to wherever she had gone. They must've had some thin walls in the building because I could hear him call her name, and she answered. Not that I was eavesdropping or anything. Was it my fault that sound carried all the way out here?

As I took another big bite of burrito, Pesto said something

about NAD and how he was destined to become a demon catcher. I couldn't make out what his mama said back to him, but from the tone, she didn't seem as proud of him as he thought she'd be.

Curiosity got the better of me. Silently, I slid out of my seat and tiptoed around the corner. I peered into the storeroom, then jerked back.

Found them.

"Listen to me, Mamá, I know how you feel about NAD."

"What about your *padre*, Pesto? Look what working for those *locos* cost him."

Pesto didn't want to hear it. "But the roux line worked like a charm. That proves I'm ready to make my first snare."

"It is too dangerous, *chiquito*," Mrs. V yelled, sounding so frustrated and angry, like she wanted to beat some sense into him.

"Crossing the street is dangerous. Being alive is dangerous. Driving is dangerous. Eating Aunt Rosalita's cooking is dangerous. I cannot be your little boy forever, Mamá. I have met my destiny."

"You're wrong. Rosalita is not such a bad cook."

Their voices got more quiet, so I tiptoed back to the table. So Pesto and his mama didn't see eye to eye on everything. Good to know.

I ate the rest of my meal and finished off the *horchata*. It still tasted good, but some of the flavor was gone. In a few minutes, we were going to have a séance, and just the thought of talking to Papa C was giving me all kinds of butterflies because I wasn't sure how I felt about him anymore.

I was about to find out.

# CHAPTER 14

# La Bruja and the Pearl

My mother, who I called Mita, joined the army at age eighteen and was stationed at Fort Bliss. Everybody says she was a little stick of dynamite, which is about the best compliment a woman could wish for, I think. She was just a corporal, but she had what it took to go up in rank real quick. Her career was on the fast track, until she met my birth daddy, Charles Smoot III, a tall, light-skinned brother with good hair, a wide smile, and a silver tongue. They hooked up, and in a couple of months, Mita was mad crazy in love and mad crazy pregnant. Turned out, Mita wasn't the only woman that my birth daddy had been hooking up with. When Mita found out about it, she showed up at the low-down, two-timing player's house with a cane pole and wore him out. That was the last she, or anybody else, saw of Charles Smoot III in El Paso.

Without a husband, Mita quit the army to take care of me, which meant she had to accept WIC and food stamps, and had to move into the worst projects in El Paso. She kept our place spotless, though, like an army barracks. Every Saturday, she scrubbed the apartment with Ajax. We kept plants, too—sage, mountain laurel, coyote mint, sand verbena, and marigolds, which she called spirit flowers. Because she was a Tejana, she raised me to speak Spanish and English. She dressed me in frilly clothes and put my hair up in ribbons for mass, which I hated so bad I used to cry and spit.

After she got burnt up in that fire, I used to lay in my bed at night, wondering what it'd be like to talk to her again. Now, here I was about to answer a call to the afterlife, and it wasn't her I was trying to reach. It didn't seem right.

"Ready?" Pesto's mama said, rushing in and drawing back a curtain that led to a hallway. "This way to the séance parlor, *por favor*."

She had changed clothes. Her whole outfit was black—black velveteen pullover with long sleeves, black ankle-length skirt made of crinkly fabric, and a black scarf with a silver diamond pattern. She'd turned into La Bruja, which freaked me out more than I wanted to admit.

"Your mama don't mess around, does she?" I said under my breath so that only Pesto could hear me.

"She likes to dress goth for séances," he said softly. "Don't let it bug you. Get it? Bug you."

"Got it." I punched him between the shoulder blades. "Now, I'm giving it back."

Mrs. Valencia led us down the winding hallway that separated the house from the store. At the end of the corridor was a paneled door with an antique crystal knob. We stopped in front of it, and Mrs. V reached up the sleeve of her pullover and pulled out a tarnished bronze skeleton key. The lock squeaked when she turned it and let the door swing open.

Stale air that smelled of dirt and old paint wafted out.

"Uh," I said, sniffing, "what's this?"

"The cellar."

"Cellar?"

"*Sí,*" she said, sliding the key back up her sleeve. "We do all the séances here."

I grabbed the doorframe like my fingers were a vise.

"Something wrong?" Pesto said behind me.

Hell yes, there was something wrong. Didn't they watch horror movies? Dark cellars were bad places where psychos in hockey masks hid under the stairs with chainsaws waiting for folks to come down a set of wooden, squeaky stairs. "Wrong?"

I said, clearing my throat. "No, no. Nothing's wrong with me."

Mrs. V pushed a button switch nailed to a wall stud, and above us on the landing, a light flickered on. The bulb hung from the ceiling by a thick black wire.

"Oh, look," I said. "Stairs." Wooden, rickety stairs that led down to a dark cellar full of cobwebs and other stuff I couldn't make out because there was only one more light, another bare bulb that hung over a second paneled door.

"Follow me," Mrs. V said, and took the first two steps. The wooden treads squeaked loudly.

"Oops. Changed my mind." I backed up, bumping into Pesto, who was blocking the doorway to the hall. "Forget the séance."

"Dude, don't freak out. It's safe." Pesto slipped past me and his mama and pounded down the stairs. "See? When I was a kid, I used to play games down here all of the time."

Play what games? Hannibal Lecter hide-and-seek? All right, girl, get over yourself. I took a deep breath and followed Mrs. V down to the packed dirt floor. It wasn't so bad once you got past the rotting smell and the dusty cobwebs and the way the naked light cast dark shadows across everybody's faces.

"Why the cellar?" I asked Mrs. V as she unlocked the second paneled door, which was half the width of the first one.

"Ambience," she said.

"It's closer to the plumbing," Pesto said.

Ambience I could buy. But what did plumbing have to do with the undead? Oh, he's messing with me, I thought. I checked their faces. Oh no. They were both serious.

Mrs. V swung the door open and clapped her hands to turn on the lights.

"Whoa!" I said, and shielded my eyes. "That's what I call white-white."

Inside, a small crystal chandelier hung from a low ceiling over a white oak pedestal table. There were three white high-backed chairs around the table, which rested on a white tiled floor. From the smell of the room, the walls had just been painted. They were white, too.

Mrs. V took off her heels and waved us in. While me and Pesto were slipping out of our shoes, she locked the door behind us.

"Uh," I said, crinkling my toes on the cool tile floor, wondering what I'd got myself into. "I can trust y'all, right? 'Cause this whole cramped-room-in-a-dark-cellar thing's starting to creep me out a little."

Pesto rested his hands on my shoulders. He whispered, "It's all part of the séance. Mamá thinks the spirits can hear us better when our auras turn pink with fear."

Speaking of fear, I pointed at the oak table. A shallow

crystal bowl, a bottle of olive oil, and a sewing needle rested on a white lace doily in the middle of it. "What's the needle for?" I asked.

"For your blood," Pesto said as we gathered around the table.

I laughed because I thought he was clowning, like it was part of the aura thing. Then I saw him nod, a serious frown on his face.

"For real?" I said.

"For real," Pesto said as he pulled out a chair for me. I was so shocked, I sat down without saying thanks. He took the chair to my right.

"Let us begin." Mrs. Valencia swirled olive oil into the bowl. "The oil and crystal bind the spirit world to ours, creating a portal. The blood of the Seeker cleaves the spirits to her. Bug, may I see your finger?"

"Just how much blood are we talking about?" I said, eyeing the sharp tip of the six-inch needle she picked up.

"A droplet is all we will need, *mi'ja*."

I squinted my eyes shut and gave her my hand. "That thing's sterile, I hope. I can't be getting no lockjaw. Ow! Damn! Thought you said it wouldn't hurt."

"I never said that." Mrs. Valencia held my finger over the bowl, squeezing one droplet out into the oil. It plopped down and spread out like cream in a cup of hot coffee. "Focus your thoughts on the bowl, Bug. Imagine the voice of the person who you love, the voice you long to hear."

"Ain't we going to touch fingers or something?" I said. "In horror movies, they always hold hands."

"It doesn't work that way," Pesto said.

His mama shushed him. "Bug, imagine the voice. Hear it in your heart."

So I tried to recall the little things about Papa C— his voice, his laugh, the way he still called me Jitterbug after everybody else had shortened it to Bug. How we drove the Cadillac way out in the desert on spring days, with the cool air in our faces, the wind whispering in my ears. Papa C, I chanted silently. I accept your call from the afterlife. Papa C, I accept your call from the afterlife.

Seconds passed.

Nothing happened.

Dang it, Papa C, I accept your call. How many times have I got to say it? You sent me the freaking fortune cookies. Show your face. Now!

The oil in the bowl started swirling.

"They're here," Pesto whispered in a high voice.

"Shh!"

The oil swirled faster and faster until a little funnel formed in the middle. The funnel started rising out of the bowl. It shot up to about four feet tall, and it glowed green and yellow, like it was made out of antifreeze. Then before Pesto could duck, it twirled into him, covering his body from the waist up in slurry gel, which now looked more like snot than olive oil.

He threw his hands high into the air, jumped to his feet, and hollered out, "Hallelujah! I feel the Earth move under my feet! Praise be! Praise be!"

"Aunt—Auntie Pearl?" I said, swallowing hard and staring into Pesto's eyes. "Is that you in there?"

Pesto beat his hands together and then shook his fingers in the air. "Eunice Catalina Smoot, what do you think you are doing playing with witchcraft?"

Yep, that was my Auntie Pearl. Dang it, this was the last thing I had in mind, Auntie catching me in a séance in a witch's house. It was like ordering fried ice cream and getting boiled okra instead. "But I was calling for Papa C. We got this fortune cookie message from him and—"

Pesto's head lolled around and then popped back up. He dropped into the high-backed chair and fanned herself. Er, himself. "Child, I'm offended. All those cookies was from me."

Only I would have an aunt who came back from the grave to stick her nose in my business. But having an elderly black woman's voice coming out of Pesto's mouth? I had to bite my knuckle to keep from snickering. Especially when he started adjusting his girdle.

It only got worse when Pesto put one hand on his hip and cocked the other wrist. He shook his shoulders like Auntie, too, and he even did the bendy neck thing while tilting his head.

"That no-good brother of mine," Auntie said. "Any man that'd sell his soul for a car ought to have his behind beaten, you know that?"

I couldn't argue. "So you know about the contract?"

"Child, I know lots of things." She winked. "Auntie's still got connections."

"Any of your connections know where I can find Papa C?"

Auntie shook Pesto's head. I could almost see her neck fat wobbling. "You ain't going to find Charles nowhere. He's planning to hide out until after Halloween so the contract will be null and void, and he'll get to keep his soul. It's part of a side deal he cooked up."

"Side deal? With who?"

"Listen here." Auntie puffed up real big and stuck out Pesto's chest like he had a pair of 38Ds attached. "I'm a good Christian woman, and I ain't about to have 'messing with demons' on my ledger."

She threw Pesto's arms in the air and waved her hands, saying her Glory Hallelujahs, just as if she was back in church. All that was missing was her light pink dress and matching jacket with lapels piped in gold lamé and her hat, a big-ass, wide-brimmed thing topped off with a foot-long ostrich feather.

I got tickled and had to cover my mouth. My good humor didn't last, though, because I finally understood what she was saying: Papa C really had deserted me. It was useless to keep looking for him. That left only one question.

"Auntie, what did you want? Why'd you send me the fortune cookies?"

She shook Pesto's oil-covered finger at me. "I came here to warn you, child."

"Warn me about what?"

"To advise you against working with witch women and their lawyers, that's what. Folks like this will lead you down the path to destruction, mark my word."

"What folks?" I rolled my eyes. "What path? Who said anything about destruction?"

She tapped Pesto's wrist. "Goodness, look at the time. My flying class is starting up, and the instructor, my-my-my. He's got wings like an angel. Bye-bye child."

My heart sank. I wasn't ready to let her go yet. "But Auntie, these are good people—"

"And it wouldn't hurt you," she said, her voice fading out, "to go to church once in a while. You need some positive role models in your life, if you know what I mean."

"Wait!"

There was a popping noise, like bubble wrap getting squeezed, and Auntie Pearl was gone. Pesto's head lolled to the side. He started snoring.

A minute later, Mrs. Valencia and my boy came to. Pesto sat up looking all confused, his whole body covered in slurry olive oil. Hair poking up in all angles like somebody had dunked his head into a vat of rancid French fry grease. He smelled like it, too.

"What happened?" he said, rubbing his head.

Mrs. Valencia laughed. "*Mi'jo*, the spirit chose you as a proxy, rather than me. Which is *afortunado* because this dress is very difficult to wash. Off to the shower with you. I will bring you a change of clothes. Bug, stay with me, *por favor*."

Pesto shrugged when I looked to him for advice. Should I stay? He shrugged again and pushed the stinky gunk through his hair, which made it look even wilder than before.

"See you in a couple minutes, dude." He wobbled up the stairs after Mrs. V unlocked the paneled door.

"A'ight," I said, though I wasn't that happy about staying behind to chat. What could she want?

Mrs. Valencia picked up the bowl and other stuff. "Did it go well, the séance?" she said. "I always miss the best gossip when

I am the Seer. You will have to share with E. Figg any information you got."

She headed up the stairs. They squeaked with every step she took.

I followed on her heels, checking over my shoulder for psychos with chainsaws. "Not much to tell." I didn't want to share Auntie's warning about witches with her.

"You didn't make contact with your *abuelo*," she said, handing the bowl to me so she could lock the door in the hall. "I can tell by your worried brow."

I touched my forehead. Did I look that worried? "It was my Auntie Pearl who sent us the message and talked through Pesto. She's real pushy."

"*Sí*," she said, nodding like it made sense. "Pearl Smoot, I remember her well. We used to be neighbors. Yes, very pushy."

Ice water ran through my veins. "You—you know who I am?"

"Of course!" Her laugh echoed down the hallway. "Am I not La Bruja? So, *dígame*, what did your aunt say?"

So she knew all along about Auntie. And she still let me in her house, which meant her heart was bigger than mine, that's for sure. I picked out one detail from the conversation I could share. "She said that Papa C made a side deal on the contract."

She nodded like she understood. "This is a very crucial detail."

"That's all you wanted to ask me?" I said after a couple of

seconds. "Because I was thinking I'd wait for Pesto outside or something."

"Not quite," she said as we reached the kitchen. She set the bowl in the sink and filled it with soapy water. "Pesto says it has been hard for you to make a living alone. So, you will live here. There is a little apartment above our store. It is not much, two rooms and a bath, but it is clean, and the price is right."

"But I already got an apartment."

She wagged a finger at me. "Rule number one, no profanity. Rule number two, E. Figg will take care of the lease on your apartment, which I understand is in a very dangerous neighborhood. Rule number three—"

I drew back from her. Who did this woman think she was? "Don't be making up no rules for me."

*"Número tres,"* she said, being the cyclone again, "no hanky-panky with Pesto. No boys allowed at all. You have your reputation to protect, *sí?*"

Now wait just a damn minute, Mrs. Cyclone. "I'm a free woman!"

"You are still a *chica*, not a *mujer*." She spun me around and pushed me out of the kitchen. "You can wait for Pesto in the living room."

I tried to lock my heels, but she got leverage on me. "I ain't moving in, Mrs. Valencia."

"Don't be stubborn. I know what it is to be forced out of your home."

Ouch! That hurt. "If you're trying to make me feel guilty, it ain't going to work."

She grabbed my palm and traced my lifeline with her finger. "Ah, I see your future, and it is your destiny to take the apartment. It will be a place of peace and reflection. Which is exactly what you need to face the terrible fate that awaits you."

# CHAPTER 15
# A Red-Letter Day

Pesto showered and changed so fast, we were outside on the street before you could say *rápido*. As we drove back to my place, I gave Pesto the highlights of the séance.

"So when are you moving in?" Pesto said. "The *barrio* is such a righteous place to live."

"Hold up, dog. Don't be rushing me into nothing."

I'd been living under my own roof for months, and I didn't need a mama cyclone running my life.

"Dude," Pesto said, "I'm not rushing you. No way. You're your own woman, right?"

"Damn right." I folded my arms and humphed. Then I sneaked a sidelong look at my boy, who winked at me.

Traffic was rush-hour thick. Pesto got stuck behind a

caravan of small vans that was taking a whole retiree home to Yolanda's Cafeteria Buffet. The speedometer needle was stuck on thirty miles per hour, and I was itching to reach across and stomp the gas pedal down. Damn, I hated not being able to drive. Going slow made me crazy. Not Pesto. The boy sat behind the wheel, tapping out a beat with his thumbs and whistling *"De Colores."*

"How can you be so freaking calm?" I barked. I stomped the floorboards and bounced in my seat. "Move! Why do old-people buses go so slow?"

"Dude," he said, "chill out. It's not a race, *sí*? The traffic will break soon, and is it so bad to spend some time together?"

Easy for him to say. He didn't hear the sound of a clock ticking in his head.

"So, dude," Pesto said cautiously, because I was still fuming, "it was your aunt who sent the fortune cookies. That's a good trick."

"Uh-huh."

"Your grandfather made a side deal with another demon?"

"Uh-huh. Maybe I should make a side deal myself, go hide out and duck my obligations, too. Let somebody else clean up the mess for a change."

"Dude, that would be such a bad idea. You're just frustrated."

"I was only teasing, dog," I said, and turned to watch a

daytime haze settle over the city. There was a grove of winterberry trees between the road and a neighborhood, and I could catch their fruity scent on the wind. Behind the trees, there was a whole street full of houses painted bright white with candy-apple red roofs. The siding was adobe-style stucco, which made the houses look solid, stable, like they could last three lifetimes.

My throat turned dry and thick. In El Paso, you didn't go nowhere without a water bottle, so I took a warm sip and turned on the radio. One of my favorite songs was ending, and I listened to it until the news came on. The second news story caught my ear:

"Three local schools are closed today due to an outbreak of lice. Hundreds of students in the west unified neighborhood were sent home yesterday, and the remaining county schools will be conducting examinations of all students in hopes of preventing a similar occurrence. In other news, local chile farmers are reporting multiple outbreaks of thrip swarms, which threatens to—"

More news about pests was not what I needed. I clicked the radio off.

When we got to the crib, Pesto hung out for a few minutes. He said he wanted to check on the roux line to make sure Beals was still captured. That was fine with me, I didn't mind the company.

146

Until I saw a red slip of paper nailed to my front door. I knew what it meant—eviction. Guess Mr. Payne wasn't playing after all.

"Oh damn," I said, pulling the slip of paper down.

Pesto joined me on the stoop. "What?"

"With all that was going on, I forgot to pay the rent." Which wasn't exactly correct. My pride wouldn't let me admit that I was broke.

"This is illegal," Pesto said, reading over the notice as we went inside. "He can't put you on the street for thirty days. E. Figg can help us put him in his place. Or like you say, tell him where he can shove his eviction."

"Don't talk to me about E. Figg. She wants money, too, remember?"

I flopped down at the table. I needed some time to get my mind right. There wasn't no way I was living under Mrs. Valencia's thumb, but I still needed a home. All my stuff could fit into three cardboard boxes, so moving was easy. Finding a place, putting down a deposit, clearing a credit check, that was the hard part.

"Dude, you don't need to stay here," he said, sitting down beside me and dropping a backpack on the floor. "The apartment over the store is totally yours for the taking."

"I don't want nobody's charity." I turned my back to him. "I don't need nobody's help."

Pesto took a long look around the apartment. "Bug, I'm not arguing with you, but help is not a four-letter word."

He stood up and held out a hand. I eyed it for a second like it was diseased, then I sighed. He was right. There wasn't nothing left for me in this apartment, in this life I'd been living. My head was spinning from all the junk that had been dumped on me, but I had sense enough to grab hold of something good when I got the chance.

"A'ight," I said, and took his hand. And hung on to it until he smiled, which made me really not want to let go.

"Before I leave," he said after a few seconds, "I have a small present for you." He bent down over the backpack, blocking what he was doing from my view.

His hair hung down over his collar, so black that in the light, it looked steel blue, and I could smell his grapefruit-tinged shampoo from three feet away, which made my nose feel all tingly. The rest of me, too.

"What you up to?" I said, leaning over him.

He hunkered forward, and I grabbed both his shoulders, intending only to pull him back. Instead, he grabbed my wrist, then tickled me under the arm.

"Stop!" I squealed but didn't mean it. I found myself looking right into his turned face. His lips parted, and all I could think about was what it'd taste like to kiss him.

My earrings dangled forward, making a sound like chimes, which broke the spell, and I snapped back to reality.

"Wow," he said, letting go of my hand. "You're really ticklish."

"Uh-huh. You just caught me off-guard, that's all. Now, show me that surprise before I kick your ass."

He laughed. "Dude, you know how to sweet-talk a guy, that's for sure." He held up a strip of red paper and then started unfolding it. As he did, a cutout of a rose appeared. It was huge, as big as my hand, and it was almost 3-D.

"This is *papel picado*," he said. "Made it myself."

"For me?" I said as he offered it.

He nodded. While I was holding this perfect rose in my hands, he bent down, patted my shoulder, and said good night.

Before I could help myself, I planted a wet, sloppy kiss on his cheek.

He jumped back, he was so shocked.

Girl, I told myself as we stood there looking at each other all awkward, you done messed up again.

After he left the apartment, my knees started shaking, and I had to sit down. I set the rose on the table and stared at it. A tear rolled down my cheek. I felt stupid crying, and I didn't even know if it was because I knew why he jumped. I was too disgusting to kiss.

The doorbell rang, and I ran to answer it, thinking Pesto had forgot something. When I pulled open the door, though, Mr. Payne was standing on the stoop. He was holding a rake.

"Well, Eunice," he said, grinning through his snuff-stained teeth. "I reckon you got my—Ow!"

I slammed the door on his beak-shaped nose, bolted the locks, and crawled into bed, the *papel picado* rose on the table beside me.

# CHAPTER 16
## Get a Job Redux

She was my lifelong enemy, but somebody else, some asshole in second grade, had nicknamed her Tangle-eye. Her real name was Tanya, but she had this funky lazy eyeball that spun in its socket like a loose marble. It made her eyes look like they were all tangled up, which people teased her about, which made her mean, which made her a brutal player in the post.

For a while.

Back in the day when we all played AAU ball, she was the biggest, nastiest sister on the floor. Then we all got faster, and she stayed slow. She switched positions from forward to center so she didn't have to run so much, and the only reason she made the Coronado High team at all was because she was so damn mean. Sure wasn't for her shot. At El Paso High, we used to call her the Undertaker, because her shot hit the boards so hard, the rebound about killed you.

That all changed halfway through her senior season. That dead shot turned dead-on, and her passing game turned from *a* bomb to *the* bomb. Her coach moved her to the point, and she showed out. Dog, she could make any pass look easy peasy:

Behind the back.

Alley-oop.

Crosscourt.

Upcourt.

And all the way down the freaking court. The change in her game was so unusual, it was unnatural.

She single-handedly turned a team that couldn't win into one that couldn't lose. Except to us. We kicked their ass twice early in the year. When we played for the third and last time, it was regional playoffs. The winner went to Austin for State. The loser went home.

Our team was good that year. Everybody kept talking about how we were a team of destiny. Each game, the stands had college recruiters crowding into them. At first, they were from community colleges and little schools. As the season went on, some assistant coaches from I-A schools were showing up. Letters from recruiters poured in, and Papa C got all excited because his Jitterbug looked like she was going to win a full-ride athletic scholarship. A sports writer for *El Paso Times* called me a female version of Muggsy Bogues, the shortest NBA player to ever dunk a basketball.

It looked as if my life was on the fast track to success. Until Tangle-eye f'ed up my destiny.

At game tip-off, me and Tangle-eye were the point guards. I had a sweet little jump shot, but I was always looking to make a good pass instead. Tangle-eye, she had the big head and had given up on passing, thinking she could win the game all by herself.

The whole game, I couldn't shut her down on defense, but I contained her, made her bust ass for every shot she took. It wore her out: Sweat poured from her whole fried-egg smelling body, and at the end of the second half, she was putting up wild threes. Didn't none of them go in, either.

In the last minute of the game, we were up by seven, and Coronado got the ball. I stuck to Tangle-eye like gravy on a biscuit.

"You want some of this, Coyote?" she said, growling as she walked the ball up, dribbling all high, just tempting me to go for the steal. Which was exactly what I intended to do.

The word *coyote* stung like scorpion poison. "What's this? Your game ain't got nothing left, Tangle-eye, except a junk shot and some rubber legs. You got any reservations?"

"Reservations about what?" she barked.

"Reservations for the next game," I said, "because you're going to be sitting in the stands watching Bug win the state championships."

I made a move for the steal. For a second, I felt the leather on my palm, and my body was already making the turn for the break. Then out of the corner of my eye, I saw Tangle-eye reach in crazy fast and flick the ball away.

She laughed, popped up for a jumper, and put in a three from downtown—no, from the 'hood way past downtown.

Bottom.

We were now up by four.

"Whose shot is junk now?" she said, pointing a finger in my face.

I took the ball on the inbounds. Thirty seconds left, and all I had to do was control the tempo, work it up the court and dish—

Damn.

Tangle-eye stripped the ball right off my hip. Her hands moved so fast, I took a stride before noticing I was dribbling air. She took two steps, not even past the half-court line, and *blam!*

String music.

The El Paso High crowd died.

The Coronado fans jumped up and hollered, "Tang! Tang! Tang!" Like she was some kind of powdered orange drink.

"Yo, Kool-Aid," I hollered at her as I ran downcourt to take the pass, "they're calling your name."

"Naw," she yelled back. "That's the sound of my travel agent making your reservations at states. Two seats on the last row for you, Coyote. Right next to the cockroaches."

I pointed at the scoreboard. Five seconds left. "Read it. We're up by one."

She laughed deep, sounding like a grown man, and dropped off to cover our other guard. How stupid could she get? Five seconds left, and she backed off the press. I ran ahead, caught the pass, and slung it down the court, where our center stood wide open for an easy layup.

That's when the sickest thing I ever saw happened. The ball dropped like a brick, way short of the center line. Tangle-eye came flying out at the top of the key and snatched the ball like a frog gulping down a fly.

She put up a jumper.

Even before the ball left her hand, I knew it was money.

I turned my back and started walking to the locker room. When the ball hit the net, the sound of leather on nylon felt like a firecracker going off. The Coronado fans in the crowd busted out on the floor, screaming their freaking minds out.

My stomach felt like it had slumped down to my knees. I wanted to cuss, to cry, to punch something, to hug somebody, to thump my chest, and to run away and hide all at the same time. Instead, I zombie-walked off the court. I passed by our bench, all of my teammates looking like their dogs had got run over or something. And there was Papa C next to the scorer's table, sagging like a heavy load.

I had let everybody down. I had let him down. I never will forget the look on Papa C's face, all twisted like he'd eaten something bitter. He was rubbing his arm and wincing.

The next day, he had his heart attack, then a stroke, and it all went downhill from there. I quit school to stay home with him, and when he was back on his feet, I started delivering pizzas because he had to go on disability. Four hundred dollars of Social Security on the first and fifteenth wasn't enough to even pay for his drugs.

Pets' Palace was one of those big pet superstores with hundred-pound bags of dog food that cost more than a month's rent. They sold everything for your pet, including personal hygiene products and dental care items. Damn, I found myself thinking, while the assistant manager, Meredith, showed me around, some folks spend more on their animals than the government spends on health care.

Fifteen minutes after I reported for work, the manager introduced me to Porsche, a standard poodle. It took about three seconds to decide me and Porsche wasn't speaking the same language. Mine was English. Hers was poodle.

A half hour later, I was aiming a water hose straight at the Porsche's snout. "Dog, you're getting a bath, even if it kills you. And if you open that mouth again, Bug's going to floss those stanky teeth with this high-powered hose."

That's when the damned dog jumped out of the aluminum washtub. My arms were already covered in scratches from that mean-assed, Garfield-look-alike orange tabby I'd just half-drowned, and my mouth was so full of poodle fur, I could've coughed up three fur balls. So if Princess Porsche had decided she was too good to stay in the tub, I had something to make her rethink her decision.

The poodle growled, daring me to do it. I always was a sucker for a dare.

I blasted her yappy mouth with twin jets of high-powered spray. The water caught her right in the chest and knocked her back. But Princess Porsche wasn't playing, neither.

She rolled with it, got to her feet, came right at me. I tried to duck, but the floor was slippery from a flood of soapy water. One of my work boots slid, and I did a Chinese split for the first time in my life.

Ow.

I heard two ripping sounds. The first rip was the noise of my jeans splitting at the crotch. Cold water poured into my panties, and my bottom got wetter than a baby pissing its diaper.

The second rip was the sound of Princess sinking her teeth into the yellow raincoat I was wearing as she tore loose a big square of cloth. If all poodles were vicious as this one, Lord help the poor groomers who had to clip their hair into the shape of a coconut bonbon.

"Damn it!" I yelled, and grabbed at the dog's snout, even though my thighs were screaming. "That's it. I'm drowning your ass, Princess."

Before I could aim the hose again, the bitch jumped me. I held up my free arm to hold her off, but she juked, going underneath and coming up right on top of my throat, mouth open, her teeth pointed at my jugular.

I heard a pop, and the room filled with an awful stink. The air burned with fire and brimstone. Princess jumped back like somebody had just let a sour fart off in her face. She yipped and ran back behind her kennel carrier.

I had to take cover, too. The fumes stung my eyes and burned my nose, even through the lapel of the yellow raincoat, which I had pressed up against my face. As I pulled my shirt up over my mouth and nose, I saw a familiar face smirking at me.

"Did you miss me, Miss Smoot?"

"Beals!" I hollered. How did that happen? He'd been standing in the carport, waving bye-bye, when I left home this morning. "You escaped the roux line?"

"You noticed. And to think my employer said you were not very bright," he said. "Kudos to you and the handsome young man for a job well done. It held me quite well for a while, as well as I have been captured in many centuries."

"How'd you get loose, you owl-eyed turd?"

"Tut, tut," he said, mocking me. "Perhaps you recall seeing your landlord with a lawn tool last evening?"

He was right. When Mr. Payne had busted in on me last night, he was holding a rake in his hands. "So?"

"Rake. Flour and salt. As you would say, Miss Smoot, do the math."

That son of a bitch. He'd let Beals loose from the roux circle, probably trying to clean up his ugly-ass yard. After months of doing nothing, he picked last night to spruce things up? "Payne messed up everything."

Beals laughed, that deep, ringing cackle I hated so much. "He did, I'm pleased to say. The roux circle did indeed unbind me from the automobile." He held out that same length of slender gold chain then twirled it. "Now that I've escaped the circle as well, I am free to roam as I wish. You and I will be closer than ever before."

At first, I started to freak out, but then it occurred to me that Beals was way too happy about this. "What's your boss think about you roaming free in here while the Cadillac is unguarded out there?"

Beals looked like he'd swallowed a diamondback. His almond-shaped eyes glowed coal red, which set Princess off again. She charged him, fangs bared, flecks of foam flying from her mouth.

"Bad dog," Beals said, shaking a finger in Princess's face. "Sit. Please allow Miss Smoot to finish her business in peace." The dog laid down on the floor, not even twitching her tail. "No need to thank me," Beals said to me.

"I wasn't planning to." Asshole. I put up the sprayer hose and called for the groomers to come get their next victim.

"She's done?" the assistant manager answered.

"Oh yeah, her ass is done, a'ight."

"It's, y'know, only been, like, five minutes."

"Well, y'know, like, somebody better get in here," I said into the intercom, "'cause I'm, like, done with this crazy-ass dog."

"Are you sure she's clean?"

"Look here," I said. "My ass is sopping wet, the crotch of my best jeans is torn all up, my drawers is ruined—"

"But is she, like, totally clean? We can't groom a dirty dog."

I was about to tell her what she could groom when I saw the corner of Beals's mouth turn up. Oh, so he thought it was funny to see me get all crazy mad. Damned if I was going to give him the satisfaction. "You want to know if the dog is clean? Here, let me ask her. Yo, Porsche, ready for your coconut bonbon treatment?"

The dog whined. I walked toward her, and she started backing away.

"See?" I hollered back through the intercom. "Your girl says she's ready to go. Now y'all, like, come get her, y'know?"

"Well," the assistant said, "you don't have to be rude. I'll send someone to pick her up."

Some team leader. I wondered if she always let somebody else do the dirty work.

"One more thing?" the assistant manager said. "If you're going to be, y'know, employed here? You should work on being nicer? Because we're all a team."

Like she knew what being a team was all about. Team meant practicing hard, working out hard, running drills until you could do it in your sleep. Until you did do it in your sleep. It meant having your girls' backs, and them having yours. There wasn't nothing about hosing down some mean-ass poodle that made you a team. Ain't no dog in team, dog.

"Go away," I told Beals. I hated him seeing me pissed off, since he was enjoying it. "And take your fart stank with you."

But he wasn't budging. He looked at the wall like he could see right through it and said, "I shan't miss this for the world, or the underworld, for that matter."

The door opened, and Tanya walked in.

It was Fate coming back to give me another kick in the pants. Tangle-eye was as tall as ever. Ugly as ever, too, with that one wandering eye that made my skin crawl.

She took a deep sniff. Then a second one. Her lips started moving and she twirled around, looking for something in the air. "What you doing here? I thought I was through with you," Tangle-eye said to nobody in particular. Her voice shook, and I could hear the fear in it.

Since when did Tangle-eye start being afraid of me? "I'm washing that mean-ass dog," I said, holding up the hose. "What do you think I'm doing, selling Mary Kay?"

"Huh?" Tangle-eye said, as if she'd just noticed I was standing there. "Aw, no, not you. Don't tell me you're the new girl. They didn't say nothing about hiring no coyote."

I pointed my finger up to her face. "They didn't say nothing to me about no loud-mouth, fat-assed, brick-laying cheat working here, neither. If they had, I would have done been out the door."

"You still sweating over that game? Coyote, don't you know, you can't change it, so just live with it."

Of all the lousy luck, to find a job where the person I hated most in the world was already working. Maybe I could hang on a couple days until I had a chance to find something else where I didn't have to deal with bitches all day. And I wasn't thinking of the dog kind.

When I didn't move, Tangle-eye held up her hand. There was a ring on her finger, a big gold, state championship ring. A ring that should have been mine. "You got any idea what this ring cost me? What I got from it?"

"Yeah," I said. "It got you a place on the All Cheaters Team. Hope it was worth the price."

Her eyes narrowed into slits. "If I was you, I'd shut that damned mouth."

"If I was you, I'd duck."

Tangle-eye was a foot taller and a hundred pounds heavier than me. She was strong, I was quick. So I sprayed her with the hose.

She cussed and tried to slap at the water. That didn't work, so she charged me. My reflexes were quick enough, so I should've sidestepped. Instead, I held my ground, and when she slammed into me, it was like she'd stuck a shoulder into a steel door.

How did that happen? I glanced at Beals, and he winked.
"You did that?"

He yawned.

Tangle-eye fell onto the wet floor, holding her shoulder while writhing around and getting soaked. Seeing a new target, Princess charged out from behind the kennel. She sunk those sharp teeth into the cuff of Tangle-eye's jeans and started tugging.

"I know you're in here! Leave me be!" Tangle-eye screamed, turning her head back and forth and crawling back against the wall for safety. She paid no attention to the dog, who was growling and ripping the denim to shreds. "What else y'all want from me? You got everything. You hear me? Everything!"

The look in her eye was so wild, it made me sad. I looked back at Beals. He looked all smug, and I knew why—Tangle-eye was a soul enchilada, too. It didn't take an Einstein to understand what she'd meant about the price of the ring.

"You are beginning to connect the dots, Miss Smoot. Perhaps you are not so dull-witted after all." He mock-saluted me and popped out of the room, leaving a methane cloud behind.

"This job stinks," I said.

I had never quit nothing in my life, but if being employed at Pets' Palace meant working side by side with a fool who sold her soul for a high school championship ring, my perfect record was about to end. I tossed my yellow raincoat on the floor next to Tangle-eye. Princess let go of her jeans cuff and attacked the coat. I helped Tangle-eye get to her feet. I handed her my name tag and headed for the exit.

"Where you going?" Tangle-eye said. "You can't be leaving this placed all messed up."

"That's what you think," I said.

"Wait, there's something I got to tell you." She reached for my arm, but I slipped away.

"There ain't nothing you got to say that I want to hear." I grabbed the door handle and yanked hard. "I quit."

## CHAPTER 17
# Get Rid of Beals Do-over

I slammed out the door of Pets' Palace, soaked to the bone. It felt good to know the truth about how Tangle-eye won that championship. In a fair fight, we would've taken Coronado down, and we would've gone to State.

"You suck," I told Beals, who was sitting in the car reading the *World Weekly News* like it was as important as the CNN Web site.

He didn't even look up at me. "Oh bother, did all not go well after I departed? Pity."

"Don't talk to me." I put a hand up in his face like I was stopping traffic. "You helped Tangle-eye cheat me."

"Not I. A fellow employee was responsible for that feat, a

demon named Stan. I believe you remember him. Wish fulfill-ment is, frankly, beneath me."

"Like repoing is frankly beneath you, too? Was that before or after Scratch demoted your ass?"

The tabloid dropped out of his hands, and he faced me, smil-ing through teeth that looked like ivory ice picks. "Why even bother finding employment, Miss Smoot? This account will be settled at midnight tonight, and your fate will be sealed."

"My Papa C—"

"Your grandfather was a vain, selfish man in life and in death. In fact, I rather doubt he is capable of love, especially for the bastard child of a dead soldier and a high school dropout who didn't remain in town long enough to see his daughter born. You have no chance at redemption. Surrender. Accept your fate in this life, as well as the next."

My breath caught in my chest like I'd been sucker punched. Beals was pure, grade-A devil.

"Don't nobody tell me to surrender," I screamed at him. "I am a grown woman who knows her own mind, and I am free to make my own decisions. Maybe they ain't good ones, but they are mine! Do you hear me?"

"What a lovely sentiment," he said, stifling a yawn. "Your mother held a similar philosophy, I believe, until she carelessly ignited herself."

"Shut up! Don't you talk about her. Not now. Not ever."

I put the car in reverse and stomped the pedal down. We rocketed backward out of the parking spot. I jammed on the brakes, almost snapping Beals's head on the dash, and jerked the gearshift to Drive. I floored it, Beals pinned against the seat.

"Slow down!"

"Shut up!"

As I whipped the car out on to the highway, I thought, I'm finished—the Cadillac isn't worth the torture anymore. Beals can keep the damned car for all I care.

At the next street, I turned into the lot of a deserted mom-n-pop convenience store. I parked and then jumped out of the car, slamming the door and leaving the engine running, the keys in the ignition.

"Where are you going?" Beals called.

I paused at the entrance. "I'm dumping your ass."

Inside the store, the air felt all muggy warm. It stunk like a mix of soured milk and stale cigarettes. The smell made me gag. I coughed, which the cashier took as a hello.

She was middle-aged, round like a rain barrel, and wore a bleached-out blue smock. She stood behind the counter, which ran along the front of the store. There were four aisles of candy, chips, and other stuff. The drink coolers on the back wall were full of Cokes, milk, and beer. Mostly beer.

The cashier greeted me. "*Buenas dias*, hon."

"I don't speak Spanish," I said.

She narrowed her eyes. "You sure look Mexican to me." And then checked me out in one of the antitheft mirrors. There were mirrors in all four corners of the store and a fifth one over the register. No cameras, though. Bet they got robbed a lot.

"'S'up?" I nodded into the mirror, and she saw me watching her watch me. She pretended to look away, but it was obvious she thought I was a thug.

At the back of the store, I took a Coke out of the cooler. I held the door open, let the cold air sweep over my face. It felt like a kiss.

The cashier cleared her throat. "Shut the door, hon. You're buying the drink, not the air-conditioning."

"Sorry." I fished in my pocket for loose change.

As I headed for the counter, the door opened by itself and a heap of dust blew in.

The cashier covered her mouth with a tissue. "The wind's bad today."

I stopped, midstride. It wasn't wind. Just a load of hot air.

Beals strolled inside, dust clouds whipping around his feet. He walked past the cashier, ignoring her. "Return to the vehicle, Miss Smoot. This instant." He blocked my aisle. "You left the keys in the ignition."

I shrugged my shoulders like, So?

"With the engine running."

I turned heel and walked to the next aisle.

He moved to block me. "El Paso has an extremely high automobile theft rate. If the vehicle were stolen, why, that would be tragic. Don't you agree?"

I shrugged like, I don't give a damn, and went on to the third aisle.

"Do you think it so easy to flee?" He blocked the way again. "Our fates are inexorably intertwined. You could not escape me, even if I wished it. And as you can see, I have no such wish."

I waved him aside. He didn't budge.

If I'd been able to touch him, I would have knocked his ass silly for not letting me by. Don't nobody herd me like a sheep.

So I got right up in his face, as close as I dared. I clenched my teeth and hissed, "Step aside."

"Look into my eyes," Beals purred.

They turned oil black.

"So cold—" I murmured.

My gut told me to get away, fast. But I felt weak, almost paralyzed. His eyes, his eyes, so cold.

"You will return to the vehicle with me," he said.

It felt like an answer was being forced out of me. "Yes."

"You will remain with the vehicle until midnight."

"Yes."

"Something I can help you find, hon?" the cashier said.

"Find?" I said, the sound of her voice clearing the cobwebs from my brain. "Yeah, find." With a shudder, I shook off Beals's control.

Sensing the change, Beals got up in my face. "My eyes, Miss Smoot."

Ain't happening, demon, I thought. You're not fooling me twice. I pulled away, grabbed the first thing I could lay hands on—a pot of Mocha Blaster coffee—and threw it into his face.

"No!" Both hands flew to his face, and he growled in pain as though the coffee was acid.

"Mocha," I whispered. "Chocolate."

Covering my ears, I backed into the latte machine and knocked a stack of cup lids onto the floor, but I was free now, scrambling to get away.

I dropped the metal pot, and the cashier yelled, "Hey!"

Seconds later, Beals lowered his hands. His whole face was scorched and swollen, like he'd been punched with a hot iron. He turned his head side to side, birdlike, trying to catch a sound. "My eyes! I can't see, you despicable urchin."

I felt a pang of pity—

"You'll pay for this affront!" he shrieked. "Hide if you can. I shall find you. Even without sight."

—until he tried to gut me with his claws.

Blindly, Beals swatted the cappuccino machine. His fingernails slashed open the flimsy front door and plastic drink hopper inside. Milky brown glop poured out, pooling on the floor and filling the store with a sticky-sweet odor.

"What the hell is going on?" the cashier yelled.

"This freaking machine's sprung a leak!" I said, hoping she'd stay put.

"Leak, my butt," the cashier argued. "You ruint the machine!"

"No, no, no," I said. "It wasn't me."

Right then, Beals took a long drawn-out breath. He wretched twice and regurgitated a dark mass the size of a softball and coated with mucus the color of snot. It hit the floor with a squish.

My jaw dropped. My breath caught in my throat. I stood paralyzed as the mass stood up on six legs, shook the mucus out of its wings, and took flight.

A black fly. Bigger than both my fists.

Beals cooed at it, "Yes, my pet. Help Master find the urchin."

The fly lighted on the window, buzzing crazy loud. It fanned its wings, drying them out, clicking its scissored mandible at me.

"Nasty," I whispered.

The cashier. Could she see it, too? My eyes flicked back to the counter.

No, she was standing tiptoed, craning her neck to see what I'd done. Like she couldn't decide whether to stay behind the register or come investigate.

"You got a mop?" I hoped to distract her, keep her from getting mixed up in this while I figured out what to do next.

Then I glanced up and saw a flapping movement in the antitheft mirror behind the counter. I could see the reflection of a second theft mirror, which was reflecting a picture of me, the spreading brown puddle, the huge fly, and something so nasty, so vile, so hideous, I almost threw up in my mouth.

"Ain't. No. Freaking. Damn. Way."

Beals the owl-eyed nerd was gone.

Beals the demon loomed before me. He stood seven feet tall, with a V-shaped head and twisted horns of an antelope. The skin on his upper body was pale red, almost orange, with ink-colored veins that rippled underneath like black worms. His lower body was covered in bloodied, matted fur. He had the legs of a bull with cloven hooves, and his fingers ended in claws shaped like eagles' talons. Two leathery wings beat the air.

"You got wings?" I said. "And horns?"

Beals laughed. "You've discovered my corporeal form. Beautiful, aren't I? Care for an encore?"

He wretched again, his body convulsing.

I turned and ran. But I heard a louder buzzing—a swarm of flies spewed from his mouth. They hit the floor in a mound of mucus. Quickly, a few dozen insects dried out and flew. They formed a black cloud that swirled around his head.

"Punish her," Beals said. "Bring me blood."

Dozens of flies shot down the aisle. They buzzed straight for my face. I swatted and ducked, and I slapped my own arms and head trying to beat them off me.

But there were too many.

Some got past, and one bit the hell out of my cheek.

"Ow! Damn it!" The wound burned like a fire ant sting.

Beals pointed straight at me. "Found you, little mouse. Your squeak betrayed you."

I darted to the end of the aisle, cut a sharp right turn, and fell flat on my ass. My head conked the tiled floor, and I looked up at the flickering fluorescent lights.

Flies landed on the lights above. The fixture turned oil black, like Beals's eyes.

"Run, run, as fast as you can," Beals called singsong. He walked slowly down the row, feeling the shelves, somehow not knocking any merchandise off.

"You ain't catching me." I scrambled to my feet.

"There you are again." Beals turned down my aisle, laughing.

The cashier headed toward us, shaking a cordless phone at me. "You're crazy! I'm calling the cops!"

"That obtuse bovine herd animal," Beals said, turning his head toward the cashier's voice, "is disturbing my hunt. No matter, my pets will enjoy feasting upon her flesh."

"No!" I said.

"You could have avoided this, Miss Smoot." Beals spread his wings and beat the air. "Her blood will be on your hands."

On command, the insects attacked.

I couldn't let Beals hurt the woman. "Get down!"

As the swarm poured over the top of the shelves, I dived forward, grabbed her waistband, and yanked her down.

"Get offa me!" She conked me with the phone.

Ow! That's the thanks I got?

I ripped the phone out of her hand. "They sting, stupid!" I whispered.

"What stings?"

"Them! They do!" Think fast, girl. "The bees! The whole store's infested."

*Bees*, she mouthed. I could see the gears grinding in her head. "Help me! I'm allergic to bees!" She kicked loose and crawled back to the counter.

"Kill the woman." Again, Beals beat his wings.

I vaulted the counter and then pushed the cashier to the floor.

*Splat!* The swarm hit the shelves above us. A few were smashed against the cigarette display. The others took off immediately.

They circled the store.

Once. Twice. Three times.

Faster and faster until they blurred.

Down the aisle, Beals called out, "Come out, come out, wherever you are."

His voice was quiet, almost sweet, and I had to fight the urge to answer. He made his way toward us, turning his head, tasting the air with his forked tongue.

I hauled the cashier up by the collar. "Outside. Not safe in here."

"Hold your horses. I don't see no bees." She tried to look. But I held her collar tight.

"That's because"—I shoved her out the door and threw the lock—"they're invisible."

"Ah, there you are." Beals turned to face me, his eyes still swollen shut. "Attack!"

The flies soared to the ceiling.

Then dive-bombed me.

I snatched a newspaper from the rack, folded it up, and swung hard.

The bodies of a dozen bugs exploded against the paper.

Their guts melted down the newsprint, and I swung again.

The flies roared past and a few splattered against the locked door. More bloody innards dripped down the glass.

"Yes!"

Beals howled. "My pets!"

I grabbed a can of SPAM, took aim at his head, and let it rip.

*Thunk!*

It bounced off his skull. He roared, "You little bitch!"

Hold up. Don't nobody call me a bitch. Before, I'd have been happy just to get out of here in one piece. Now, it was on!

I yanked more ammunition off the shelves—buns, bread, canned chili, pork and beans, and Vienna sausages. I fired the projectiles, one can after another.

*Ping! Ping! Ping!*

Beals stumbled back toward the cooler.

"Cease!" he bellowed. "You will be punished for this insult."

Keep down, girl, and keep quiet. If he can't find you, the flies can't sting you.

I grabbed two cans of EZ Cheez spray and crawled to the end of aisle three.

There he stood, my little owl-eyed man, his glasses tilting to one side, eyes puffy and swollen. He turned his head from side to side, listening.

A purple-colored goose egg was rising on his forehead.

Serves you right, I thought.

I flung the cheese cans at him and sprinted to the drink cooler. I cut hard to the left. Ducked behind a beer display for a second to catch my breath and then squat-ran to the next aisle, behind the health, beauty, and car care section.

I checked the antitheft mirrors.

Beals's hide glowed blood red, and his triangular face was contorted in a mask of rage.

He stood surrounded by a pile of busted jars, bottles, and cans. Impaled on one of his horns was a loaf of bread. Strands of spray cheese decorated his body like a string of saucy garland.

I snorted—it just slipped out.

"Ravage her!"

Ravage? I stood up. "Hold up, asshole. The contract didn't say nothing—"

Before I could react, the monster-sized fly jetted across the store. It smacked my face, bit my hands when I shielded myself. It lighted in my hair, latching onto my dreads, and sunk its jaws into my scalp.

"Goddamn it!" I screamed and cussed.

I slapped at it, clawing and scratching to get free.

Half-crazed, I scanned the shelves of motor oil, filter

wrenches, air fresheners, zit cream, rubbing alcohol, and cans of hair spray for something, anything I could use.

Wait a second.

Hair spray?

I grabbed a can of Super Hold. Shut my eyes. Clenched my lips. And doused my whole head.

The fly dropped like, well, a dead fly. It hit the floor with a crack, the sound of a brick falling.

I raised my foot. And stomped.

The insect's body crumpled, like a chunk of burned coal.

"Smoot!"

That's my name, don't wear it out, I thought. Try to find me now, asshole.

Quietly, I armed myself with more Super Hold and sneaked over to the next aisle. Then the next, keeping an eye on him in the mirrors.

Beals was standing three feet from me, only the display racks separating us. My heart raced with excitement and fear. It terrified me to think of what Beals would do if I failed. But the thought of nailing his ass made me so happy, I almost giggled.

I rose from my crouch with a can of hair spray in each hand and aimed carefully, my fingers on the nozzles ready to fire.

Beals sniffed. His forked tongue licked the air. "Ah, my little mouse has come to its senses."

He turned to me.

The tongue tasted my scent.

He raised a taloned hand toward my face.

"Fire!"

Hair spray shot out of the nozzles in a thick, double mist.

Beals threw back his head and bellowed, a shock wave of sound that rattled the store windows. His wings smashed into the ceilings and his talons tore the air. He swung at the spray cans, but I ducked as he swiped, and then I sidestepped, unloading the contents.

When I was through, he was a statue. A giant, ugly, vandalized living sculpture that smelled like potted meat, farts, and processed cheese. But a statue just the same.

I snagged a full can of Super Hold hair spray from the shelf, and I victory-danced around him.

"How you like them apples, Beals? Now who's the bitch? That's what you get for messing with Bug Smoot. That's right. Uh-huh."

Another few sprays, and all of the flies were history. When the Super Hold hit them, they shriveled up and dropped to the floor, hard chunks of ash. I finished them off with a few satisfying stomps.

"That'll hold your ass for a while."

Time to go—I wanted to be miles away when Beals unfroze.

# CHAPTER 18

# The Deal Breaker

I took off in the Cadillac and in a few seconds, the store and Beals were in my rearview.

"Yo, Pesto," I said when my boy answered his cell a few minutes later, "is that apartment over y'all's store still available? I'm ready to move in. Right now."

He let out a whoop, and then I told him about affixing Beals.

"Righteous!" he said. "Just make sure you're nowhere near when he unfreezes. He's likely to be a little angry."

I felt a little sorry for the mess I'd left for the cashier. "I froze his ass in a convenience store. I'm going to be miles away."

"That's cool. I'll report the incident to the NAD," he said, "so they can send in a sanitizer crew. Oh yeah, before I forget,

E. Figg's been calling looking for you. She found something in the contract and needs to see you ASAP. Her words."

"That don't sound like good news," I said. But I was too pumped to care.

We agreed to meet at the car wash, then take Pesto's car to the law office. There wasn't no way of knowing how long Beals would stayed affixed, even covered in two whole cans of Super Hold, so I wanted to park the Cadillac at the Rainbow to throw him off the trail. He could probably follow me anywhere, but I wanted him to have to choose between guarding the car and guarding me.

On the way to the law office, Pesto told me all about E. Figg. Check that, told me all he knew, which wasn't that much since he got it all secondhand from his mother.

E. Figg was a mystery. She had law degrees hanging on her office wall, but they were from the 1940s, and no way was she that old. Pesto said the diplomas were fake. She was a lawyer because she had passed the bar exam, but Pesto said she had been a doctor during World War I, a suffragette in New York, a buccaneer in the Caribbean, a French revolutionary, and even the queen of a small Mediterranean country.

There was a pattern with E. Figg's jobs. They all gave her the chance to steal without getting caught, and they gave her the chance to help folks who didn't have nobody in their life to help them. Folks like me.

Nobody knew how old she really was, though some people had their suspicions, and nobody in Pesto's line of work paid much mind to it. Two-thousand-year-old people weren't unusual, and everybody knew that demons and angels were immortal. They did know that she'd been making noise about leaving town soon. They also knew that she had a grudge against Beals and had been waiting for the chance to get him in a beatdown.

Pesto thought that was why she took my case. I was one of the "downtrodden," and it gave her a chance to get a little payback on the demon. When I asked him why E. Figg hated Beals so much, he didn't know the answer. She kept her own secrets.

"She's going to help me, right?" I asked Pesto as we got to E. Figg's office door.

"If she can't, dude," he said, opening the door for me, "nobody can."

"Have a seat," E. Figg said, pointing at a couple of high-back chairs. She cut right to the chase. "I've got bad news and worse news. Which do you want first?"

"Bad," Pesto said.

"Worse," I said.

"Bad it is. We established the fact that your grandfather offered both the Cadillac and his soul as collateral for the loan." She cleared her throat. "Instead of fulfilling the terms of the contract, his soul somehow found a way to escape capture. That triggered the repossession clause, which calls for the car to be returned to its owner on a certain time and place. That time is October thirty-first, at the stroke of eleven fifty-nine P.M., and the place is Smuggler's Gap at the top of the Trans-Mountain Highway."

"Okay," I said. "What's the worst part?"

"The worst part is," E. Figg said, "my colleague deciphered the hieroglyphics and found an unusual clause there." She grimaced like my Auntie Pearl about to yank off a Band-Aid, so whatever E. had to say, it was really going to sting. "It states that if the original signer refuses to surrender his soul, the cosigner forfeits all rights to collateral, including the cosigner's soul."

"But I'm the cosigner." My lip quivered. "The collateral is my soul? *My* soul? That ain't right."

E. Figg spun the contract around. "This is your signature?"

"Yeah, but—"

"You were thirteen years of age at the time of signing?"

"Yeah, I—"

"Which means you agreed to surrender your soul if your grandfather reneged on the agreement. In short, Miss Smoot, you made a deal with the devil."

No, I didn't; Papa C did. He was always hocking something to get some extra cash. I never dreamed he'd hock me, too.

"The signature is legal," she said. "The contract is binding."

I slapped the big oak desk. The contract, a pencil holder, a cup of paper clips, and E. Figg's nameplate all jumped about a foot. "That . . . that . . ." I let out a string of four-letter words that could have blistered paint. "He pawned me."

"You're referring to?"

"Papa C! That asshole pawned me! The one person on this Earth who loved him."

E. Figg straightened up her desk while looking straight into my eyes. "Unfortunately, your grandfather chose to involve you in this."

It still wasn't making any sense. I asked, "Why would you need a cosigner on a soul, anyway?"

"Maybe your grandfather's soul wasn't of sufficient value to cover the cost of the vehicle. Or perhaps he had a history of not honoring his debts."

I couldn't argue with that. "But I ain't done nothing wrong. I ain't hurt nobody, stole nothing, or had premarital relations. What else is a girl supposed to do? I can't lose my soul for eternity. Think of all the church-going I'd be wasting."

Pesto stood behind me, hands resting on my shoulders.

"Dude, don't give up hope. E. Figg knows how to break the contract. Right?"

E. Figg didn't flinch. The woman could play World Series poker, her face was so straight. "The best option," she said, "would be for your grandfather to honor the terms of the contract. Mrs. Valencia tells me that you tried to make contact?"

"Didn't do no damn good," I said. "He's skipped out, and even my Auntie Pearl can't convince him to turn himself in. She used to be able to make him do almost anything." Except stop drinking. He did that for me.

E. Figg muttered, "Men" under her breath. "Okay, there is one way to break this contract, but only at great cost. There is a common-law escape clause left in the language, because Scratch has a legendary weakness for competition. Are you familiar with the musical tradition of two musicians challenging each other to a competition?"

"Yeah, it's called cutting heads," I said. "But I ain't got a musical bone in my body. I don't even own no instrum—"

"It doesn't have to be an instrument," she said, interrupting me. She kept checking her watch, which meant she was either calculating my bill or had a deadline. "Do you have any particular skill at which you excel?"

Basketball, I thought, except it'd been forever since I touched a ball. "No."

"None?"

"Not no more."

"Think, Miss Smoot. What do you do best?" she said.

Pesto cleared his throat. "Dude, what do you spend all of your time doing? Hint, hint. Car. Hint, hint."

"Driving," I said, not appreciating his tone. "Delivering pizzas. That's about all I can do."

"Pizzas?" she said.

"I am the bomb when it comes to delivering pies. Ask my asshole former boss, Vinnie."

"Pizza. It's unorthodox, but Mr. Scratch likes a challenge." She got up, showing us the door. "I'll contact his attorneys, and we'll negotiate. If they agree, I'll let you know what they say."

"But Beals keeps on saying I'm running out of time. Makes a noise like a clock ticking."

E. Figg rolled her eyes. "Don't fall for that old trick. He's been doing it forever. Thinks it adds a sense of urgency."

Damn right it does, I thought.

Outside, she smiled, showing off two rows of perfect dental work. "Enjoy your Halloween. I mean that." She winked. "Eat lots of chocolate."

"Wait," I said. "What about your fee? We ain't—"

She waved me off. "I'm taking your case pro bono."

"My name's Bug, not Bono."

Pesto said softly, "'Pro bono' means for free."

Oh. "Why?" Why did she make a big fuss about her fee when she knew I didn't have the cash? Maybe I didn't want no charity from her.

"When we met, I didn't realize that your soul was in the contract, too. Call me naïve, but I assumed your case was about a car and an irresponsible male. When it's an innocent girl, that changes my perspective. I owe that snake Beals a little payback, and if I can stop him from doing his job, it will bring me great satisfaction."

"A'ight then," I said, holding up a fist for a little dap. Anybody who wanted to bust Beals was straight with me. She smiled, shook her head like it was the silliest thing, and gave me some dap back. Maybe E. Figg wasn't so uptight after all.

"Since you're my lawyer now—Vinnie wrote me a bad check," I said, reaching in my pocket, then handing the check to her. "Ain't that against the law?"

E. Figg took it. She read it hard for a few seconds, then smiled. "I would like to buy this check from you."

"The lady at the bank says it ain't worth the paper it's wrote on."

"To her, maybe." Before I could turn her down again, she ducked inside and returned with her wallet. She pulled the money out and paid me the face value of the check. "My people will take care of this."

I hoped that meant *The Sopranos* way of taking care of things.

"One more thing," E. Figg said. "I've heard through the grapevine that Beals is unbound from the car and from the roux line."

When I nodded yes, she said, "Be extremely careful around him, Bug. An unfettered demon is dangerous to all of us." With that she smiled, like she knew a secret she wasn't telling, went inside, and locked the door.

# CHAPTER 19

# Home Again

After we left E. Figg's office, I went into a blue funk. I had to get used to the possibility that I could lose my own soul, and that ain't an idea that you can wrap your head around. It's not like finding out everyday bad news, like a sprained knee's going to keep you on the bench for two weeks or Medicare has decided it ain't paying for the stroke medicine your granddaddy needs. A few years ago, a few months ago, hell, a few hours ago, that was how I categorized bad news. Losing your soul to the devil took bad news to a whole new level.

Being me, though, I decided not to fret about it. There's a chest in my brain where I can lock the blues away. It was a skill I learned playing ball because you've got to clear everything else out of your mind and focus on the game. Not even the game but the play, the pick, the shot, your fingertips kissing the pebbled surface of the basketball.

So I folded that funky mood up like a blanket, put it into the chest, and turned the lock. "I want to move into the apartment over the store," I had told Pesto as we inched through traffic on the Trans-Mountain Loop. "Right now. You willing to give your girl a hand?" In my experience, staying busy was the best way to keep the chest locked.

"We should've gone back to the store," Pesto said as we parked in the carport next to my apartment, "to get the truck."

"Why we need a truck?" I asked as Pesto followed me inside the building.

"So we can move your stuff to the new place in one trip, right? There's, like, no room in the Jeep for your furniture."

Since Mr. Payne rented the apartment furnished, I told Pesto we didn't have to worry. "All I got is my clothes, some pictures, and a couple pots and pans for cooking."

It took about fifteen minutes to get my whole wardrobe and my pictures into four plastic garbage bags. We loaded the kitchen stuff into a wooden box that I had used as an end table, and then we were ready to catch fire out of that mug.

"Do you want to, you know," Pesto said when I said it was time to go, "look around, say *adios*?"

"To who? The cockroaches?" I said. "Hell, no. I can't wait till the door hits me in the ass."

I pushed the door open with my foot, swung around with the loaded box on one hip, and rammed into the paunchy potbelly of Mr. Payne, who had appeared out of nowhere, right in my path. The force of the collision knocked him backward onto his butt, and the bottom of the box fell out, spilling the kitchen stuff into the rocks and dirt.

"Watch it!" he yelled.

"Watch it your damned self," I said, throwing the box aside. "Look what you did to my stuff. Ain't enough you're evicting me, you got to get up in my grill, too."

He didn't get off the ground, just laid there like somebody was going to offer him a hand up. That'd be a cold day in hell.

"I saw you'uns sneaking off without paying what you owe me," he said. "Just like you people."

"What kind of people would that be?" Pesto, who had followed me outside, set down the bags, and started collecting the things that had dropped.

Mr. Payne gave him a hard, long look with his good eye. "A Mexican. I might've known, I might have known. Can't find a feller of your own kind to shack up with, Eunice?"

I picked up my best pot and swung it at his head. He zagged at the last second, and the bottom of the pot glanced off the peak of his skull. It knocked off his lame comb-over, which turned out to be a cheap, moth-eaten toupee and not a comb-over at all. I would've swung again if I hadn't been laughing so hard.

Mr. Payne took that chance to get to his feet. He mumbled something under his breath and spat on his palm. He rubbed the spit on his head and then slapped the toupee back in place.

"Bug," Pesto said after I dropped the pot back into the box, "could you go to the Jeep, please. I'll take care of the mess."

"Why?" I said. "You about to kick his ass, dog?"

Mr. Payne shook his fist at us. "Hold on one cotton-picking minute. Take one step, and I'm calling the deputy with the Taser back out here."

"You want money, here, take some money." I pulled out the cash E. Figg had given me and counted out enough to cover the days I owed for. Then I wadded up the bills and fired them one at the time at his face. "Take your freaking money. I don't give a damn about money or this apartment or you, you bigoted, lying, bullying piece of armadillo shit!"

"Bug," Pesto said, "please."

The tone of his voice didn't have please in it. "A'ight then," I said through ragged breaths, because I was about to cry, and that's the last thing I wanted to let Payne see me do.

I took the bags from him and walked around to the carport.

I dumped the bags into the back of the Jeep and got in the front seat. Arms crossed, I frumped about not being able to make out nothing they were saying, though I heard the murmur of their voices.

A few minutes later, Pesto joined me and started backing out.

"Ain't you going to tell me what's up?" I said.

"I had business to settle with Mr. Payne," he said, and then his lips clamped tight, meaning he was done talking about the subject. I didn't feel like talking about it, either.

As we pulled out, the headlights of the Jeep shone on the side of the yellow-bricked row house. Standing in the shadows was the coyote, its eyes reflecting the light. Its head was sagging, and all of its ribs showed through its fur. After telling Pesto to hold up, I jumped down and ran around to the garbage cans. To keep animals out, Mr. Payne had tied down the lids with bungee cords, which I popped off every cover, right before I tipped the cans over on the ground.

"Happy Halloween, dog," I said as I jumped back into the Jeep.

"You up for some trick-or-treating?" I asked, grabbing Pesto's hand and lacing my fingers between his, hoping he didn't pull away. Which he didn't. "Thought we might take E. Figg's advice about eating lots of chocolate."

"Maybe," he said. "I know some outrageous neighborhoods for chocolate bars."

"Dude, that would be so righteous," I said, grinning as I imitated him, and we headed out to enjoy what could be the last free night of my life.

# CHAPTER 20

# Running with the Devil

By the time eleven o'clock rolled around, the whole backseat of Pesto's Jeep was full of plastic bags of candy. The clock was almost done ticking, which made me excited and sick to my stomach at the same time. Maybe it was the chocolate.

"Look at the sky," Pesto said as we drove through the *barrio*.

While we'd been trick-or-treating, the sky had been clear with a full moon throwing shadows, the light was so bright. But as we got closer to the Rainbow Auto Wash, a thunderhead rolled in. The cloud blocked out the moon and stars. With a crack of thunder, the sky opened up, dumping a boatload of hail on the street. No little hail, neither. These suckers were the size of gum balls.

"That came out of nowhere," Pesto said.

He hit the wipers, and I pushed up the cloth top of the Jeep to keep the ice from collecting.

Then as quick as it started, the hailstorm quit. The thunderhead rolled away, and then the moon came out again. Me and Pesto traded a look.

"What you thinking, dog?"

He tapped the steering wheel anxiously. "At ISIS, there's been *mucho* buzz about anomalous phenomena. Weird weather patterns, unusual animal behavior, seismic activity."

"Meaning what?"

"I'm not sure. It's probably bad."

Probably bad. The boy had a gift for understatement, that's for sure. I took a deep breath and stared out the window. The weather was changing, again turning colder, with a bite in the air. The palm trees planted in the median twisted in the growing wind, which made the dead fronds clatter like bone chimes. Every house had window boxes stuffed with damianita, chocolate daisies, and oversized roses that bloomed as big as your hand. For some reason, I couldn't smell them as we drove by. They had no scent at all.

We found Beals in the front seat of the Cadillac, acting like he'd never left it. He was pissed about the whole hair spray thing, I could tell, but he didn't go all demonic on us like I'd expected. He didn't even speak until Pesto locked the Jeep inside the car wash, and we piled into the Cadillac with our bags and bags of Halloween candy.

"How," Beals said, "did you spend your last free hours, Miss Smoot? Hazarding pedestrians? Overindulging in fatty foods? Wallowing in self-pity?"

I answered his snotty question with a, "None of the above." I pulled onto the highway headed toward the Trans-Mountain Loop. "Tonight is Halloween. Me and my boy Pesto went trick-or-treating."

"What a splendid way to enter a race for your soul, engorged with trans fats and cocoa butter. But wait, aren't you too old for that charming but antiquated ritual?" he said.

"Mr. Beals," I said, "ain't nobody ever too old for some chocolate."

He made a gagging sound but kept right on jawing. "What is next on your agenda, a lovely visit to the *mamasita*'s plot on All Souls' Day? Dressing as a corpse for the Day of the Dead? Perhaps as your own grandfather? Oh, forgive me. I'd forgotten that these are your last hours on Earth. There will be no more celebrations for you."

"Dog," I asked Pesto, catching his eye in the mirror, "are all demons huge assholes?"

"Yes—but not this huge."

"Ticktock," Beals murmured.

Like I needed a reminder.

So I drove the highway up to Smuggler's Gap on the top of the Franklin Mountains to meet my fate. I was as quiet as a graveyard.

After Papa C's heart attack, the doctors at the health center kept saying he had the wrong cholesterols. He had all of the bad kind, and none of the good. When they wrote him a prescription for some pills to balance it out, he didn't have the money to pay the drugstore to fill it. Keep this up, they kept telling him, and your ass is going to die of the heart attack. But it wasn't a heart attack that took him. It was a MeMo's chicken bone. MeMo's was a restaurant down off the Boulevard, back up in the neighborhood where Papa C stayed when he was a boy. It's got what Papa C used to call soul food, which meant collards and chitterlings. The smell by itself was enough to make me sick to my stomach. Papa C loved it, though, because he said it smelled like home.

Last year, two days before Christmas, Papa C drove us crosstown in his Cadillac for our Day Before Christmas Eve dinner. Papa C wore his hair combed slick with pomade. Murray's Original was the only brand he'd buy. It came in a tin, which he'd put on the stove to warm up and then dab some on a brush to run through his hair. Once it got in, that pomade wasn't coming off, and it made his head smell like the Cadillac when we changed the oil.

Every time we went to MeMo's, he ordered the special, which was wings and gizzards with sides of greens, fried okra, and biscuits with chowchow. I wasn't hungry, so I got a bowl of rice pudding and some sweet tea. It was too hot in there to eat, even with ceiling fans going overhead. My mind was still stuck on losing that game to Coronado, and Papa C was trying to talk me out of having the blues.

"That hootchie mama ain't got nothing on you, Bug. Just got lucky, that's all."

I leaned back in the rickety chair, tugging on the edge of a red-and-white-checkered plastic tablecloth. "That's what I'm saying. God was on her side that night."

Papa C pulled out a hunk of chicken wing with his false teeth. "Don't be saying that. It's blasphemy."

"All I'm saying is, it was like there was an angel sitting up on the rim making her sorry-ass shot go in."

"Bug, let me tell you something, and it ain't something you need to be repeating around Christian folks." He leaned in close to me, whispering through the hunk of chicken he was chewing. "They wasn't no angel helping that girl, it was the dev—ack! Ack!"

Papa C's eyes got so wide they about popped out. He clawed

at his throat. When he tried to talk, nothing came out but pan-icked air. That's when I knew he had inhaled a chicken bone. Back in freshman year, we learned about the Heimlich maneu-ver, so I ran around to his side of the table, meaning to use it on him before the bone got stuck.

Before I could reach him, this big-bellied fool wearing a garbage man uniform came out of nowhere. I tried to squeeze around him, but he was the size of a sumo wrestler, and I couldn't get by.

"Hold on," he said, getting right behind Papa C. "I'll fix you right up."

He slapped Papa C on the back hard three times. That was the way they tried to unchoke folks back in the day, but in my class they said backslapping was just as likely to make some-thing stick as it was to get it out.

"Step off, fool," I said, pushing the garbage man.

He smiled with shiny teeth. "Just trying to lend a hand, little miss."

After wrapping my arms around Papa C, I jammed a fist in his belly below the rib cage. I pulled sharply as hard as I could. Two times I tried, and nothing happened. Papa C was fighting for breath now, and he twisted and clawed like a cat dipped in water.

The third time, the last time I yanked, there was a popping

sound. A plug of wing meat came flying out of his mouth. I was a hero. I'd saved my Papa C's life.

"Thank the Lord," I said, expecting Papa C to take a big breath.

Something was wrong. He didn't breathe at all. Instead, he went slack, and I had to hold on to keep him from falling into the biscuits and chowchow.

"Help me!" I screamed, looking around for the garbage man, but he was gone.

I stumbled back, crashed into the table and chairs behind me, and landed on my butt on the floor. Papa C was still in my arms, and I was trying to get my fist back down for another Heimlich when his body went limp. There was a bunch of hollering and yelling, and folks came running to help. It was too late. Papa C was dead.

Turned out, the wad of meat wasn't the only thing stuck in his throat. There was a piece of wing bone down in his windpipe. The doctors in the hospital said they'd never seen one down so far before. When I told them about the fat-ass garbage man whacking Papa C, they said that's what probably forced it deep. I wanted to kill that garbage man, and I wanted the police to arrest him. The cops didn't do nothing about it. They said he was just being a good Samaritan, and anyhow, nobody at MeMo's remembered seeing a man the size of the Franklin

Mountains. It was like he'd never even been there.

It's funny how memories come to mind at the weirdest time. But it wasn't really weird for me to think of Papa C's death, under the circumstances. It was the circumstances that were the really weird thing.

When we got to the turnoff for Smuggler's Gap, I decided to keep on going, just to see what would happen. Beals was ready for me, though. The car braked by itself, and the steering wheel moved in my hands. The blinker signaled the turn I was making against my will.

"We mustn't arrive late for our date with destiny," Beals said.

"You suck," I told him.

"There, there, Miss Smoot, do not despair. Damnation isn't so terrible, once you've grown accustomed to it." He laughed behind a hand. "Of course, it does smart a tad when your soul is ripped from its mortal cage, but the pain fades, it fades."

"No matter what happens," I snarled, "you still suck."

I checked the rearview. Pesto stuck out his tongue while making horns with his fingers. I laughed out loud.

"We have arrived," Beals said, keeping me on task. "Turn left here and take the first space."

I pulled into a parking area. There wasn't anybody else around, though, except some coyotes howling nearby and a sky full of stars overhead, until E. Figg pulled up in a gold Mercedes.

Me and Pesto got out to meet her. Beals stayed in the Cadillac, but I could tell he was watching E. as she touched up her makeup and then got out of the car. She held up a red document. It was tri-folded, with a black wax seal.

"Scratch accepted the offer," E. Figg said, waving the document like a trophy. "With one contingency."

My knees sagged in relief. I was a bundle of nerves. How could somebody be happy about having to race the devil? But I was. Pesto must've known I was worried because he put an arm around my shoulder and pulled me close.

"What's the contingency?" I asked.

E. Figg patted my shoulder, too, which made my knees sag again because it had to be bad news. "Scratch insists on your free will as the wager."

"My what?" I said. "My soul's already on the line. What good is my free will?"

Pesto groaned. He explained that even when Scratch had your soul under contract, you at least had the rest of your life to live, as long as you kept your free will. "If you give that up, you're enslaved to Old Scratch, and you go work undercover for him, helping to collect souls."

"Listen carefully, please," E. Figg said. "The rules must be followed to the letter." She went on to explain the setup: It was a two-driver race. Both drivers would get an address to deliver a pizza to. The first one to the house was the winner. If I won, I got to keep the car and my soul. Plus, Papa C would be released from the contract.

"What if I don't win the race?" I said.

Beals stage-whispered, "It's a trade secret."

"You little snake, it is not." E. Figg cleared her throat then said, "The terms are very clear. If you fail to win the race for any reason, you lose everything. If you make a wager with Scratch, it's all or nothing."

"I accept the terms," I said, because I knew in my heart that I could win.

"The die is cast," Beals said.

That's when we heard the deep throttle of an engine, and everybody fell silent. I recognized the car as it rounded the corner, a black BMW E38 735i. It rolled into a parking spot, and the door opened. The air turned cold. I caught my breath. It felt like I had just swallowed an icicle, and goose bumps popped out all over my arms. I could tell Pesto felt it, too. His arm shivered, and I could see his breath freezing in the air.

I don't know what I was expecting. A giant diablo with red skin, horns, black goatee, and a long tail like Beals. Or maybe a Paul Bunyan–looking man, with crazy-ass hair and a beard, somebody who could snap your spine in half with his pinkie. Or maybe an evil leprechaun with a pot of gold for buying souls. Whatever I was expecting, this wasn't it.

Old Scratch didn't look old at all. His hair was jet black, and he wore it slicked back and pulled into a short ponytail. He had a goatee, which was trimmed neat, and he was average height, not much taller than Pesto. His suit was white, double-breasted, and his shoes were so polished, they shined white in the moonlight. When he stalked toward us, it was like seeing a jaguar move, muscled and powerful, watching, gauging us, ready to strike any time it felt the urge.

"Miss Smoot," he said in a low country accent, taking my hand and kissing it, "*ma chère*, we meet again."

The skin on my hand burned. "Again?" I blushed. For a demon, he was dead sexy. Him and Beals wasn't nothing alike.

"You and I were acquainted when your grandfather signed the contract for his Cadillac. I trust he was satisfied with the vehicle? It was the finest of its day, as I recall."

Then I remembered. "But he was fat and—"

He smiled, and I felt something light and warm in my belly. "And how are you feeling? Full of vim and vigor, I hope."

"I'm fine, no thanks to you," I said, pushing that warm feeling away. I want to stay good and pissed off, ready to poke his eyes out. "So fine that I'm ready to kick your ass right now."

Scratch's smile fell, like he was disappointed that I wasn't buying his line of bull. He snapped his fingers, and Vinnie—my freaking boss, Vinnie—hopped out of the BMW, two large pizzas in his hands. He wore the heavy leather jacket and boots, along with a black bandana tied pirate-style over his head.

"Vinnie?" I said. "You sold your soul for a pizza joint? Dang, that's just sad."

"Up yours," he shot back, "you lazy little c—"

"Vincent, mind your tongue. Young ladies shouldn't hear such language." Scratch snapped his fingers again, and Vinnie's red Indian Four bike appeared, along with a sidecar. "He sold his soul for a motorcycle. And his free will for a lifetime supply of gasoline, bless his heart. He didn't own the pizzeria, either. He only managed it for me. A little white lie on his part."

So Vinnie and Papa C had something in common—they both loved machines and they both were stupid.

"Beals," Scratch said, and handed him a copy of the red document. "I leave the matter in your hands while I seek an adequate position from which to watch the show. Ms. Figg, lovely to see you again, *ma chère*."

One more snap, and he was back in the BMW, roaring out of the parking lot. Beals sighed, like it was all a big burden on him. But when nobody but me was looking, he winked.

Before I could react, Vinnie gunned his bike. "Let's do this thing," he said, trying to sound confident. His voice was shaking, and I could tell he was just as worried as me.

"We're waiting on you, Vinnie." I held out my hands to take a pizza from him, but he flipped it to Pesto, who was busy sipping from a bottle of water to wash down all that chocolate.

"Dude," Pesto said. "I don't eat pizza."

That's when E. Figg stepped in. "In order to make sure that Vinnie runs an honest, aka nonsupernatural, race, we agreed that an innocent soul would accompany him. So, Pesto will ride with Vinnie, and Beals will ride with Bug."

Beals sighed. "Why must I suffer the bad driver?"

"Shut up," I told him. "I got the worst end of this deal."

"No way," Pesto said. "I got the worst end of it. I have to ride with Vinnie Soprano here." On his way to his spot on Vinnie's bike, he touched my neck and leaned in close to my ear. "Be careful," he whispered. "Don't trust Beals."

"I don't trust anybody," I whispered back and then said, "See y'all at the bottom."

Vinnie gunned his bike again. The sky above him filled up with blue smoke. It made the whole parking lot stink like exhaust. "I said, let's do this. It's midnight already."

E. Figg took a pizza from Vinnie and dropped it onto Beals's lap. He picked it up the way you hold a dirty diaper and set it on the floorboard.

"The address is on the box." E. Figg patted my shoulder, then gave me a quick hug. I could smell her jojoba shampoo and a hint of perfume. It reminded me of roses. "Best of luck," she said. "Break a leg."

"Yeah," Vinnie said. He plugged one nostril and blew snot at my car. "Or your neck."

"Kiss my ass," I said.

Vinnie made an obscene gesture with his fist. "So, you think you're something at making deliveries, huh, girlie? Watch and learn how a man takes care of business."

He cranked up the bike. Pesto, who looked scared as hell, slid into the sidecar, holding the pizza like it was a life preserver.

Before anybody could even say, "Ready, set," Vinnie gunned it, popped a wheelie, and then his head exploded in flames. His flesh started bubbling off, dripping down his collar. My boy Pesto didn't flinch at all. He stood up in the sidecar, uncapped his bottle of water, and drained it on Vinnie's head. The fire went out, which left Vinnie's face looking like a melted bobble-head.

"That's a good look for you, Vin," I hollered.

With a scream that sounded more like a gurgle, Vinnie roared out of the lot, leaving me sitting at the starting line. I stomped the accelerator, and the Cadillac lurched forward.

"Wait!" E. Figg yelled after me. "Make sure you follow all laws—"

"No time for chitchat!" Beals bellowed right in my ear. "Vincent is escaping!"

# CHAPTER 21

# A Shortcut to the Soul

By the time I was out of the parking slot, the brake lights of the motorcycle were like two eyes blinking in the distance.

I hated cheaters.

"What's the address?" I asked Beals.

"1666 Deadrich Street," he said. "Does it matter, Miss Smoot? Even a notorious lead foot such as yourself is destined to lose. Ticktock."

"I wish you was an alarm clock so I could slap your snooze bar."

The road stretched out long, flat, and straight. The grass beside the road was mangy as a coyote's back. A cloud floated by the horizon, the only hint of moisture anywhere.

It looked like the race was already over. But I'd delivered a pie to that same address many times before. The man who lived there was a damn good tipper. The road the house was on went up the side of the mountains, and the house itself was in a ravine, which started way up on the Trans-Mountain Loop. The only way to get to the house was to go all the way down into town and then back up through the neighborhood. Did Vinnie know that? If he didn't, I could beat him just by knowing the territory, as well as a couple of cut-throughs to shave off time.

"Vincent has GPS," Mr. Beals said like he could read my mind.

"Bite me."

"Don't tempt me."

Slamming the gas pedal down to the floor, I hit ninety going down the straightaway. Beals actually grabbed hold of the hand rest, and I could see little licking flames coming out of his nose.

"Scared?" I said.

"Only of your driving."

I laughed. Serves you right, you ugly demon.

There wasn't much traffic on the Loop, but I had to keep swerving around the cars and trucks that were there. I was beginning to give up hope. How could I catch up to the devil's motorcycle?

I heard the coyote before I saw it, a long, lonesome howl that caught my attention like it was talking to me. It appeared in the rearview, running behind the car, matching my pace. What the f—? No way could a normal coyote do that.

I gunned it and after a few minutes, moved ahead of the coyote. Then I saw them, the taillights of the motorcycle glowing, just turning down onto the first stretch of the Loop. I slammed the brakes, tires squealing like a sister with a bad perm, and clipped the guardrail on the left side of the ridge.

Beals screamed, his voice high like a little girl's.

"Shut that up, you big sissy."

"Do not damage the collateral!" he said, almost spitting out the words. "I am on the verge of consummating my plan."

"Plan? What plan?"

"Mind the road!"

"Let me do the driving." I jerked the wheel, swinging wildly into the opposite lane.

"Miss Smoot, you cannot kill yourself in an accident! Shut up and drive!"

The Cadillac fishtailed. The engine pulsed, and when I whipped around the next turn, I was side by side with the motorcycle. I glanced into the sidecar, and Pesto looked like he'd swallowed his own tonsils.

"You okay?" I hollered, and took my eyes off the road for a split second.

Mistake. Big mistake.

A landslide popped up out of nowhere, and Vinnie took the chance to swerve over and push me against it. My right fender caught a guardrail. Showers of sparks flew, lighting up the night sky, and it sounded like the metal was peeling off one strip at a time.

I slammed the brakes, and the motorcycle moved ahead. Vinnie took the next turn like he was on rails. I gunned it to catch up, and that's when I heard a sound like metallic popcorn, the clattering sound of the engine. Damn.

Vinnie was way ahead now, almost finished running the Loop. No way would I ever catch him, especially if he kept running me off the road, and he had to know I wasn't about to slam into him with Pesto in the sidecar. In a few minutes, he'd hit the EP and from there, get to the house ahead of me. No shortcuts could slice that much time off.

Past the highway, I could see down into the ravines that led to the city. The lights from El Paso were like a beacon that I couldn't follow.

Then I heard it again, the coyote howling. It was running with us, this time on Beals's side. As we hit a sharp curve, it sprinted ahead and jumped up on the retainer wall.

"Turn there!" Beals commanded.

I didn't think, just reacted. I slammed the brakes, yanked

the wheel to the right, and headed into the ravine.

The coyote jumped in front of the car, barking insanely. I swerved hard to miss it, and we flew toward a dry creek bed. The Cadillac took flight. Beals screamed. I screamed. I bet the car even screamed.

And like a rock, we dropped down the ravine and landed in the creek bed with a loud crash.

"Yes!" I yelled as I gunned it. The Cadillac roared down the sandy, hard wash, bouncing like we had beach balls for wheels and throwing tons of dust into the air.

"Vinnie's got GPS, but I got mad skill," I said as the lights of 1666 Deadrich Street appeared over the bank.

Ahead, the coyote was standing on a boulder. I took that as a lucky sign. I drove out of the wash and across a short stretch of scrub. The Cadillac bounced one last time when we jumped the curb and landed at the foot of the driveway.

# CHAPTER 22
# 'Tis But a Scratch

The house on Deadrich Street had about six thousand rooms, three front porches with columns that reached up to heaven, and a swimming pool so big, my whole apartment building could take a bath in it. There was a line of big palm trees in front, all along the driveway that snaked down to the street. I pulled up to the garage, grabbed the pizza out of Beals's stunned hands, and ran up to ring the bell. When a middle-aged white man with a potbelly, dressed in a navy blue silk bathrobe, came to the door, I handed him the pizza.

"That was fast," he said, and gave me a wink. "You always was a lead foot."

Even though I'd delivered to this man at least once a week

215

for the last year, there was something different about him. That wink. That voice. So familiar.

"Papa C?" I whispered. "Is that you in there?"

"Who you think's been giving you a twenty-dollar tip once a week for almost the last year? Of course it's me. Shh." He put a finger to his lips. "We got to talk, Jitterbug. It's about a side deal I made. But I think the deal's gone bad. He's up to no good, this Beelz— You!"

"Ah, Mr. Smoot, you've revealed yourself," Beals said. "It's just as well. The man I arranged for you to possess will be so grateful to see you go. I trust you are prepared for your journey to hell?"

I ignored Beals and went straight for Papa C. "I can't believe it! You're alive and in the flesh and answering the doorbell? I ought to knock your fool head clean off! You got any idea what you put me through?"

"Bug, listen," he started. "I sold my soul to the devil to get that car, but then this Beelzebub here, he come to me saying he knew a way I could duck the repo. All I had to do was hide out for a year, and the contract was null and void. But that ain't so." He showed me his palm. A jagged, black scratch covered the lifeline. "The year ended at midnight, and Old Scratch still owns my soul."

"Indeed he does." Beals snapped his fingers, and Papa C

froze. "And when I extract it, it will finish my bound duty for this particularly rewarding project."

The demon leaned in, put his lips on Papa C's mouth, and sneezed twice. A purple aura appeared around the white man, a shadow of light. The aura took a human shape. It grew taller and thinner. Beals sneezed a third time, and the man's body fell backward onto the grass. Standing in his place was Papa C. Except he was purple and see-through, and looked like he was sleepwalking.

"Did you know," Beals said, "that the human soul weighs less than an ounce?"

I closed my mouth, which had fallen open. "That's Papa C's soul?"

"No," Beals said, "it is the shadow of his soul. His spirit is invisible to you."

"Papa C?" I reached out for the purple shadow, and my hands went right through it, like he was made out of steam. The aura dissolved into thin air. "Papa C," I called three times, but he wasn't nowhere to be found. "Beals! What kind of trick is this?"

"It is no trick," Mr. Beals said. "It is the termination of repossession. Since he is already dead, your grandfather's soul is now ready for transport to the underworld."

"What?" I said. "He's not going nowhere—I won."

"You did not win the race."

"Are you out of your mind, Mis-ter Beals? I finished first. Me, I did. I beat Vinnie down the mountain. Almost killed us both trying, too."

"No. You violated the terms of the contest, so you have forfeited your wager by leaving the highway, which E. Figg tried to warn you not to do."

"I—I—"

He got up in my face. "You—you did not listen. You—you acted impulsively, predictably. You—you cheated to win, the very act you profess to despise so much."

"What are you talking about? How did I cheat?"

"You turned off the highway. How many times must I explain this? Leaving the road is against the rules. You may not leave the road. It destroys the vehicle. It endangers the collateral. Leaving the road is a bad thing, Miss Smoot. A very bad thing, and you are a very bad girl who deserves to be punished."

"But you're the navigator. I was following your directions—doing what you told me."

"You listened to a demon? How unfortunate." Beals snapped his fingers, and the contract appeared in his hands. The stink of fire and brimstone filled the air.

Beals stuck a big magnifying glass beneath my nose. He held

the contract under it. "It says clearly on line number 123,666 that at no time during the race will the driver of the second part—that's you—"

"Don't be discussing parts without my lawyer here."

"—place the collateral in peril by commission of rash acts such as running down pedestrians, avoiding roadkill, or leaving the roadway."

He grinned, letting it sink in.

"Asshole. You set me up!"

"I merely provided the opportunity. You chose to seize it. Free will is a bitch, Miss Smoot."

"No, no, you're the bitch! How was I to know the rules? Didn't nobody tell me! I ain't the cheater here, Mr. Beals. You are! You did this! You planned. It. All." I screamed in frustration.

"Alas," Beals said calmly, "I have once again lived up to my reputation."

I kicked the ground, knocking a plug of dirt loose. I booted it again, wishing it was Beals's head. "That's so, so . . . wrong! I had a deal with Scratch, and you messed it up. Why you always hating on me?"

"I don't hate you, Miss Smoot. I'm rather fond of you. One might say that I've had my eye on you for quite a while, since the tragic death of your mother, in fact. You have all the traits I desire in an acquaintance—loyalty, determination, self-reliance, and passionate desire to exercise free will. It is those very qualities that make you so desirable and so easily controlled. That's why I manipulated Scratch into giving me this assignment, because I knew it above all others gave me the best chance at escape."

"So why didn't you run off the minute you got free, instead of dogging my ass?"

"And miss the fun? How could I, after I worked so hard for so long to engineer this, this whole extravaganza. The repossession. The race. The roux line. I orchestrated it all."

He threw his arms wide like a conductor in front of a symphony. That's what he was, wasn't he? The conductor.

And he'd played me like a drum. No, more like he played me for a fool. "You bastard." I covered my mouth and tried to breathe deeply.

He bowed. "If I had a conscience, I would be overcome with guilt at this moment. Since I have none, you'll have to forgive my lack of remorse or compassion. You do have my thanks, however, for freeing me from the endless control of that vain fool Lucifer."

"*I* set you free? You're crazy. How did I set you free?" Then I remembered the roux line.

"Now I am free to wander the earthly plane, doing the work that I love so well."

I was almost afraid to ask him what work he was talking about. "What work?"

"Oh, you know," he said, "the usual biblical stuff—blood, locust, darkness. Nothing too original, I assure you. How did you enjoy the frogs and hail, by the way? Just a little warm-up exercise, but it felt good to do mayhem again."

"You are such an asshole."

"You and I are very much alike, Miss Smoot, bound to a duty that we abhor, unable to pursue our own ambitions, defeated by an opponent who played fast and loose with the rules."

"I ain't nothing like you. I got—"

"What? Morals? Ethics? Hunger?"

I shook a finger at him. "At least I got a soul to lose. You got nothing inside but evil. And ugly teeth."

"Soon you will know the irony of that statement. I wonder, however, why you think I've no soul. If I had none, I could not exist in any form. Do not think of me as a power-starved demon, but as a tortured soul who wants to serve no master but himself, to be a slave to none. And now that I am free, I can use my unfettered powers to do what nephilim do best—collect an army of souls to overthrow Scratch. And you, Miss Smoot, will be my first collection and because you have lost your free will, I will take that as well. You will become my slave and I your master. You will serve me, much the way that your former boss, Vinnie, must serve his master."

He snapped his fingers, and two dogs appeared out of nowhere. They were black shadows, with only their green eyes shining and their mouths wide open and bloody red. They looked like two big Rottweilers, except they each had a long tail like an alligator with quill-shaped spikes sticking out at the tip.

"I hate dogs."

"This I know, Miss Smoot. Unfortunately, where you're going, there are thousands of them, all at my command."

One devil dog grabbed a hold of my left ankle, and the other closed his mouth around the right knee. I felt them growl through the bone and muscle of my legs and heard a sound like a grape skin popping as they sank their teeth lightly into my skin.

"There is a contract law," Beals gloated, "and there is Old Law. Contract law grants Scratch the rights to your soul and your free will. But Old Law, what you might call the nephilim version of finders-keepers, allows any unfettered demon to lay claim first. If the demon is fast enough. If he is clever enough."

Beals cackled like a demented fun-house clown. I gritted my teeth and tried to twist my legs free long enough to roll away. But the dogs clamped down hard, and I screamed. Bone-jarring. Razored pain cut through my legs and into my belly, and I fell face-first onto the grass.

"Ow!"

"Oh hush," Mr. Beals said. "You have a pathetically low tolerance for pain." He grabbed my left hand and scratched the palm with a fingernail, leaving a thin line of blood. I felt the throbbing wash from my belly into my arms and down my hands.

"Ouch," I said, even though the pain was scalding.

Then Beals bent over and punctured my thumb with a fang. He licked the blood with his forked tongue. Fire ripped up my arm and into my face, and my head felt full of white-hot flames.

"A taste of what is to come, for you now belong to me, soul and will, and I shall relish every excruciating moment it takes to extract them from your body," Beals said. He clapped his hands, and the pain went away. "Better? You may thank me later."

"Like hell I will," I spat out, and fell to one knee. His words swirled in my mind like a dust devil in the sand.

He held up a short length of gold chain. "Do you know what this is? It's adamantium, also known as demon iron. After one of my projects went awry, Scratch sentenced me to the Fiery Pit. As I dangled from adamantine shackles above the penal flames, I hatched an escape plan. I would volunteer to work as a repossession agent, one of the most humiliating of all demon jobs. Next, I would find a contract that offered the greatest opportunity for escape. It was difficult at first, and I failed on previous attempts, but then your grandfather's case came to my attention. It led me to you, and the rest is history, just like my shackles." He pushed the chain into my scratched hand. "After I've gone, give this to Lucy for me, won't you? That's a good girl."

"Who?" I tried to argue, to tell him to deliver it himself. Instead, I put the chain in a pocket and got to my feet.

"Old Scratch. He's about to make his grand, but oh-so-predictable, entrance."

On cue, the BMW screeched to a halt in the street. Scratch backed up, then roared up the driveway and parked a few feet behind the Cadillac. The sound of music—Nat King Cole—drifted out as he opened the door. He strolled around the Biarritz, clicking his tongue and shaking his head while looking at the damage. I'd really torn the car up. The right side of the front bumper was crumpled like a paper wad, and there were deep grooves cut along the passenger's side from where we kissed the guardrail, with long, curled metal shavings clinging to the back fender. Scratch bent down by the trunk for a closer look, and the muffler fell with a bell-like clang onto the pavement.

"The damage certainly lowers the resale value," Scratch said. "Pity. Beals, contact Lloyd's to file a claim." He snapped his fingers, and the Biarritz disappeared, busted muffler and all. "Thank you for the automobile, *ma chère*," he said to me. "As well as for your grandfather."

He snapped his fingers again. Steam rose up next to me, taking the shape of Papa C's body. Papa C looked like he had for most of my life, spindly legs and potbelly included. If I hadn't been able to see right through him and if he didn't stink like toe jam, I would've thought he really was alive again.

Papa C grabbed his face. His head swelled up like an angry boil, and his mouth opened big and black and empty. "N-o-o-o-o," he screamed. It didn't really make any sound. I could feel it in my mind, though, and it was damned pitiful.

Scratch snapped his fingers again, and Papa C was gone. A puddle of glop was all that was left behind.

"Just one freaking minute," I yelled. "This ain't right. Beals tricked me into taking a shortcut. Truth is, I beat your ass fair and square."

"Fair, perhaps, but not quite square. Beals?"

"Indeed, master," he said sarcastically.

"Thank you, Beals." Scratch looked at him funny, like he wasn't sure of how to make out the situation, and snapped his fingers. Beals evaporated into the night.

A couple seconds later, Vinnie and Pesto pulled into the driveway.

"Dude!" Pesto yelled as he finally got out of the sidecar of the motorcycle. "You won the race." He ran up on me all arms wide open until he saw the look on my face and the Rottweilers from Hell dribbling slobber down my high-tops. "What's wrong? Why are you crying?"

Man. I hadn't even noticed that tears were rolling down my face. My bottom lip stuck out pouting, too. There was a heavy weight in my legs like I'd run a hundred laps around the court and a heavier, sinking-sick feeling in my belly.

"They took Papa C," I said as he finally hugged me. "They took the car over a stupid-ass technicality that was so small they had to magnify the magnifying glass to see it."

Not that I gave a damn, but Vinnie looked scared to death. He looked especially terrified when Scratch called him over with a finger.

"Vinnie," Scratch said, sighing, "how disappointing."

"But—but, master," he blubbered. "It's not my frigging fault. A frigging coyote tried to bite my tires, and the Mexican blocked my GPS with the pizza box. The girl cheated, anyhow. I saw her drive off the side of the frigging road."

"Vincent," Scratch said calmly, almost bored. "Such language. How many times must I take you to task about the profanity?"

"Please, master. Don't." He got down on his knees. "I'll do better next race."

"There will be no more races, Vincent. You simply don't have the heart of a gladiator, but I blame only myself for that. Well, off to slave reeducation camp with you."

He snapped his fingers. Vinnie was gone.

"I fear," Scratch said, clearing his throat and waving Pesto away, "that things did not turn out as well as we'd hoped. Thank you for the race, Miss Smoot. It's—oh, yes, one more thing."

He snatched my left hand and started to draw a fingernail across it. "My goodness, what is this?"

"Goddamned Beals scratched me," I said. I handed over the piece of gold chain. "And he said to give you this."

"Beals?" he said. His voice sounded calm. He held the chain in his palm. It melted into a puddle of gold, which turned into a glop of egg white.

Then he threw back his head and bellowed, "Beals! How dare you steal my prize!"

The shock wave of the sound threw me and Pesto backward, and we held on to each other to keep our feet.

A bright light shone from his body, a cold light, almost neon. Scratch's face changed, turned blood red, and two massive ram horns curled out of his skull. Fur sprouted from his face, forming a mane, and metal claws grew from the ends of his fingers. A long tail of thick muscle wrapped around his legs, and the tip oozed liquid, like a scorpion stinger full of poison. The tail whipped around my chest, binding my arms, and he pulled me close.

"Get that nasty tail off me. I ain't that kind of girl."

"Let her go!" Pesto shouted, and reached for me. Scratch wagged a finger, and Pesto froze mid-step.

"I can damage you, *ma chère*," he said, "so be still."

My body turned rigid, and my muscles wouldn't, couldn't move. I couldn't even blink.

The air turned frigid, but his breath didn't freeze in the air. He stared into my eyes, and my whole self went cold. It felt like a Popsicle headache all over my body.

"I see his plan now. He tricked your grandfather into defaulting on the contract and then escaped my binding spell. He stole you before I could claim you. How easily he manipulated you and the boy into freeing him. Now he is loose upon the Earth unchained, and there is no means for me to bind him. You are a very foolish, very prideful girl."

"Pride goeth before the fall," I said through chattering teeth when he released me.

He grimaced. "You do not understand what forces you have unleashed. Since antiquity, I have controlled the balance of power between Earth and the underworld. Call me what you will, but I have preferred to recruit souls from those willing to trade for material goods. It is more civilized, more dignified, and it keeps Him from meddling. Beals has a different business model. He sees an Earth in which souls are harvested by the hundreds of thousands with earthquakes, storms, grinding wars, and pandemic. The Black Plague, the Great War, these were only two of his little projects, and if I had not chained him . . ."

He let go of my wrist. "You are nothing but a half-bred El Paso peasant, a soul I thought barely worth pursuing. And you set him free. Ah well, that is the way of things. Be thankful I am prevented from slaying humans, Miss Smoot. If I could, I would render your flesh into fat and burn it like a candle."

"Oh," I said, and caught my breath.

"What a shame. If your free will belonged to me, I would allow you to live out your natural life. I might even offer you a sporting chance to win your freedom back. Beals, tragically, will make no such offer. The Great Deceiver likes to play with his food before he kills it. *Bon chance, ma chère.* You are going to need it."

He snapped his fingers, and *pop!* He was gone, the BMW along with him.

# CHAPTER 23
## Going on a Beals Hunt

I was shaking so hard, I thought my chattering teeth were going to crack apart. I sat down on the curb, and Pesto put a warming arm around me.

"Dude." Pesto stuck a bandana in my hand. "Wipe your nose and eat some of this." He pulled out a chocolate bar.

"What's the use?" I said. "Ain't no demon to chase away now."

"Chocolate fights depression. Your brain's got receptors that are hardwired for chocolate. Girls have five times as many as dudes." He snapped off a chunk and set it gently on my lips. The chocolate started melting, and so did I.

"My thumb is killing me," I said, sobbing.

Pesto's lips kept moving, but there wasn't any sound.

His face got fuzzy, and I felt my eyes roll back in my head.

I didn't remember much between eating the chocolate and Mrs. V putting me to bed in my apartment above the store. She got me undressed, tucked me in under a quilt decorated with a patchwork Virgin Mary, and talked me into taking a few sips of bitter camomile tea.

That night, I dreamed about being a spider dangling over a pit of fire. I could see a hand above me, pinching a line of silk and bouncing me up and down. The flames kept licking at me. My legs got scorched, then curled up, and Beals started laughing, high and screechy like a witch. The echo of his voice filled my head: "Rise and shine, Miss Smoot. Your fate is at hand."

I woke up to stinging pain in my hand. The predawn light shone through the open curtains, and I held up the thumb for a look. A stream of blood trickled down the knuckle to my wrist, and when I gasped and sat bolt upright, Beals's face was six inches from mine.

There was blood on his lips.

I felt his breath on my face, and the rancid-meat stench of it turned my stomach. I threw up in my mouth, and I spat it in his face.

"Get out of my bedroom, you cloven-hoofed son of a bitch."

He wiped his face with a handkerchief. "Think of that as what you would call a freebie, Miss Smoot. I have come—"

"To harass my ass and drink my freaking blood." I yanked the covers under my chin and pulled my legs up into a ball.

"I have come to make an offer. The taking of a human can be quick and merciful, or it can be drawn out for hours, even days, which is excruciating for you but is a singularly exquisite process for me. I so enjoy it. In fact, I'm quite well known for my unique method—I suck out your soul, your will, and life in equal measures."

I tried to sound brave, even though I was freaked out. "And I should care why?"

"Because you can avoid a great deal of anguish by agreeing to become my consort. You will be taken swiftly and painlessly, and I will give you a seat in my earthly court when I have over-thrown that weak, arrogant Old Scratch. Think of it, Miss Smoot. You will reside in a palace, drive the finest cars, and dine on the most exquisite gourmet meals until your stomach is no longer empty."

With every promise, a vision flickered in my eyes. I saw myself in a mansion so big, it made the houses on *MTV Cribs* look like double-wides. I saw myself cruising the Loop in a Maserati with pimped-out spinners. I saw a table filled with food and a butler chopping up my steak and feeding it to me. It would be a lie to say I wasn't tempted.

"But I'd be dead."

"A trivial detail, I assure you."

One look at the bloody gash on my thumb was all it took to bring me back to reality. I held my scratched palm up at Beals. "Why don't you just kill me if you want it over with so fast?"

He sighed. "Oh, when will you start listening? I do not wish to kill you. Yet."

"Yet?"

He licked his lips. My head spun, and I heard a rushing sound in my ears. I went down again and hit the wood floor like Auntie Pearl feeling the spirit at a Sunday service.

"As Solomon had his Sheba, I shall have you. Ruminate on my offer, Miss Smoot. But be warned, the longer you wait to surrender, the more horrendous your pain will become. Don't call me. I'll call you."

With the smell of egg farts, he was gone.

I knew Beals wasn't telling the truth about me being his consort. He was the Great Deceiver. There had to be something more he wanted, something he couldn't just take. Or he would've done it, no matter what he said. Think, girl, I told myself, as I lay on the floor. What would a demon full of blind ambition crave?

My head felt like a dried-out sponge. Papa C's alcoholism left me with no reason to drink, but how he looked with a hangover was how I felt. My tongue was all sticky, too, like the floor of a dollar movie theatre. It had been a bad night, but morning finally brought the sun. It also brought a breakfast of *huevos motuleños*, which was tortillas covered in eggs, black beans, and cheese. Pesto took *salsa picante* on his. I ate mine straight, all five of them. I was hungry as a mad dog. Thirsty, too. I emptied Mrs. Valencia's store of *horchata* and then moved to ice water.

As I ate, Pesto kept shaking his head in wonder, saying he'd expected me to wake up depressed. Mrs. Valencia cut in and said it was good to eat after a tragedy.

"It is your body's way of getting on with trauma. The past is past. You have to now look to the future."

"It's not like I got much of a future to look to," I said, emptying another glass of ice water. Damn, girl, quit whining, I thought. You know you're pathetic when you get tired of hearing yourself piss and moan.

"Do not say that," Mrs. V said. She got a mortar and pestle down from the cabinet. "E. Figg once told you that there is always something to lose. Listen to me now, *mi'ja*." She shook the pestle at me. "There is always a future, always something or someone to live for. Isn't that right, Pesto?"

"*Es verdad,*" Pesto said through a half-eaten tortilla.

The TV in the corner was turned to the morning news on KINT, the Spanish version, so I didn't have any idea what the anchor was talking about. Mrs. Valencia watched while standing at the kitchen counter and mixing herbs. She made a clucking noise with her tongue, and I glanced up to see a whole bunch of dead fish in the Rio Grande. Thousands of fish, maybe hundreds of thousands, floating belly up. The reporter was talking and waving her arms toward the factories across the border, the humongous *maquiladoras*, which were so big, they blocked the horizon.

"What happened to the fish?" I asked her as I wiped up tortilla crumbs and loose beans from my place at the table.

"*La niña* says the *maquiladoras* killed them by spilling chlorine into the river. What a shame. This is what happens when the capitalists make the laws. Even then, they break them, no?"

"I heard that," I said, agreeing with her. On TV, sanitation workers in bright yellow suits were scooping out the fish with big nets. I leaned over to Pesto. I said softly, "There's a bunch of weird things going on—frogs, dead fish, the hail. After the race last night, Beals said something about messing around with biblical plagues. Like he was practicing."

"Practicing for what?" he said.

"You're the NAD wannabe, you tell me."

"This Beals thing is all new to me, dude," Pesto said. "Okay, I'll touch base with Castor. The boys at NAD have to know something, right?"

I still wasn't too sure about the NADs. "You passing the buck?"

"Being smart, that's all." His voice sounded wounded. "I'm in over my head with biblical plagues. I don't want to do anything to get you hurt."

"That's sweet," I said, because there wasn't nothing else to say. Like I told Mrs. Valencia, I didn't see much point in worrying about a girl whose life wasn't worth a damn anymore.

After breakfast, I cleaned the kitchen, mopped the floors, and took the garbage out to the Dumpster in the alley behind the grocery store. The alley stunk like a drunk man's vomit, and the ground was littered with all kinds of pieces of garbage. The edge of the Dumpster was over my head, so I had to toss the bags in. If the second bag hadn't caught on a piece of metal and ripped open while I was slinging it up, I never would've seen the coyote.

She was crouched in a space between two buildings, hidden by the shadows. When the bag broke, a couple of half-eaten steaks fell out, and that was too much for her. She dashed out, grabbed the meat, and scrambled back to safety. I barely saw her do it.

"Hey, dog," I said. Hands on my knees, I bent down, trying to get a good look at her. It's a bad idea to approach an eating animal, so I kept my distance. I could tell from the white markings on her front paws that it was my coyote.

"You got my back, huh?"

The coyote growled through a chunk of steak. Then she yipped a couple of times, which was enough to make me back all the way to the end of the alley.

"Guess that answers that question. I'll be going then." I didn't know what made a coyote adopt me or how she'd followed me all the way across town, but I was glad she was there.

# CHAPTER 24
# The Other 1/10 of the Law

"What kind of crack-house law firm are you running?" I said across the table to E. Figg, Esquire. "I lost my free will because you didn't think to check all of the stipulations? I had that race won."

E. Figg had stopped by the store to check on me. To see how I was holding up. That's what she said at first, before she admitted to thinking I must be dead already. Beals had a habit of getting the owners of souls he snatched killed right away—a car accident, a plane crash, bad Chinese food. She thought he must have something special in mind for me.

*"Por favor,"* Mrs. Valencia said. "Be respectful."

Pesto's mama was on the right, I was on the left, and Pesto

sat between us. He held both my hand and hers, like a chain.

"I did read all of the stipulations," E. Figg said, "and I tried to warn you, but you drove off too soon. Help me understand why you left the highway."

I crossed my arms and stared at her earlobe hard enough to give it a second piercing. "The engine was giving out, Vinnie was way ahead of me, and Beals said to turn. I should've stopped for that coyote. I played right into Beals's hands."

"A coyote?" Pesto interrupted.

"Yeah."

"Dude, remember what I said that the Navajo say about coyotes? That they're guardian spirits who transform instead of going to the afterlife?"

"Drop it."

"But—"

"I said, drop it."

Mrs. V cleared her throat. "What can we do to help Bug now?"

"Nothing," E. Figg said, pushing her glasses up. "Old Scratch has his hands full dealing with Beals, who is attempting a coup, so he's probably not in the mood to negotiate. The truth is, there is nothing I or anyone else can arrange. Unless you know an innocent who's willing to wager himself for you."

Pesto opened his mouth to speak. Both me and Mrs. V squeezed the snot out of his hands.

"*¡Cierra la boca!*" she said.

"Shut your mouth!" I said. "Don't you even think about it, Pesto Valencia. That ain't happening."

Pesto looked at me with those big brown eyes, and my insides melted. Damn, I was going to miss him.

"Look on the bright side," E. Figg said, breaking the tension. "While Beals and Scratch are fighting, Bug is relatively safe."

Her bright side wasn't all that bright. "How many times've you lost your free will, E. Figg?"

"Please, Bug," E. Figg said. "I would help if I could."

"No, I'm serious," I said. "There's more going on here than you been letting on, and since you keep wanting to preach, it's time you came straight with me. How many times've you lost your free will?"

"Bug," Mrs. Valencia said, "*por favor*, show—"

"It's fine, Mariposa." E. Figg took off her glasses, folded her hands on the table, and smiled at Mrs. Valencia. Her voice cracked a little when she said, "The answer is, once. Beals was the collector, then, too."

That explained why she hated him so much. "How'd you get it back?"

"You're quite the bulldog," she said. "Well, someone I love sacrificed himself for my sake." She took a deep breath, put the glasses back on, and stood. "If something else comes up, I'll contact you immediately. In the meantime, enjoy the rest of your day."

"I'm sorry," I said, standing up. "I didn't mean to get all up in your business. Even if things didn't work out, I want you to know I appreciate everything you did. You and me, we're straight, right?"

"Right," she said.

We all shook hands and said thanks. I didn't mind her kicking us to the curb. There wasn't nothing else to say, and it was time for me to suck it up and take care of business. In junior English, we read this book about a mean-assed old lady who made this neighbor boy come over and read to her every day. Turned out, she was addicted to morphine, and she was using the reading to help kick the drug. She didn't want to pass on in debt to anybody or anything. That's exactly how I felt. I didn't want to end my life beholden to anybody. But I didn't want to give up trying, either. If I could only find somebody, anybody who could stand up to Beals the way that Old Scratch did.

Bingo.

"Wait," I called, following her to the door. "How about you arrange a meeting for me. With Beals *and* Scratch."

"I don't understand."

"Everybody keeps saying that demons can't turn down a bet.

Let's do a sit-down with the two biggest ones. Maybe turn them against each other. See what they'll go for."

E. Figg paused at the door, half in and half out, thinking. "It's unorthodox, but it's worth a try, I suppose. It may go nowhere, too, so don't get your hopes up. Let me handle the sit-down, though, for your protection. I'll be in touch."

I watched her go. By the time she crossed the street to her Mercedes, she was already working the phone. Her car was parked next to a flower-seller's donkey cart, and she bought a bundle of roses from the old vendor. His cart was overflowing with marigolds, dahlias, lilies, and roses. The open windows let in the sweet smell, which chased away the smell of the street and the dust. I felt a little tug of hope inside and went back to the kitchen.

"*Oye*, Bug," said Pesto, who was sitting at the table. "You and me should drop in on the NAD boys together. I've got a feeling that they're lonely."

Mrs. Valencia, who was washing dishes in the sink, threw her hands in the air, flipping suds everywhere. "Ay, the Abyss? No! No! Pesto, I told you not to go back to the Abyss. It's *muy peligroso* for normal people. You risked enough taking Bug there before."

"Mamá, it's no big deal. It turned out fine. Castor and Pollux gave us some good advice."

"Their advice set Beelzebub free, *mi'jo*! How can you trust them now? No! I am putting my foot down, Pesto. I don't want to hear about NAD again. *Nada! Nunca más!*"

And with that, La Ciclóna swept into the other room, leaving Pesto looking all windblown and crumpled in her wake. I didn't say nothing because he looked so pitiful, but I was right there with Mrs. V. Their home brew had let Beals loose, and they weren't doing a damned thing to help put him back.

# CHAPTER 25
# Bug Got Game

It was All Saints' Day, and folks were still shopping for Dia de los Muertos. Las Cruces Mercado was jumping. Me and Pesto stepped in to help out. The work kept my mind off Beals for a little bit.

While we were stocking up, two women from the health department came in the store. I saw them talking to Mrs. Valencia and then pointing toward the back. I thought they were after me until they took a handful of plastic bags from Mrs. Valencia.

"What's up with all this?" I asked Pesto, who asked his mama the same thing in Spanish.

One of the women, who obviously also spoke Spanish,

answered as she stuffed all the bags of spinach from the cooler into the plastic bags. "You don't watch the news? Five children in this county have been hospitalized for E. coli food poisoning. We've got at least a hundred confirmed milder cases, and it's getting worse."

"From spinach?" I said. "Isn't it hamburger or something that—"

"Vegetables can carry the bacteria as well." She dropped the double-bagged spinach into a thick white bag, along with the latex gloves she'd been wearing. Her partner closed the bag and sealed it with tape. "Here are instructions for cleaning the shelves and storage area," she said, handing Mrs. Valencia a yellow sheet of paper. "Follow them to the letter."

"*Sí*," Mrs. Valencia said, nodding. "We will do as you say."

'Thanks," the women said, leaving the store with the spinach. "We'll be in touch."

"Those girls were hard-core," I said, making sure I didn't touch the shelves. Last thing I needed was some deadly bacteria killing my ass.

"Ay, *cinco niños* sick," Mrs. Valencia said, crossing herself. "What is this world coming to?"

A big mess, I thought. Then I heard a little moan come from Pesto. When I glanced over at him, he'd gone pale, and he looked like he was about to pass out.

"You okay?" I mouthed, not wanting to disturb Mrs. Valencia, who was giving her rosary a rubdown. "What's wrong?"

He shook his head and mouthed back. "It's Beals. You were right, dude. These are the plagues of Egypt."

"You mean like Moses and the pharaoh in the Ten Commandments, right? The story where the last plague is the death of every firstborn child?" He nodded, and it hit me like an elbow to the gut. I'd let Beals loose on the Earth to do his dirty deeds. The first plagues were just a warm-up. They were getting worse every time, and if the bastard followed the pattern, he was planning on killing thousands of kids in El Paso.

If I hadn't been so pissed, I would've gotten sick to my stomach, right in the middle of the aisle. To think that a couple days ago, my biggest problem was a dirty car and a stupid boss. I took Pesto's hand and gave it a squeeze.

"I'm going to find a way to stop him. I can't be having this on my ledger."

Me and Pesto talked quietly about what we could do to find Beals and kick his ass.

"Dude," he said, "I still think we should seriously consider me putting my soul up in a wager."

"No!" I smacked him hard enough to get the customers' attention. "I told you before, I'm not letting you do any such thing."

246

He decided it was time to sweep the stockroom. He grabbed a broom and headed to the back of the building.

A couple minutes later, I was by myself. For a girl who doesn't like nobody telling her what to do, I got this thing about empty spaces. It's the quiet. I scooted out of the produce section, trying not to walk too fast, and went over by the stockroom. Soon as I heard Pesto's voice, my heart stopped pounding.

But my heart didn't like what I heard. He was arguing with his mama. About me.

"We can't just let this happen," Pesto said. "Not stand by and do nothing."

"Sometimes, *mi'ja*, nothing is the best medicine we can take." I could tell by the strain in her voice that Mrs. V was about to go off. My mouth runs too much, but deep inside, I can't stand to see folks fight, not really fight, which is different from just making noise and cracking on somebody, because when you really fight it means you're hurt, which makes me hurt.

I swung my hands out, knocking a jar of sweet pickles off the shelf. It hit the tile floor and busted into big chunks of thick, green glass. Gherkins scattered everywhere, and when I heard Pesto and his mama coming to check out the sound, I knew I had done the right thing.

247

After we cleaned up the pickle mess, Mrs. V threw us out of the store to get some fresh air. Over my protest Pesto took the chance to set up a meeting with Castor and Pollux, and in less than a half hour, we stood crammed into the NAD command center, watching the computer screens light up like slot machines.

"The demonic activity has been off the charts," Pollux said. "ISIS has been slammed with furlough requests. All the pipes are backed up, and you know the problem. All of the flow is going directly from the main line right into the El Paso system. It's overwhelmed. The whole place is going nuts."

"What's up?" I said. "What's causing it?"

"You are," Pollux said. "You and your power-hungry demon boyfriend."

"Are you whack out your mind?" I said, and popped Pollux on the head. "You best watch that mouth before I tea-bag you in real life. I ain't playing. Do I look like I am playing with you? We both got the same problem. So how about y'all tell me how me and Pesto can banish Beals once and for all?"

Castor shook his head. "We talked about this last time. The difficulty with banishing a nephilim is that the process isn't cut-and-dried, like saying abracadabra. It's complicated. Because you need three things: first an object bearing the Seal of Solomon."

"Like the thing on your hat?"

"Good eye, good eye. The second thing you need is the Testament of Solomon, but like we said, we think the correct phrasing was lost in translation, so nobody at ISIS has been able to make it work."

"The last agent who attempted it," Pollux interrupted, "ended up a pile of skin flakes."

My stomach did a little twist. "Forget that idea, then. How else are we going to stop this?"

"I've got an idea. If we—" Pesto began before Pollux interrupted him.

"Not we. You two. ISIS is officially neutral, like Switzerland. We can only extract demons for visa violations, and since Beals is a nephilim and has diplomatic immunity—*Eek.*"

"*Eek? Eek?* A demon is about to bring the whole city down on our asses, and all you got to say is '*eek*'? Damn. I think somebody's lost part of their manhood, if you know what I'm saying. If you NADs think of anything, give my boy Pesto a holler, huh?"

A red light on the command center started blinking. On one of the monitors, an alarm graphic popped up, and the screen flipped from one head shot to the next. It stopped on the picture of a man with a fat face and a lame-looking toupee.

"Yo," I said. "I've seen that ugly mug somewhere before."

Castor jumped back into his seat. Pollux reached for the alert screen, and Castor smacked his hand. "Looks like a runner. Level Thirteen djinn with an expired work visa. The cleaners haven't been able to find him. He may have changed his appearance. What do you think, Poll?"

"I'll suit up."

"Even if he did alter his form, he's barely a Level Thirteen, though. Hardly worth the trouble. Let the next shift handle it."

"No. It's our extraction."

"Good idea. Let the next shift handle it." Castor printed the info from the screen and acted like he was sticking the paper into a file. Instead, he folded it up and slipped it to Pesto.

"Hey," Pollux said. "I saw that. Technically, you're violating security protocol."

Castor smacked him in the head. "Technically, you're still a noob. Bug, Pesto, *vayan con dios, mis amigos.*"

"Wait," I said. "Castor, you said we needed three things to banish Beals. What's the third thing?"

"Love," Castor said. "It's the one thing demons can't abide."

After leaving the Abyss, we drove around a long time, chatting each other up about nothing much and listening over and over to the greatest hits of Captain and Tennille, which was his only eight-track that still worked. Finally, Pesto's Gremlin started overheating, so we pulled into a community center next to a tennis court with a couple of ball rims on one end. There were a few folks standing around talking, setting up booths of some kind.

On the wall of the building was a mural that caught my eye. In the center of the mural was a Tejano man with a thick moustache and shoulder-length hair. The profile of a man with an eagle mask grew out of the left side of his head, the eagle's razor-sharp beak opened, with a rattlesnake writhing out of its mouth in place of a tongue. The snake curled around under the head, its fangs bared, and it was facing down a jaguar, which also was showing its fangs. The jaguar's tail twisted up to form the profile of a conquistador. I liked the way everything in the picture grew out of something then came together again, and I would've spent more time admiring it if Pesto hadn't popped the car hood and tried to take off the radiator cap while the engine was hot.

"Ain't you ever worked on a car?" I said, smacking his hand away. "The water in the radiator's about six million degrees. You can't pull the cap till the engine's cooled off. What were you and your mama fighting about?"

Pesto looked shocked for a second. "Slipped that right in, didn't you, dude?"

"Spit it out." Don't be me, don't be me, don't be me.

"It was about you. And my *padre*. He died trying to capture Beals, did you know that?"

What? He what? "No," I said in a quiet voice.

"Just found out myself, dude. Suspected it, but this was the first time she confirmed it." She wouldn't give him no details, though. All anybody knew was him and some other agents went out to bring a demon in, and it turned out to be Beals. He took them all out before Scratch stepped in.

"This changes everything," I said. My knees wobbled.

"It does not." He pulled a basketball out of the hatch of the Gremlin. "The situation is exactly like it was before. Exactly. How about a little one-on-one?"

What did he think he was playing at? Changing the subject on me. "I ain't into basketball no more."

He jogged over to the court, and when I wouldn't follow, he tried spinning the ball on a fingertip. "If memory serves, dude, you were, like, this amazing point guard at EP High, right? All-city, all-district, all-region—"

"All tired of running up and down a court chasing a bouncing ball," I hollered, and moved closer. "Basketball is a game, and I'm too grown to be playing some game."

Pesto dribbled twice. The boy carried the ball too high. Stealing from him would be too easy to be any fun.

"I know, dude, you're over the hill," he said, "and totally quaking in your shoes. Your boy Pesto's got righteous game."

I got up and slow-walked onto the court, made him wait. "Game? The only game you got is Monopoly."

"Oh yeah? Well, the only game you can play is chicken." He flapped his arms like wings. "Rusty chicken."

"First, my game ain't rusty. Second, even if it was, the only thing you can run is your mouth. Third," I smacked the ball across the court, "you palm the ball too damn much."

"Nice one," he said. When he came back with the ball, Pesto was smiling. "Play you to ten."

"Forget you."

"Bet I can kick your butt."

"Now, how am I going to bet money? Ain't like I got Benjamins falling out of my pockets."

He tried to spin the ball again and hit himself in the nose. "I'm not talking money, dude."

"What you got in mind?"

"A kiss."

"What if I win?"

"The same. A kiss. It's a win-win proposition."

I scoffed. "Sounds like lose-lose for me."

"Dude, that's harsh." He smacked a twenty on the blacktop. "If you win, you keep the cash. If I win, I get a kiss."

So it was a win-win for me, either way. "I'm going to hate taking your money." I flicked the ball away and scooped it in the cradle of my elbow, holding it back so he couldn't reach, even with his long arms. "Just like I took this ball."

He reached in. I smacked his hand. I spun away, took three steps, and put the rock up on the board. It rimmed out and bounced right into Pesto's hands.

"Rusty," he said. "Rusty chicken."

"Who you calling chicken? You wouldn't know a chicken if it pecked you on the ass."

"*Bwock, bwock.*"

He tried to pop a shot, but I was in his face before it rolled from his fingertips. I flicked the ball away, picked it up with a cross dribble, and pulled up for a baby jumper as he skied by, expecting the layup.

Bottom.

Aw, jump! "Who's eating chicken now?"

It was make it, take it. He checked the ball to me.

"So what kind of chicken you like?" I dribbled between the legs. "Wings?" Behind the back. "Legs?" Low cross, with a stutter step.

"Breasts."

"Breasts?" I said. "Best get your head in the game and off chicken, boy."

As he cut off my stutter-step move, I bounced the ball between his skinny-ass legs, picked it up behind him, and laid it in with a pretty little finger roll I released just three inches under the rim. I banked a jumper off the board and in. My shot needed some work. I'd meant it to be all net.

"I wasn't talking," he said, checking the ball, "about chicken."

I rifled the ball into his belly. The wind popped out of him like somebody snapped bubble-wrap. "That's why you're getting played. Concentrate."

"It's hard. To concen—" He sucked in mouthfuls of air. "—trate when a dude. Tries to remove. Your appendix. With a basketball."

"Check."

He looked all hurt because I wouldn't play his flirting game. See, when I stepped into a game, it was on. I don't play. I work. I win. I hate losing more than anything. I hated Tangle-eye taking my team out of the playoffs. I hated losing the car race. And it wasn't just about losing my Papa C, the car, or my soul. It was about getting beat again by somebody who wasn't playing fair.

"It's on," I said, my teeth all gritted up and tight when Pesto checked me the ball. I felt the muscles in my jaw working hard, like I was chewing up glass Coke bottles.

"Whoa," he said.

I didn't even mess around. No talking smack, no showing him my moves. I just took the ball and took it home, every time. Pesto didn't score. He didn't even touch the ball, except to feed it back to me. I gave up keeping score after 15–0, just kept taking the ball and taking it home, until I was so tired, my legs felt like I was running knee-high through the blacktop. I went up for the last shot and hung there, the ball still in my hand.

"That's enough," I said.

I'd already beat Pesto, so there wasn't nothing to prove by making the next shot. It wasn't him I was playing against, anyhow. It was Tangle-eye and Old Scratch, Beals and Papa C. Anybody who had ever cheated me. My boy Pesto wasn't here to cheat me.

"Game over," I said, and let the ball fall out of my hand.

"Aw, dude," he said, laughing, "I was just about to make my move. My strategy was to get you exhausted and then charge hard down the lane."

I laughed through the sweat streaking down my face. The boy was amazing. He gets his ass handed to him, and he can still crack a joke. Too bad I found him too late.

While Pesto snatched up the ball, I spotted the twenty still on the pavement. I folded it and shoved it in my back pocket.

"You're keeping my money?" Pesto said.

"Damn straight," I said. "I won it, right? I'm hungry, let's get something to eat."

"We just ate breakfast."

A few minutes later, we were driving across town, after I had used the twenty to buy us lunch. A bag of McDonald's was on the floorboard, full of three Big Macs, an extra-large fries, and an apple pie. The pie was for Pesto.

Pesto turned down the Captain and Tennille on the eight-track. "Are you in a hurry to get home? Because there's this ISIS thing I've got to do, and maybe you'd like to give me a hand. If you want. No pressure."

"What you up to, dog?"

"Your old apartment building. To visit Mr. Payne."

I drew back like something stunk. "Why drive all across town to see his ugly ass?"

He pulled an empty mayonnaise jar out from under the seat, along with a can of Super Hold hair spray. "Y'know that photo of the runner Castor slipped me at NAD? It's Mr. Payne."

"No way!"

"Way, dude, big-time," he said. "Your old landlord is a demon. Know what else? He works for Beals."

# CHAPTER 26
# Stuck on You

Mr. Payne's apartment was on the opposite end of the building from mine. The sun had set, and the weather had turned cool. Goose bumps rose on Pesto's arms. Mine were fine. I felt hot and flushed, even though Pesto said my cheeks were red from the cold.

We parked in the street the next block over and, armed with the jar and the hair spray, crept back to the yellow-brick building. When we reached the corner, Pesto stood watch while I checked the windows. I spotted Mr. Payne in the kitchen, wearing a ratty robe over a dirty wife beater and a pair of boxers. He was also wearing red cowboy boots.

His back was turned to me, and he was scraping ice off the

inside of the freezer and eating it with a spoon. Auntie Pearl used to do that in the summertime, and I always thought it was nasty. Now, though, my mouth was dry, and that ice would've felt good on my throat.

Pesto whistled. I gave him the thumbs-up, and he waved me around. While he waited at the corner with the jar, I knocked on the door, holding the hair spray behind my back.

"Rent!" I hollered, banging hard on the door.

Inside, the freezer door slammed, and I heard heavy footsteps crossing the floor. I waited until he had time to stick an eye up to the peephole.

"Rent!" I hollered louder.

A string of cuss words came from inside the apartment, and he was still spitting out profanities when he swung the door open wide.

"Nice pants," I said with a straight face.

He yanked the ratty robe closed. I couldn't help but wonder why demons always picked the form of bony white men.

"What in tarnation do you want?" he yelled at me.

"Rent!" I yelled back. "You want it?"

"You got it? Then let me have it."

It was almost too easy. I raised the can to eye level, aimed it at his face, and pressed the button down. And—damn it!—the freaking thing jammed.

His eyes got wide, and as I pressed the button again, he realized what was happening. He stepped back and slammed the door, which hit the can and knocked it flying across the sidewalk. I heard the deadbolt slide as I banged my shoulder into the wood, trying to force it open.

"What happened?" Pesto said, jumping onto the stoop next to me.

"The button stuck," I said. "He got away, and he's locked the freaking door."

"Stay here," Pesto said, then sprinted to the corner of the building. "I'll check the windows in the back of the house."

I grabbed the hair spray and put the button back on, since it had fallen off when it hit the concrete walk. I jammed the button down as hard as I could and squirted hair spray all over my pants.

"Shit," I said, slapping at my pants and jogging to the corner. From there, I could watch Pesto and the front door, too. One problem—my boy wasn't nowhere to be seen.

"Pesto?" I called out, worried. If Payne had hurt him—

Then from the back of the building, I heard the crash of glass breaking, a man yelling, and a dog growling. Pesto! I sprinted around to the next corner, and when I turned it, I saw Pesto sitting on the ground, rubbing the back of his head. A big cowboy boot was lying next to him, and the other one was still on Mr. Payne's left foot. He was on the ground, too, but on his back, with the jaws of a coyote stuck to his throat.

"Call her off!" Mr. Payne squealed. "Call off your mutt."

"She ain't mine," I said, helping Pesto up, "and she ain't no mutt." But she did have a taste for garbage, and she wasn't about to let that demon loose.

"What happened?" I asked Pesto.

"Plan . . . worked . . . perfect."

The boy had a funny idea of perfect. "You still got the jar?"

He held it up with one hand and rubbed the sore spot on his head with the other.

"Get ready to do your thing, then." I whistled, and the coyote let go, scooting away into the shadows as I aimed the Super Hold. Payne gasped as I sprayed his ugly face, affixing him with his eyes rolled and his tongue lolling out. "How much do I spray?"

"Cover his hands and feet," he said. "I'll take it from there."

After I yanked off the other boot, I did just what Pesto asked. When I was finished, the demon looked thinner and flatter, like I'd ironed him out with starch.

"Want some help with him?" I said.

"No." His jaw was set, and he had his game face on.

Pesto unscrewed the lid of the mayonnaise jar. He set the mouth of the jar against Payne's bald spot and pushed down until the whole head popped inside, sounding like a juicy zit exploding. Yellow fluid filled the jar, and Pesto stood it on edge while stuffing the rest of the demon's body inside. It shrunk down fast, the arms and legs shriveling up like hot plastic.

"Don't close the lid." Payne's voice drifted out of the jar. "I can help with that problem of you'uns, if you know what I'm saying, Eunice."

"The name's Bug," I barked. "How can you help me? Get me evicted from hell?"

"No," Payne said. "But I know a way to banish Beals for a thousand years."

"Liar," Pesto said.

"Let me out, and I'll tell you."

"Tell us now," Pesto said, "and I'll think about letting you out."

"You first," Payne said.

"Too late."

"Wait! Wait! You win, son. You win. All you'uns got to say is this incantation, '*By the name of the one God whose true name is Yahweh and the Greeks call Emmanuel, I strip you of your wealth. By the number 644 which the Hebrew call* kaf mem dalet, *I strip you of your power. And by the name of the Spirit, who the Romans call Eleeth, I banish you to the pit.*'"

I pulled the iPod out of my pocket, then made him say it

three times over so I could double-check the text. "Payne, you ain't told us nothing we didn't already know. We got the whole Testament right here, and it didn't work on Beals. I tried it."

"No, no," the demon protested. "Listen, it's professional courtesy. A demon can't directly tell a human how to banish another one, so you got to switch it around."

"Switch what?" I said.

"The name! You got to switch it around, you ignorant hussy!"

"Lid," Pesto said, holding up the jar. The whole thing was full of the yellow fluid, and hot vapors were pouring out the top.

"Just a cotton-picking minute, you lying piece of trash. You said you'd let me loose!"

"I said I'd think about it," Pesto said. "And I think you're going back to hell."

Payne let out a streak of profanity so long and harsh, it could peel paint.

"Bug," Pesto said, "now!"

I slapped the lid on, and he screwed it down. "Dude," I said, imitating him. "That is so righteous." So was he. Pesto wasn't no basketball player, and he couldn't drive to save his life, but when it came to being a demon catcher, he'd chosen the right line of work.

"*Muchas gracias.*" Holding the jar like nuclear waste, he walked back to the Gremlin with me.

"Think he's telling the truth about the incantation?" I said.

Pesto sighed. "Probably not, dude."

"Thought so."

We wrapped the jar in an old sweatshirt. Pesto pulled out something like a remote control and pushed a button. While we were sticking Payne into the glove compartment, an orange strobe lit up our faces. A half-ton pickup truck roared down the street, flashing its high beams and honking. I held up a hand to block the lights as the driver of the truck whipped across the lane and slammed on the brakes. It stopped an inch from Pesto's bumper, just as I was about to scream.

"The NADs are here." Pesto snatched the jar from the glove compartment.

He got out of the Gremlin and walked over to the truck, which was painted lime green and had Looney Tunes cartoons painted on the doors, the hood, and the utility boxes. The words WE'LL PLUMB THE SEVEN SEAS were written on the panel of the truck bed.

Pollux stayed behind the wheel. Castor jumped out of the passenger's seat. He waved at Pollux to turn off the lights, which were still blinding us.

"Quick, quick," Castor said, after congratulating Pesto on

capturing his first Level Thirteen, "give me the entity. We have to get him in storage ASAP."

Pesto handed Payne over, and we followed Castor around to the back of the truck. He dropped the tailgate, revealing a rectangular black safe as wide as the truck bed. It was solid stone, made of the same stuff as the NAD command center, with a door and a combination lock in the middle. I expected Castor to spin the dial. Instead, he put his palm on the door, and it swung open. A green light poured out, turning us all green, too. Castor pulled out a clear tube that looked just like the one they use at bank drive-throughs. He slid the mayonnaise jar into the tube, set the tube back inside the safe, snapped the door shut, and gave the dial a hard spin.

"I love doing that," he said. "It's a complete fake, of course, but the way the dial clicks makes me smile." He shook both our hands. "Good work, both of you. Pesto, *hombre*, stop by the office in the next couple of days. I'll give you a hand with the application for NAD."

And then, as quick as they showed up, the demon catchers were gone. It had happened so fast, there were still ghosts from the headlights dancing in my eyes.

# CHAPTER 27
# Time to Make the OFRENDAS

My eyes popped open. My nose was burning from the stink of smoke. I searched the apartment—nothing. Then I ran downstairs to the unlit Mercado. I stared into the darkness, searching with my eyes and nose, but found nothing. But there was smoke. There had to be fire. I had to find it. Fire in the store would ruin the Valencias. Fire in the building would ruin my home. Fire in the *barrio* would destroy the neighborhood. The same way fire had destroyed my life with Mita.

I felt him in the room before he said anything.

"Think of it as my cologne," Beals said.

Then before I could find him, I was driving across the Loop, the sun burning red as it set on the horizon. On a rise beside the road, the coyote sat watching, huffing, howling. Ahead, the road appeared like it'd been unzipped along the yellow line. The pavement caved into a sinkhole that opened, a mouth that ate up everything in its way. Until the demons came. They were right out of the Bible—red bodies, leather wings, horns like rams, cloven feet like goats. A whole flock of them flew out of the sinkhole, a swarm of demons migrating. In the middle of the swarm was Beals, in the same shape I'd seen in the convenience store.

On order, the demons swung toward me. I screamed as they lifted the Cadillac off the ground and carried it high into the air. Their bodies were pressed against the windows, red flesh oozing maggots out of their pores. I crawled into the backseat, trying to get away, but there was no escape.

"We shall dominate this world, Miss Smoot. My rule will be kinder than Scratch's, happier. He enjoys extracting small doses of misery from billions, while I prefer to kill thousands with plagues and wars—quick, dirty, self-contained."

"I don't want no part of your brand of 'kindness,'" I said.

"Join us," Beals commanded. His voice rang long and deep like the sound of a church organ.

"Up yours," I said, but my voice was small and tinny. I showed him a quick, dirty middle finger.

He swooped in and grabbed me by the thumb. He slit the

skin with his fangs. Blood poured out, and he held it over his mouth to let the blood drip into it. His body quivered in ecstasy. Fiery pain raced up my arm and exploded in my head. I saw bright lights, yellow fireworks, then darkness.

"Hey, you okay in there?"

Somebody was knocking on my door. I felt hot and dry mouthed, as if I had a fever. At first, I thought I was back in my old place, and Mr. Payne was coming to collect the rent. One look at my bloody thumb brought me back to reality. I wrapped it up in a tissue. The wound was deeper than before, and it burned more than it hurt.

I opened the door looking like hell, but Pesto smiled like I was the sun rising on his day.

"*Buenos días, bonita.* Time to make the *ofrendas.*" Carrying both an empty box and a second box full of bamboo sticks, tissue paper, tape, glue, yarn, ribbon, and scissors, he slid by me into the room. I had just enough time to pull an old dress shirt over the thin T-shirt and shorts I had worn to bed.

"What's that for?" I asked him when he put the box onto the floor. "Hey, this is my old stuff. What're you doing with it?"

He handed me a beat-up cigar box. "I got it out of the closet. Hope you don't mind."

I shrugged.

He started sorting out the items from the Mercado. "For making *ofrendas*, the offerings for the dead. It's Día de los Muertos, remember?"

I yawned. "Dog, I ain't much on celebrating today. Got anything to eat? I'm hungry as a mug."

"Mamá is cooking biscuits and sausage," he said, "But she won't let us eat if we don't finish."

My stomach growled, which was as good as me agreeing. "I still don't get this whole *ofrendas* thing."

"The *ofrendas* are homemade altars built to tempt the dead to return," he said. "We put all the things they loved on the altars, like for my *abuelo*, we put out Snickers bars, Pabst, *machacado con huevos*, and *horchata*. So his spirit will smell all this delicious food and come back to us."

"When they come back, what happens?"

"They eat because they're tired from their journey from the afterlife, and then we celebrate with them."

"Celebrate?" I said. "They're dead, what they got to celebrate?"

"Dude, to the Aztecs, sleeping on a grave or breaking bread with dead was—"

"Freaky."

"—just another way of honoring their loved ones. So you're going to build an *ofrenda* for your loved ones?"

I opened the cigar box. "Dog, you really believing this? That the dead will come back?"

He cocked an eyebrow at me. "A maggot-filled demon sucks the soul out of your body, and you don't believe that the dead walk the earth? Come on."

I closed my fist on the black mark Beals had left there. The thumb wasn't bleeding anymore, so I balled up the tissue and tossed it in the garbage before Pesto could see it. "You got a point."

Pesto showed me how to cut out the designs for a *papel picado*. He folded a piece of tissue paper into squares and then drew a picture of a laughing skull on the outside.

"Here, cut this *calavera* out, and I'll do one of Catrina, the queen of Calaveras."

"Dang, boy, you got some talent. If this demon immigration officer thing doesn't work out, you could get you a job doing art."

He blushed. So cute. "Me? I'm nothing. You should see the old men in the *barrio* making these. They get about fifty squares of paper and then hammer out the designs with an awl or a little chisel. I should only hope to be that good."

"Keep practicing, then," I said, "and you will be. Ouch!" The tip of the scissors nicked my thumb, and blood smeared on the tissue paper. "Damn. Now I got to start all over."

I started to tear the *papel picado* up, but Pesto caught my hand. Don't let this happen, girl. You know there ain't no future in it. But dog, the way he looked at me with those round, doe eyes . . .

"Don't throw out our work, it's bad karma. Besides, the dead don't mind a little blood."

After we finished, we strung up the cutouts using tape and yarn. I tied one of Catrina across the arch on Papa C's altar, because he always did like the ladies. I set the other *papel picado* aside for my second *ofrenda*.

In my stuff, I had a picture of Papa C in his favorite suit. I put the picture into the *ofrenda*, along with the name tag from his uniform. Pesto helped me arrange a box of Raisinets, a cigar, and some sugar mints. We put the picture on top, surrounded by votive candles.

"You'll light the candles tonight," he said as we both stepped back to take a look. He leaned close to me, and I felt the heat from his body. My hands started shaking, and it wasn't because I was nervous. My breath shortened, and a knot tightened in my belly.

"This is a good *ofrenda*. Simple. Humble."

"You saying my altar's lame?" I said.

He took my hand and kissed it. "It wasn't an insult. My own *ofrendas* are simple, too. Those huge *ofrendas* totally turn me off, and you don't need twinkling lights to attract the dead.

A strategically placed cigar is just as effective."

"Sorry," I said, and I was. "Everybody says I'm too defensive."

"You don't have to defend yourself from me."

Oh yes, I did. Him standing there with those long eyelashes, flicking the hair out of his face, smelling like a mix of cologne and cilantro. I knew if I let our relationship go any further, it was going to hurt even more to let him go. "You want to help me with this other *ofrenda*?" I asked him. "I need to get some stuff from the grocery, and I won't know what I need until I look around."

"Oh, a mystery, huh?" He rubbed his hands together. "Who's this one for?"

I thought for a second before telling him. Oh, well, he was going to find out eventually. "My Mita," I said, and watched the smile dawn on his face.

# CHAPTER 28

# Be with the One You Love

There wasn't much to Papa C's funeral. He was a veteran, so they buried him for free at the Fort Bliss National Cemetery, where all the graves are the same size and all the headstones were practically identical. From a distance, the graveyard looks like rows and rows of rounded white teeth poking out of the ground. Wasn't nobody there but me, the preacher from Auntie's AME church, and the preacher's wife, plus two workers standing a few yards away next to a backhoe, sharing a cigarette. After it was over, I was all alone.

Mita's funeral was different. We had it in a cemetery with headstones taller than me, and I played hide-and-seek around them until Auntie Pearl made me stop because it was disrespectful to play in a graveyard. Mita's grave was beside the trunk of an old tree. Somebody had carved a woman's head into the top of the trunk, along with a pair of long arms and a basket. The basket was full of climbing roses, and they were spilling down onto the ground.

So when Mrs. Valencia told me that her Pesto was going to help clean my family's graves and have a little party in the cemetery, I knew which grave we were going to clean. The National Cemetery took care of the graves, but Oaklawn Cemetery was a private graveyard, so there was nobody to take care of the graves except family. When I was a little girl, every time Auntie took me to visit Mita's grave, I cried my eyes out, and I wouldn't quit for hours. That's why she stopped taking me, and why it had been years since I'd been back to visit, ever since Auntie Pearl passed and was laid down to rest close by.

Pesto and his mama picked me up at the side door of the store in Mrs. V's Ford pickup.

"Bug," Mrs. V said as she put the truck in Park. "Would you like to drive? Pesto thinks it would cheer you up."

"Nah," I said, "Thanks, but I've lost my taste for driving."

They exchanged a look, but didn't say anything else about it. I dropped a bag with my stuff in the truck bed, which was full of yard equipment like rakes and hoes, hedge clippers and flower pots. Then I slid in next to Pesto in the front seat.

"You stink," I said, because he smelled like a sports bra rolled in dirt. He'd already been working in the sun to get us ready for the day, while I got to nap, which I'd done until a half hour ago. My appetite was still off the chart. I had eaten six enchiladas and downed two quarts of orange juice.

"Dude." He lifted up an arm and fanned his pit. "You haven't smelled nothing yet."

"Pesto!" Mrs. Valencia swatted him in the belly. "*Mi'jo*, that is no way to treat your girlfriend. She deserves respect."

"Girlfriend?" we said together.

Mrs. Valencia started humming and then backed out on to the street without even looking. She almost backed straight into a Buick. When the driver laid on his horn, Mrs. Valencia just waved like she had every right in the world to be running over folks.

"Dude, you all right?" Pesto said softly. "Your aura's kind of purply brown."

"Me and my aura's fine." I shook my head. "It's the enchiladas I had for lunch. Too many peppers." That was the thing about spicy food—you could blame just about anything on it.

When we got to the cemetery, I knew we'd find Mita's grave covered in all kinds of brambles and roots and leaves. How was I going to explain to folks that had supper on their families' graves every year that I had neglected my own mother? I was a no-good dog of a daughter, and that was the truth.

We pulled through the double iron gates of the cemetery and took a right turn down a dirt path. It wound around the side of the graveyard where all the rich people were laid to rest, across a rickety wooden bridge, and down the hill to an area where they buried the poor folks.

"Ah, what a beautiful day for work." Mrs. Valencia turned off the engine. She left the AC power on so we could listen to the radio. A song by Selena was playing, and Mrs. V was humming right along.

We unloaded the stuff from the bed of the truck. I grabbed a hoe and a shovel, and Pesto picked up three big flats of marigolds. Seemed like neither of us was in the mood to talk. That was okay by me, because the sun was shining, and the air had a crisp bite to it. The wind carried the spicy smell of sumac, a plant that grew all along the wall of the cemetery.

We were moving too slow, so Mrs. V started shooing us along. "Put the marigolds over there, *mi'jo*. Bug, where is your *madre* resting? We will start with her grave."

It took a few minutes to find the grave. I remembered the carved lady with the roses was by a small tree, which was a big tree now. She looked more weather-beaten, though somebody has just put on a fresh coat of whitewash. The roses had grown mad crazy, spilling all the way to the ground and spreading out like a huge wedding veil of flowers. Mita's grave marker was covered with dirt, and like I expected, the grass was grown over with little cacti sprouting up.

"Ah," Mrs. Valencia said, "what a lovely headstone. Your *madre*'s name was Catalina Rose? What a coincidence. My *mamacita's nombre* was Rosa. We will have to make this grave *muy especial* then, *sí?*"

"*Sí,*" Pesto said emphatically, and started attacking the little cacti with a hoe.

Mrs. Valencia handed me a spray bottle and a boar-bristle brush. I went to work scrubbing the headstone, washing off years' worth of grime, keeping my back turned to them so they couldn't see how ashamed I was.

When we got done, Mita's grave looked better than any grave up in that place. The grass was trimmed, the headstone was shiny, and there was a little row of river rocks around it, a border that Pesto made. We had gathered the rose vines together and brought them closer, encouraging them to grow in her direction.

Holding a rake, I stood up to stretch my sore back. It had taken us a solid hour of hard labor. My hands had blisters in the palms, and I was sore in places where I didn't know I had places.

Mrs. Valencia pushed a tray full of marigolds into my hands.

"These are the flowers of the dead, which the Aztecs called *cempasúchitl*. We place them on all of the graves."

"All of the graves?"

"*Sí.*"

I took the flowers and started arranging the little plastic pots of marigolds in the shape of a cross. Pesto and his mama stood back until I was done. Normally, you would put a picture of the loved one on the *ofrenda*. All my pictures of Mita had burnt up when the apartment burned. I could picture her in my mind still. Mita had a small smile but full lips. She didn't wear makeup much, except when me and her was going to do the shopping and then it was only lipstick. Dark red lipstick, the color of ripened cherries. Her eyes were hazel brown with little crinkles on the lid under them, and I remember tracing the crinkles with a finger, wondering why she didn't iron the wrinkles the way she pressed them out of my dresses.

This one time, Mita pushed the couch out of the middle of the room and rolled up the Navajo rug she'd once got from her grandmother. We pulled off our shoes and rubbed the soles of our feet in the dust on the stoop to make them slide easy, which I loved 'cause Mita never let me even play in the dirt, much less track it into the house. She tuned the radio to a Tejano station and cranked up the volume. "Let's dance!" she said, and spun me around like a wood top. I landed in her arms, laughing, and she spun me out again, our arms unwinding like a string. We danced the Mexican polka and another dance, the Cumbia, Mita telling me, "roll your hips, shake your shoulders," and both of us laughing and spinning, the music blaring, Mita with a smile on her face. We didn't quit until we were both covered in sweat and the neighbors were beating on the wall.

Shaking as I placed the last pot of marigolds on the grave, I lost all control of myself. I started bawling like a baby. I almost never cried, and now, it seemed like I'd never stop.

"I'll give you a few minutes alone," Mrs. Valencia said, rubbing my shoulder.

After she left, Pesto said. "It's going to be all right."

Tears and snot poured out of me, and I let loose with this growling coyote sound. Then Pesto had me. He wrapped his long arms around my shoulders, holding me to his chest so tight and hard, I felt like a little girl again, safe and protected. He kissed me on the forehead and told me things that were so far from the truth, it wasn't even funny—like it was all going to work out, he was going to help me fix it, and he loved me.

I wiped the funk off my face and looked up at Pesto. I could give myself to this boy, body and soul. But I would never have that chance. My soul was in *hock*. You know how humiliating that is, to be in hock like somebody's old china or a guitar they never learned how to play? Castoffs. Like me. "There ain't no hope for us."

"There's always hope when you love someone."

"Boy," I said, wanting to bury my face in his chest, "you don't even know what love is."

"I do love you, Bug." He took my hands and pressed them warm into his. "I want to be with you, always."

Then he tilted down to kiss me, and I pulled back wondering how this fool could want to smooch a girl with a face puffed up from crying, and then I leaned in because if a boy was willing to do that, he must really love you. His lips were soft and gentle, like I expected them to be, and then I realized that I'd been thinking a lot about how this would feel.

Know what? It felt even better.

"You think you're slick, huh?" I said when he opened his eyes.

He scratched his head. "What are you talking about?"

"I'm on to you," I said, teasing him and barely holding in a smile. "Couldn't handle my A game, so you taking advantage of me when I'm down, stealing that kiss you couldn't win."

"What kind of person do you think I am?"

"A good one." He was getting all hurt, so I grabbed his shirt and pulled him down to my level. "I'm just messing with you, dog." Then I laid my own kiss on him, and his eyes popped open. He was gentle, I was fierce. He was calming and damn, I was hot, 'cause I kiss like I play ball—all out.

"I want to be with you, too," I said, letting go of his shirt and then grabbing it again.

Wow, he tried to say, but no words came out. That's when I knew. I loved him, too.

The world went white. No, brown, the color of sand. It looked white because I was standing in the middle of the miles and miles of dunes in White Sands. With the sun's light blazing at an angle, the sand looked like snow. The wind blew dirt into my mouth.

"Pesto?" I spun around, kicking up a sandy dust, searching for him. Gone. He was gone. "Pesto!" I screamed.

"He cannot hear you. He is not even aware that you're missing," Beals said. He appeared a yard away from me. He was taller, beefier, with more hair. The hair looked darker, thicker, wavier, and a week-old beard covered his face.

"This is a dream," I said. I meant it to sound like a fact. It came out like a question.

Beals denied it. "Think of this as my business office. It is where I do my work and where you will have a desk when you have accepted my offer to serve as my assistant."

"Not on your life," I said. "Or mine."

"Pesto's then."

My face burned hot. I swallowed, then said, "Like that stupid boy means something to me."

"You are too transparent, Miss Smoot." He chuckled. "Did that young man not pronounce his love for you? Did you not admit yours for him?"

I crossed my arms and turned my back on him. "Mind your own damned business."

"Rude gestures aside, understand this: Thrice I have offered rewards to take your place at my side. Thrice you have rebuffed me. I shall not make an offer again."

"Good." Maybe now he'd let me be for a while.

"Next time I shall take your life. Your life, Miss Smoot."

I waited a few seconds to answer, so he'd know I was thinking. "I'm ready."

Beals licked his reddening lips. "Splendid."

"I'm ready for you to kiss my ass. Don't matter what you offer me, asshole, the last place I want to be is at your side. Now, put me back. I got a party to go to."

# CHAPTER 29

# Love the One You Be With

*Next time, I shall take your life. Your life, Miss Smoot.* Beals's threat kept replaying in my mind the whole time we finished the work on the grave, put away our tools, and washed up in the restroom of a Mickey D's. You got to take hold, girl, I told myself after we got in the truck and drove back to the neighborhood. Put that fool demon out of your head for a little while and have some fun for once.

So that's what I decided to do as we drove down Ochoa Street into the *barrio*. Just in time for the Fiesta de Las Muertas to really start jumping.

I knew a party when I heard one. The clatter of steel drums trickled down the street, and the evening clamored with the sounds of music and laughter. The sun was a blood orange in the sky when Mrs. Valencia parked the truck at the 7-Eleven on Fourth Avenue. The three of us piled out. I hooked Pesto's arm and strolled up the sidewalk, intending to enjoy myself, just to spite Beals. And the warm, inviting smell of food—*taquitos*, frying *empanadas, sopaipillas,* and baked bread! My belly growled in anticipation.

"To avoid the traffic," she explained when Pesto asked why she was making us walk so far.

"Besides," Mrs. V said, "you can use the exercise, *mi'jo*. Your pants have been getting a little tight in the seat, *es verdad*?"

"No, it's not true." He twisted around, trying to look. "Bug, does my butt look fat in these jeans?"

"No ma'am." I laughed and then dodged as he swatted at me. "Missed me, missed me, now you got to kiss me."

Ahead, the crowd noise and the thump of salsa music got louder. The rhythms called to me, pulled me forward like a siren's song. I grabbed Pesto's hand. "Dang!" I shouted, feeling the beat in my belly button. "Hurry, dog. Don't keep a girl waiting."

"Why the hurry?" Mrs. V yelled over the noise. "There is time to enjoy ourselves."

Enjoy, yes. Time, no. Beals would come for me soon, and I wanted one last night to get my groove on.

"Mamá, where's your Latin blood? Get with the program," Pesto answered for me. "We came to party, *sí*? Don't be a stick in the mud."

"*Cada uno lleva su cruz.* That is my cross to bear." She waved us on. "You two enjoy yourselves. But stay on Campbell Street, *por favor.* The police have closed it from here to Eighth Avenue, so you'll be safe."

"*Maldición!*" Pesto said. "Why are you overprotective tonight? We can cross the street alone, you know. We're not *niños.*"

"No one said you were. But never mind that—*¡vámanos!* Have fun. There are many of my *amigas brujas* here tonight, and I must buy supplies while I have the chance."

We watched her bustle over to a clump of gray-haired *señoras,* most of them dressed in velvet gowns and wearing embroidered shawls over their faces. They were gathered under a small tent, looking more like hens than witches.

"Your mama's a trip," I said.

Pesto pulled me close and slipped his thumb into my back pocket. "*Cada uno lleva su cruz,*" he sighed, and we both laughed. "But I love her anyway."

He led me to the corner of Father Rahim Avenue, where a band played loud, hot salsa. The musicians wore skeleton costumes, which glowed greenish-yellow in the twilight. Their heads were painted like *calaveras*—white faces, with big round spots for eyes, nose, and mouth.

We plunged into a crowd of costumed partiers. I started grooving to the beat, right alongside a couple of dancers dressed in red, ankle-length crinoline skirts and halter tops. They wore pink scarves over their hair, and their faces were painted like skulls, too.

"It's the dance of the dead!" I shouted over the music to Pesto.

"Wait till you see the parade." He watched me work my hips. "Want to salsa?"

"Don't know how!" I called.

"C'mon, I'll show you." Pesto took my right hand in his left. He set the other hand on the small of my back, and I could feel the heat of his skin through my shirt. I touched his shoulder. We looked deep into each other's eyes, and—

He spun me like a freaking top.

"Whoa!" I twirled back around, and he caught me in his arms.

"Yeah!" Pesto shouted as he swung me out, then grabbed me around the waist. "Righteous! You're even more beautiful when you dance."

I did a body roll and bumped my hips into his. "Oh please. I ain't beautiful, and you know it."

"Don't try to be modest." Pesto pulled me close with a double-handhold step, and his arm brushed against my top. "How would you like it if I didn't notice how sexy my girlfriend was?"

My face blushed hot. "How would you like it if I knocked you in the head?"

"Just speaking the truth!" He laughed and swung me around, threw an arm across my belly, and set his chin on my shoulder. "Any harm in that?"

"Stop it!" Mrs. V hollered and rushed up to us. "Oye! The whole *barrio* is watching you."

She took Pesto by the wrist and hauled him away from the bandstand.

Embarrassed, I scooted off to the sidewalk. I pretended my shirt needed rearranging, but it was me that needed to straighten up. Girl, what were you thinking?

"Mamá, it's the fiesta!" Pesto threw his arms wide. "Live a little, eh?"

"This is not the time to draw attention to yourselves." She wagged a finger under his nose, then crossed her arms.

I stepped in. "Yo, dog, she's got a point." I didn't want to show up my boy, but I kind of agreed with her. Everybody didn't need to know our business. So I put a hand on his chest and said under my breath, "We can dance some other time, a'ight?"

"Come with me." Mrs. V grabbed us both by our pinkie fingers and led us down to the next block on Campbell, to where the junk vendors had set up shop. "*Mira*, Pesto, smell this. I was able to buy fresh dried spearmint leaves. It's so hard to find these days. Now, I need some beeswax."

Pesto leaned over to me. "She needs to mind her own beeswax."

"I heard that! No candy for you."

"That's okay," he said. "I've already got something sweet."

I rolled my eyes. Please. I couldn't tell if Pesto was show-ing out for his mama or had read a book of bad pick-up lines. Either way, it was irritating me, like the tags on the seam of a new shirt. "Look at all this sh—stuff," I said to change the subject.

Mrs. V drifted down the row of tables until she found one selling pots of marigolds and votive candles, along with rolls of beeswax.

Me and Pesto stopped at a booth selling every kind of cheap toy or *calaveras* T-shirts associated with Los Muertos. You could blow your whole paycheck on *mazapán*, black velvet paintings, plastic toys, and blow-up glow-in-the-dark skeletons.

"Some families save all year," Pesto pointed out, "just to buy stuff for All Souls' Day."

They were also selling palm readings. A sign offered to "bestow the secrets of your destiny" for only five bucks.

I pointed at the sign. "Think I ought to go for it? Y'know,

test them, since we know my destiny." I meant to be funny, but it came out sounding sad.

Pesto didn't seem to notice. "Don't waste your money. I can read your palm way better."

I stuck out my good hand. "Prove it."

He gently unfolded my fingers then traced my lifeline with a fingertip. "I see . . . I see . . ."

"You see what?"

"I see . . . the weather forecast."

"The what?"

"The weather. Tonight's forecast is for warmer temperatures. Very warm."

What had come over him? Since when did he start getting all Rico Suave? I balled up my hand into a fist. "Boy, you better quit trying to play me."

"Playing's not what I had in mind."

"See? That's what I'm talking about."

He scratched his head, confused. "Dude, I thought, you know, girls like that kind of thing."

I crossed my arms. "Not this girl. Damn, don't you know me by now? Don't try to be something you're not." I wanted to smack him.

Girl, you better take hold of yourself. What is wrong with you? I felt so irritated, like my clothes didn't fit right.

"Dude, it's just—"

"I don't play games. If you want something, come right out and say it."

"I do want something." He lowered his voice. "To spend time with you."

Mrs. V chose that moment to walk up behind him.

"Look!" I said loudly. "They've got sugar skulls. Want one . . . Mrs. V?"

Pesto looked like he'd snorted a nuclear-hot tepin pepper.

While Mrs. V eyed Pesto suspiciously, I dug out some money and bought three sugar skulls, one for each of us.

The booth happened to belong to the Valencias' neighbor, Mrs. Morales. "*Hola, Mariposa y Pesto. Who is this niña bonita with you?*"

"*Oh, ella es una amiga de la escuela.*" Pesto nudged me to keep strolling. "Say nothing. She is the biggest gossip in the *barrio*. I told her you were a school friend. But by tomorrow, she'll be telling everyone we're engaged."

"Engaged, huh?" That didn't sound so bad. Except that I'd never be married. There were lots of things I'd never be.

"Mrs. Morales made these herself," Mrs. V said after she caught up with us and I handed her a sugar skull on a stick.

I took a lick of mine then screwed up my face. It tasted like ammonia.

"Sour?" Pesto said.

I nodded, not wanting to offend Mrs. Morales. I took a second lick just to be sure. Nasty.

Pesto, though, took a big bite and about tore that thing up. He ripped the head in half, and little pieces of skull hung off his bottom lip, dancing around as he said, "Dude, you're doing it all wrong. Don't just lick it."

So he grabbed my stick and bit my skull in two.

I hit him. "I was going to save that."

"Ow! That hurt."

"Suffer."

Mrs. V gave Pesto her sugar skull, and he gobbled it up, too. "Ay, my son, what a pig he is. Come on, *mi'jos*. Join the procession to *las ofrendas*. The exhibition is about to begin."

As the last of twilight faded into night, we followed the slow-moving crowd a few blocks down Campbell Street. The *ofrendas* were displayed under tents around the edge of Armijo Park, which covered a whole city block. Two sidewalks crisscrossed the grass, and my eye followed them to the center of the park, where I saw a huge, dried-up fountain.

In the middle of the fountain's empty pool, there was a marble goddess holding a nocked bow. She stood on the heads of four sea turtles with open mouths. Below that were a dozen sculptures of Cupid, all of them holding water jugs.

"Look at this one," Pesto said, getting my attention.

He pointed to an *ofrenda* the size of a king-sized bed, with hundreds of marigolds and just as many candles. They put out so much heat, I could feel the burn on my cheeks ten feet away.

"Now that's an offering," I said.

"Amazing, isn't it?"

We saw hundreds more *ofrendas* in all shapes and sizes. Some were simply a cross, flowers, and an arch. Others were over the top, with all kinds of psychedelic skulls, life-size skeletons dancing together, and papier-mâché cows with flowers for horns.

"Dog, I see what you mean about spending a whole paycheck on the *ofrendas*. Dang."

Holding hands, we walked on down to the south corner of the park, where the parade started up. The first group was a company of Native girls dressed in heavy cotton skirts decorated with rolled-up cones of metal.

"Jingle dancers," Pesto said.

Next, a group of big-gutted men wearing vests and fezzes rode by, peddling tiny bicycles and waving to the crowd with orange foam-rubber fingers.

"Jingle bellies," Pesto said.

Snort. Now that, I thought, is the boy I fell in love with.

"Look, you two," Mrs. Valencia said, "the big-head puppets are next."

A line of dancing skeletons came by after that, followed by the biggest puppet ever: a black-faced Jaguar with deer antlers sticking out of its head. Its arms were so long, it took two extra puppeteers to carry them. Its wingspan took up the whole street, from sidewalk to sidewalk. In one hand, it held a pitchfork, and in the other, a whip.

"Remind you of anybody?" Pesto said.

Yeah, it did. It also reminded me that our together time was short. I snuck a quick look at my scratched palm and frowned. I squeezed my hand shut. It was wrong. Us trying to be together.

Pesto tried to put an arm around me. I shrugged it off. I tugged at my collar. Why was it so hot? I felt all out of sorts. My skin was dry and itchy and too sore to scratch. It felt tight, too, like my whole body was one size too big.

"Bug, wait," Pesto said. "I only—"

"I know, I know." I leaned in and set my head in the space between his shoulder and chest. He smelled so good, it made me forget for a minute how spiteful I felt. "I was counting on finding a way out of this by now."

"That's okay. We can go to Plan B."

"Dog, we've been through so many plans, we've used up the whole alphabet." I sniffed the air. My mouth started watering. "Do I smell *tamales*?"

Up ahead, at the corner of Eighth and Campbell, there was

a white-haired man selling *tamales* out of a cart. I loved the warm texture of the filling on my tongue, the bitter flavor of cumin. When I was a little girl, me and Mita used to make *tamales* with the family next door and then sit out on the stoop, eating and talking, passing time by finding constellations in a sky full of stars.

"*Dos*, please," I told the man, and handed over the money. I bought two, one for each of us.

I unwrapped mine from the corn-husk wrapper and took a bite. My tongue about danced in anticipation.

Oh, the flavor was ecstasy.

At first.

Then I bit down into something crunchy and felt wriggling in my mouth.

My stomach twisted, and I spat the *tamale* out on the street. Maggots. The filling was full of maggots. I dropped the uneaten part onto the sidewalk.

Pesto picked it up. "Dude, what're you doing?"

I started feeling strange, like I had the flu. My face felt flushed hot again, and my stomach made a deep rumbling noise.

"I'm going to puke," I told Pesto, and ran around the side of a hardware store into an alley. My stomach heaved again, and I vomited maggots.

I pointed to the pile of writhing white worms on the pavement. "Look! The freaking *tamale*'s full of freaking maggots!"

The only light came from a utility lamp over a door deeper in the lane. Pesto bent down to check out the mess.

He shook his head. "I don't see anything. No maggots here."

I slumped against a rusted-out Dumpster, and the stink of rotting food and wet cardboard made me puke again.

This time, the maggots were floating in something red.

"Blood," I said. My knees sagged.

"That was a dry heave, Bug." Pesto grabbed me around the waist to hold me up. "No blood, nothing."

I unhooked Pesto's arm from my waist and stumbled back against the brick wall of the alley, the middle of my palm burning like a handful of battery acid. My whole hand was turning black now, as if my blood was ink and the veins were wet with it. I tried to make a fist, but my hand was too swollen to close. I felt a spike of stabbing pain, and my thumbnail split in two.

I fell to one knee. With my good hand, I grabbed Pesto by the shirt. "Go, baby," I gasped. "You got to run."

"I'm not running anywhere." He swept me up, and I turned my face away so he didn't have to smell the sick on me.

We'd gone a couple of steps toward the mouth of the alley when the buzzing started.

Flies. My head lolled to the side, and I couldn't lift it. All I could do was watch as the air filled with black flies. They erupted out of the manhole covers, the same as the thick swarm I'd seen at the convenience store, only ten times bigger.

"Go," I rasped at Pesto because he'd stopped and was looking down at a manhole.

"Wait." He stomped on the cover, which had been lifted up a couple inches.

"It's a demon!" He squatted on the cover, keeping it down with our combined weight.

*Clang!* The demon slammed into the lid below us. *Whump! Clang!*

"Hang on! I—"

With a roar the demon threw the lid aside. Together, me and Pesto tumbled across the alleyway.

Pesto twisted to take the brunt of the impact with his shoulders, and we slammed into a row of plastic garbage cans. I landed on top of him, limp as a soggy corn-husk doll.

The djinn hopped like a frog into the alley.

"More coming," I said, and three other djinn escaped as Pesto climbed to his feet, groggy and vulnerable. He held up a wobbly fist as if to say, Bring it on.

They rushed us.

And the coyote rushed them.

Growling, she shot out from behind the Dumpster and leapt into the air. Her snarling mouth caught the throat of the first djinn and ripped it open. He fell backward into the manhole, spraying the ground with black ink.

Before the others could react, the coyote circled back around, putting herself between us and them.

She yipped, a high-pitched warning bark.

"Hurry," I begged Pesto. "She can't hold them off."

"Hurrying!" Instantly, he slung me into a fireman's carry and pulled a remote control out of his pocket. He hit it three times then took several quick strides toward the street before I heard the sound of brakes.

*SCREECH!*

Pesto staggered to the sidewalk as a lime green pickup truck whipped into the alley ahead. Its high beams flooded us, and I felt too weak to even cover my eyes. A blizzard of white dots blanketed my vision.

"It's about time!" Pesto yelled.

"Sorry!" Castor called as he jumped out of the front seat. "Bad traffic."

He and Pollux wore the same Hawaiian shirts, along with wide, leather utility belts. The pentalpha on the brim of their caps shone like a badge, and I blinked away the white dots so I could watch the action.

They pulled on bulky backpack sprayers. "Find cover!" Pollux ordered. "This could get ugly!"

We slipped behind the truck.

Pollux opened up on the djinn with his sprayers, and the demons froze in mid-step, their arms raised in defense, posed like mannequins in the window of a trendy mall store.

Pollux shouted, "Back! Back! Fiends of Hell!"

"That's not really necessary, you know," Castor said.

"Buzz kill."

"Nublet."

"What about the animal?" Pollux said, pointing his nozzle at the coyote. It slunk backward behind the Dumpster, teeth bared and growling.

Castor unclipped a plastic cylinder from his utility belt. "Out of our jurisdiction. Let it go."

I dropped my head onto Pesto's shoulder. "I'm so tired."

"Hang on," he said.

While Castor and Pollux cleaned up the mess, Pesto carried me to the center of the park. He set me down on the edge of the derelict fountain.

"Where does it hurt?" he said, checking my pulse.

"We playing doctor now?" I said. My head was clearing, but my stomach was twisted in knots, and my hand burned like fury.

"Pesto!" Mrs. V came running across the park grounds. "Is Bug injured? *¿Qué pasó?*"

"Djinn," I said.

Pesto pointed to the alley. "They're coming through the sewers."

A wave of pain hit my gut, and I pulled into a ball. Mrs. V grabbed my bloated hand and found the bloodied thumb. She pressed on the cut. Pus and blood spurted out of it.

Mrs. V pulled a handkerchief from her purse and wrapped it around my thumb. "Put pressure on this," she ordered Pesto. "Don't let go, no matter what happens."

"Mamá, what *is* happening?" Pesto said.

"It's Beals," she said. "He's coming for Bug."

# CHAPTER 30

# The Fountain of Luth

Castor and Pollux clearly didn't understand the situation. They were packing up.

"Stop!" Mrs. V demanded. "You can't leave now!"

While she charged over to them, the NADs casually pushed the four cylinders into the safe in the back of the truck and shut the tailgate.

She pointed at me, then to the alley, then at me again. Castor shrugged and climbed into the cabin, but Pollux must've said something smart because she yanked off his stocking cap and swatted him with it.

Pollux stomped to his side of the truck. He hopped inside and slammed the door. The truck clattered to life, and they probably would've driven off without another word if the earthquake hadn't hit.

The ground rumbled and shook. Up and down Campbell Street, the pavement buckled, and the concrete sidewalks crumbled. Mrs. V and the NADs raced toward us.

Manhole covers shot into the air. Then landed with a heavy *clang! clang! clang!*

Djinn leapt out of the sewers, dressed in navy blue suits, stinking of human waste. They were silent except for the high-pitched rasping sound they made as they stalked toward us.

All at once, the crowds of partiers got the message. It wasn't some kind of stunt. They ran in all different directions, wild-eyed with fear in their death costumes. They knocked over trash cans, climbed over cars, crashed into newspaper stands, and stampeded anybody that had fallen in their way, as chunks of asphalt, dirt, and sand blew into the air and then rained down.

As Pesto protected me from the falling debris, Castor and Pollux laid out a cloud of Super Hold. But there were dozens of demons now, way too many for two NADs to control.

Pesto pulled out the remote control and started furiously pounding buttons.

"No use! There's no backup crew on duty," Castor yelled. "We're on our own!"

The djinn closed in. A haze of stinking sulphurous gas clung to them.

*Boom! Ka-bloom!* The windows of the hardware store exploded, and after another low rumble, fire shot through the windows. With a concussive blast of superheated air, the doors blew open and a river of fire poured out, like lit gasoline from a pump.

The flames spread fast until the fountain green was one curtained inferno.

"Come on!" Pesto grabbed me under the arms.

No use. I was a stone.

Mrs. V pulled out a bag of dried spearmint. She crumbled the leaves, then spread them in a tight circle around the fountain. They smelled like chewing gum, but richer, stronger. Almost too strong.

*"Prisa!"* she commanded, "Get inside the spearmint line with Bug. The djinn cannot cross it."

Castor and Pesto followed her into the circle as a wave of reinforcements swept past the frozen djinn, closing in on us. They sprayed Super Hold until their tanks drained dry. But the next wave came, then another.

The last of the fixative sputtered out, and Pollux turned to Castor as if to say, What now?

The fire encircled us. It popped and cracked, electric, biting, torching the night.

Through the smell of burning, I caught the stink of rotten eggs.

Beals.

He waltzed through the flames. "My, what a lovely reception. And a pair of plumbers' helpers from ISIS as well. I am flattered."

"I'll give you a reception!" Pesto screamed, and charged.

"Wait!" Castor grabbed for him.

"Now stop!" With a wave of his hand, Beals made Pesto—and everybody else—fall silent. They froze mid-step, like affixed demons.

"See? Two can play at that game, Castor," Beals said, stepping over the spearmint leaves. "Ah, my recumbent Miss Smoot. Now I can devote my undivided attention to you."

Beals hovered above me. I was completely paralyzed. Unable to fight him off. "Sorry to interrupt your fiesta, but I sensed that your feelings for the young agent were going too strong, and I could not allow that to continue. What is that phrase human males adore so much? Ah yes, if I can't have you, no one can."

My eyes burned from his sulphurous breath as he bent low.

"How delicious you are!" He licked his lips and shuddered with delight. "The taste is always sweeter when the fruit has been denied, don't you think? Ah, Miss Smoot, when I am finished feasting tonight, you will belong to me and me alone. For eternity."

I shot him a bird with my brain.

His djinn had moved in tight against the circle of spearmint. Like they could smell the blood of a new soul. Their eyes grew wild and ashen, and they softly chanted my name.

*Don't be saying my name!* I screamed silently.

Gingerly, lovingly, Beals lifted my hand up and placed it in his. He ran his forefinger along the scratch mark, and my skin felt as if it had turned to ice. He set his lips to my thumb, tasted the air with his rattlesnake tongue. And went tumbling head-first into the empty fountain pool.

"Watch that first step," a deep voice boomed. "It's a doozy." I turned my eyes to follow the voice. Scratch stood high on the head of the goddess. He was dressed in a white suit with a white straw hat, and he carried an ivory-handled cane that he used for balance.

Stepping from the goddess's shoulder to the head of a tur-tle to the back of a Cupid, he moved to the edge of the pool and hooked the collar of Beals's suit coat with the handle of his cane.

Beals came up spitting mad, his suit covered in muck. "How dare you interfere, Lucifer?"

He sprang backward high into the air, like a supernatural

grasshopper, and landed lightly outside the spearmint line. He threw back his head. A swarm of black flies erupted from his mouth. They caught fire, creating a buzzing firestorm that attacked Scratch with no mercy, blanketing him with a swirling mass of red coals.

"Lucifer, you will feel my unchained wrath."

Scratch yawned. Like a conductor starting an orchestra, he drew his hands together to signal an upbeat. Jets of water spurted out of the mouths of the turtles. On the downbeat, water gushed from the Cupids' jars. He raised a fist, and torrents of water deluged the once-dry pool. Thick, steaming mists rose from the fountain, snuffing the fire out of Beals's black flies. They popped like tiny firecrackers and landed dead in the water, giving off the acrid stink of burnt gunpowder.

"Bless his heart," Scratch said, lowering his hands and taking a bow. "He tries, doesn't he?"

"Yarrrr!" Beals threw up his arms like, what the hell? What's a demon got to do? Then he stepped past Pesto and the others, back into the line of hissing djinn. "You can't defeat us all, Scratch. We are many, you are few."

"Stop it, you old fraud. You know as well as I that neither of us can harm the other. This is all theatre, and bad theatre at that." Scratch turned his attention to me. "Pardon me, *ma belle au bois dormant*. I did not intend to ignore your plight."

He tapped the mark on my palm, and the swelling faded, taking the throbbing pain with it. I sat up, holding the hand tight against my stomach. I felt limp and clammy inside.

I should've thanked him, but I was way past being polite. "Don't pretend you're doing this for me."

"True," he said, and snapped his fingers. "I'm doing it for all of mankind. Quite magnanimous of me, wouldn't you say?"

I got to my feet, trying to stand tall. "No, I would not."

"Still feisty." He twirled his mustache. "I like that. I see now why Beals chose you. You have that *je ne sais quoi* quality he adores so much in humans."

"Excuse me if I don't give a damn." I grabbed hold of Pesto's cold hand, trying to pull him away from the fountain. But he was as rigid and solid as the fountain statues. "Let them go!" I screamed.

"If I did that, you might escape," Scratch said. "And you mustn't leave quite yet, *chérie*. There is business to attend to."

He turned to Beals, who was standing arms crossed behind the djinn on a buckled chunk of sidewalk. His face was dark, hidden, but I could see his almond eyes smoldering.

"Beelzebub! I believe you've stolen one of my souls. Release her, if you don't mind."

Beals wailed like a gull protecting a scavenged french fry. "I do mind. Very much. My Old Law salvage rights supersede your contract rights, which you well know. Finders-keepers. She is mine. For eternity."

Scratch stepped down from the fountain and crossed to where I was still pulling in vain on Pesto's hand. The djinn murmured and scuttled away as Scratch leaned against Pollux's stony body, an elbow resting on the Super Hold backpack.

"But clearly, you are open to negotiation on that point. Why else would you take so long to claim her? So, you're using her as bait. Consider me hooked. The question is, what do you want?"

"Why," Beals said, "domination of the earthly plane, of course. With the usual terms of combat."

"Not that old chestnut again?" Scratch pulled out a cigar. He drew a nail across Pollux's forehead, and the tip of his finger erupted in flame. He took a deep puff. "I hoped you would choose something more original."

Beals snarled. "Unlike you, I am not so easily distracted from my ambition. Domination of Earth. Or nothing."

Scratch shrugged. "Have it your way. If you win, you get the Earth to do as you wish for one hundred years. If I win, you will be sentenced to one thousand years chained above the fiery pit."

"And," Beals said, "you renounce all claim to the girl."

"We have a wager."

"Hold up!" I let go of Pesto and stepped as close to Scratch as I dared. "Ain't nobody asked me what I think of this whole deal." I was the one thought of a bet in the first place. "There ain't going to be no wager unless—"

"The die is cast," Scratch boomed.

*Crack!* The night sky seemed to split, and the park filled with thick, pungent smoke that made my eyes fill with tears. I dropped coughing and wheezing to the ground.

# CHAPTER 31

# You Got to Protect This House

When the smoke cleared, my head felt like a chewed-up sugar skull. I was alone, parked on the hardwood floor of the dimly lit El Paso High gym. A single basketball sat on the floor near the center circle.

I picked the ball up, spun it on one finger, and then pressed it against my nose. The smell of the leather was better than cologne, better than the scent of a window box hibiscus on a dusty day. After Papa C died, I should've come back to the game. I missed it more than I ever imagined.

The roof of the gym formed a narrow v-shape, with a ribcage of steel trusses that curved down at the walls. On a hot day you could smell the resin in the wood and the turpentine stink of the varnish. The gym had seen better times. The hardwood was full of scratches and gouges, and the paint that marked the free throw lanes had faded out. The air inside was hot and muggy, like the furnace had been turned up to full blast.

"What the hell is going on?" I said. A small spotlight clicked on, flooding me in a pool of blinding light. I shielded my eyes.

"Exactly, Miss Smoot." After all the time I spent around Beals, his voice still sounded like fingernails on a chalkboard. He stepped into the light, but I could see his eyes glowing in the darkness before he got there.

"Where's my crew? Pesto? Mrs. V?" I said. "The NAD boys?"

"Your motley collection of friends," Beals said, "is in the stands, sitting in the silent darkness, suffering the great pain of knowing nothing."

"You're pure evil." He was still trying to mess with my head.

"Nonsense." He wiped his glasses with an embroidered handkerchief. "Nothing is pure evil. I, myself, am only three percent evil. The remainder is made up of blind, insatiate ambition, no different from any CEO who climbs the backs of his colleagues to reach the top, then rapes the environment, gives unborn children birth defects from chemical dumping, and impoverishes thousands of workers to save the pennies that purchase his golden parachute."

"Give it a rest." I bounced the ball. The sound echoed in the rafters. "You're only saying that to justify yourself."

"The need to justify inhumanity is a particularly human trait. I neither pretend nor make apologies for what I am. Or for what I want." He chuckled. "Now on to the business at hand. Scratch and I have arranged a wager. A game of basketball for control of the Earthly plane."

Basketball for world domination? "Why basketball?"

"Nephilim are incapable of harming one another, as you saw earlier. Scratch can annoy me, but he cannot destroy me. Therefore, we must use champions to fight our battles. That is your part in this wager. If you choose to play as my champion, I shall release your soul. If you win."

I spun the ball on my middle finger. "My free will, too?"

Beals's lip got jumpy. "If you win."

"What about the first contract I had with Scratch?" I did a crossover dribble between the legs. "He acts like it's still in force, too. Since you stole my soul and all that right out from under his nose."

His anger smoldered like burning tires. "Scratch agreed to release you from his contract, as well. He has repossessed both the car and your grandfather, after all."

So if I win a basketball game, I get to change my fate? I didn't have to think twice. "I'm in."

I expected Beals to cackle, but for a half a second, I saw a shadow of doubt cross his face, as if he was more worried than he was letting on. "So kind of you to agree to play for me. I do enjoy the bitter irony. It is so . . ."

"Bitter?"

". . . excruciating."

"So's your voice." I perched the ball on my hip. "Now, shut up and let's do this. And make sure we're all straight on the rules. Ain't going to be no stipulations and escape clauses."

"In due time, Miss Smoot."

A bigger spotlight popped on, bathing me in brightness. I was wearing shorts and a jersey, my old EP High uniform. The jersey was trimmed in blue, and there was a red stripe running from under the arm to the edge of the shorts. My shoes had changed, too, into a pair of Converse that matched the uniform.

"Name your second," Beals said.

"My what?"

He sighed, looking pained. "The game is two-on-two, according to the parameters of the bet. Choose a second player for your team."

Easy decision. "I pick my boy Pesto."

Beals smiled, like he knew what I'd say. He probably did because it was all part of some dumb-ass plan I was playing into. So what. I didn't give a damn anymore.

"I said, I pick Pesto. What's the holdup?"

Pop! There Pesto stood in a matching jersey. My heart did a little dance, *thump-thump-thump*, to see him.

"Bug," he said, jabbering, "I've got your back. Just you and me. We can do this if we give a hundred and ten percent."

I put a finger to my lips to shush him. "Who we playing against?" I asked Beals.

"I promised not to kiss and tell," Beals said, pretending to lock his lips. He stepped out of the light and disappeared.

"Asshole."

Seconds later, another spotlight flicked on at the opposite end of the court, and somebody stepped into the pool of light.

"It's her," I said to Pesto. "Every bad thing that ever happened to me wrapped up in a big sack of meat."

Tangle-eye stood underneath the basket dressed in her black Coronado uniform, doing nothing but waving her championship ring and staring at us hard. Like that was going to work on me.

I wanted to tell that skank, Girl, I've done looked into the maggot-and-pus-filled face of a demon. You think your ugly mug is going to scare me?

Behind her, the double lobby doors flew open. The house lights went up, and in marched the audience for the game, all the djinn from the fountain square, plus a few hundred more.

So Beals had brought his boys for backup. Funny how Scratch didn't seem to need a posse.

They filed into the bleachers on the left side of the court. The other side was empty. Where were Mrs. V and the NADs? Beals said they were here, too.

"Dude," Pesto said, moving closer to me. His face was flushed, and beads of sweat were forming on his lip. The gym felt swampy hot and smelled like wet corduroy pants. "I didn't know there would be, like, spectators watching."

"Me neither. You can hang, though, right?" I said, and then a movement caught my eye. "Well, well, look what the cat drug in. I wondered where she'd gone."

E. Figg was walking down the bleachers from the press box, talking to an older woman in a black judge's gown. They were followed by Mrs. V, who looked frazzled and worried, and the NADs, who both had buckets of popcorn. Popcorn? Unfreaking-believable.

Bringing up the rear was this tall, handsome brother with a '70s Afro and hands the size of skillets. There was something familiar about the way he looked, the way he moved. So familiar, it felt like I knew him.

Sitting in the stands behind the scorer's table were Beals and Scratch. Scratch tipped his hat to me, and Beals showed his fangs.

"Pesto! Bug!" Mrs. V shouted, sounding more confident than she looked. "You can do it, *niños*. We have faith in you."

She took a seat on the bleachers next to Castor, who shared his popcorn. Dang, Mrs. V. Not you, too.

E. Figg left the bleachers and crossed the court. She bowed her head, probably afraid to watch. Have a little faith, I wanted to tell her. Me and Pesto, we got game, and if Tangle-eye couldn't cheat, we were going to own her ass once and for all.

"Bug," E. Figg said after she'd waved us over to the top of the key on one end of the court. She had to holler over the music and noise of the crowd. "I'm sorry I didn't get in touch with you myself. By the time I contacted Scratch, Beals had mobilized his djinn, so the meeting happened, but not the way you wanted."

"You arranged this game?"

She smiled and nodded. "You didn't think I'd abandoned you?"

Which is exactly what I thought. I shrugged. "Um, well. You know how it is."

She covered her mouth in shock. "Bug! I would never desert a client."

"It's game time, counselor," the woman in the black gown said as she joined us in the key. She waved for Tangle-eye to come over, too. "Players, my name is Judge Hathorne. My family has a long history of presiding fairly and objectively over contests like these."

Then she put a ball on her hip and went over the house rules for the game. "No supernatural powers allowed. No interference from higher powers. No blood, no foul. You are playing to ten, one point per basket. Half-court. Make it, take it. One free throw equals one field goal. Any questions?"

I pointed at the tall brother with the Afro, who was crossing the court, coming toward us. "What's his story?"

E. Figg spoke, "That's the bad news. I think you'll recognize him, if you add a few years to his face."

I stared hard. "Papa C?"

He winked. "Jitterbug." He had come back as a younger version of himself.

All I could say was, "Sorry, old man. I already got my second."

"That's right," Pesto said, giving his jersey a shake. "Me."

"He ain't your second, Coyote," Tangle-eye said, stepping up next to Papa C. "He's mine."

E. Figg patted my shoulder. "On that note, I'll take my leave. Bug, Pesto. Do me a favor. Kick his ass."

As E. Figg returned to the bleachers, I stood slack-jawed, trying to sort all this out. The muggy heat of the gym seemed to be affecting my brain. It was too hot to think.

Papa C cleared his throat. He smelled like boiled cabbage. "Old Scratch made me an offer I couldn't refuse. He says he's going to give a soul back to whoever scores the winning basket."

"Your soul? What about me? I lost everything because you wanted a freaking car. You pawned your own granddaughter, you son of a bitch!"

I expected him to at least say he was sorry. That he was out of his mind with Cadillac lust. That he didn't know I was signing myself away to eternity in the fiery pit. But all he did was look at me and say, "A man's got to do what a man's got to do."

"How would you know? You ain't no man." I turned my back on him.

"It ain't got to be that way, Jitterbug. I tried to make it right."

"Kiss. My. Ass."

The judge blew her whistle. The scoreboard flickered on.

"Time to play, Coyote," Tangle-eye said.

"Shut the hell up," I said, and checked Pesto to make sure he was ready because he looked like he was about to puke, too.

"Tip-off," the judge yelled, and tossed the ball high.

With the sound of sneakers squeaking on wood, all four of us jumped at the same time. Me and Pesto smacked heads, and Tangle-eye fell over her own feet. Papa C yanked down the ball and busted ass up the lane. He went for the finger roll, and put in an easy layup.

"1–0," the judge called out.

The score was posted on the scoreboard clock. The crowd of djinn stomped the bleachers to the rhythm of "Another One Bites the Dust." I fought the urge to salute them with my middle finger.

The air in the gym felt like a sauna. It had to be over a hundred degrees. Back in the day, I had liked it that way. Heat made the other basketball teams give out, to sweat harder than we ever sweated.

But a long time had passed, and I wasn't used to the heat. Pesto was feeling it, too. At the top of the key, sweat pouring down his face, he checked the ball to Papa C, and I got on Tangle-eye's hip.

When the pass came her way, I jumped in front and stole it, then flicked it back to Pesto. He stepped up for that sweet jumper, but as soon as it left his hands, Papa C swatted it down. He grabbed the ball, used Tangle-eye to pick me, and popped the strings with a deep jumper of his own.

"2–0," the judge said.

The crowd erupted in screams and stomping. The gym felt like it was getting smaller and hotter, and Pesto's hair was soaked with sweat.

I grabbed the rebound so that me and Pesto could set up a play.

"Your *abuelo*'s killing us," he said, breathing hard.

I nodded that he was right. "Then we deny him the rock. I'll let Tangle-eye get the ball. We'll both defend Papa C and leave her wide open to lay some bricks."

We did. She did.

Three shots, three misses.

Brick. Brick. Brick.

I beat Papa C to the ball—he had height, but I had moves—and bounced it out to Pesto, who drained a jumper.

"2–1."

The djinn booed so loud, it rattled the windows. Pesto covered his ears, but I ate it up like candy—the sound of hundreds of voices in one place, the echo of the announcer's voice on the PA calling out my name, and the smell of varnish and old wood in the gym.

I always thought when I died and went to heaven, this is what it would be like.

Always bring your A game, Papa C had told me. I was about to show these lying-assed, backstabbing cowards my A++ game.

Four minutes later, I took a second to glance at the board. The score was 5–3, us. Papa C had just broke loose for a layup after me and Pesto had both put in two baskets apiece. Tangle-eye was so slow, we used her to pick Papa C every time.

He was getting mad about it. Tangle-eye was getting mad about it.

I was loving it.

Neither Papa C nor Tangle-eye was sweating, while me and Pesto looked like we'd driven a convertible through the car wash with the top down. Now, Papa C brought the ball along the arc, walking slow, catching his breath and letting the crowd get into it.

All around us, the djinn cheered, and then a deep-throttled chant started, "Tang! Tang! Tang!"

"Tang! Tang! Tang!" I chanted back, right in her ear 'cause I was sticking to her hip like cellulite on a thigh. "You're still Kool-Aid to me, cheater."

She didn't give any warning. Her hand came out of nowhere and smacked me in the mouth, her gold ring busting my lip.

"Foul!" The judge blew her whistle, and we got the ball back.

"No blood, no foul," Tangle-eye said.

The judge pointed at me. "What do you call that?"

I pulled my hand away from my mouth. There was a puddle of blood in my palm.

"Cover that." The judge threw a towel over my hand and pulled me off to the side. "They can smell blood."

"Tho whad?" I said. My lip was swelling up like a puffy-ass

balloon. The crowd of djinn got quiet, and when I scanned the stands, they were all staring at the red smear on my chin. I swear some of them were drooling.

"You've got a gym full of soul-sucking djinn, and you're saying, So what? You have more guts than brains, young lady." She finished cleaning me up. "Get back in the game."

In less than a minute, me and Pesto both scored again.

"7–3!" the judge hollered.

But the foul and the crowd had gotten Tangle-eye fired up. She started throwing her weight around. She bumped me out of the way and stole the ball when it slipped from my sweaty hands. She threw up another sad-ass brick, but Papa C was expecting it. The rebound came right to him, and he went back up and put it into the net.

"7–4."

"Quit shooting," Papa C barked at Tangle-eye.

"Shut your freaking mouth, old man, unless you want some of what I gave your Coyote girl."

Papa C's eyes narrowed. If he'd been one of the demons, lava would've come out of his pupils. "Check the ball," he told Pesto.

I ran my tongue over my lip. That shot to the face had taken more out of me than I thought. My head felt spinny, and when

I tried to cut Tangle-eye from the lane, I tripped over my own feet. I bent over, hands on my knees, gasping for wind. Trying to breathe in this heat was like sucking air through a wet washcloth.

Easy layup. Even Tangle-eye could hit that.

"7–5."

"You okay?" Pesto whispered to me as he pulled me back up on my feet.

"Switch out," I said. "Let me take Papa C next time, and you lean on Tangle-eye. Throw your weight around."

That didn't work. We let her take the pass, and she got under Pesto, slammed him with a shoulder, and knocked him flat on his ass. It was like a dance—ball, slam, bam. He hit the court so hard, his butt looked like a paint scraper.

Three more layups. Three more points.

"8–7."

"She's totally not getting through me again," Pesto said when I helped him up. He gasped for breath, which told me he was almost totally gassed. We had to finish this thing now.

Sweat dribbled between my dreads and down behind my ears. The neckline and armpits of my jersey were soaked with perspiration. "Stay low like a crab. Backpedal."

"Low. Crab. Got it."

Bless his heart, he tried to be a crab. Except he looked more like a duck. He stuck his butt out at one end, his hands out at the other, and Tangle-eye popped him right in the chin with an elbow. He fell like a bozo punch balloon with no air, and Tangle-eye scored again.

"9–7."

The crowd went mad crazy. They smelled a different kind of blood this time.

Tangle-eye got up in my grill. She shoved her ring, which was speckled with my blood, in my face. "How you like them apples, Coyote?"

I pushed her away. "You better get up off me."

Papa C grabbed Tangle-eye by the shirttail, dragging her back. "Enough of that."

"Step off!" she howled back at him.

He kept pulling her down the court until she was under the rim. That's when I noticed Pesto wasn't getting up. He was still in the same place Tangle-eye had dropped him. He hadn't moved an inch.

I dropped to the floor beside him. "Pesto." I smacked his cheeks. It was like hitting rubber. "Wake up, dog. Wake up, wake up, wake up. You better not desert me, too, boy. I'll kick your ass, you know I will." My eyes filled with tears, and my nose started running.

The judge whistled for time out. Mrs. V, E. Figg, and the

NADs rushed out to check on him. They crowded around him in the lane while Scratch strolled across the court, Beals at his heels.

I expected Mrs. V to be all freaked out. Instead, she checked Pesto's pulse, felt his jawbone, and inspected his teeth for breakage. When she was satisfied, she backed off and let the NADs help out.

I chewed on my thumbnail, nervous. "What if he can't play?" I said.

"If so," Scratch said, and smiled through his moustache, "then your team forfeits, Miss Smoot."

Beals hissed. "There will be no forfeit, you over-luminescent glory hound."

E. Figg stepped in. "Let's see what happens to Pesto before we worry about the consequences."

"Consequences never were your forte, E.," Beals said.

"Beals," E. Figg said, "if I wanted you to talk, I would have shaken a rattle."

"Still upset about the whole garden incident, eh?"

E. Figg blew him off. "See, Bug? Pesto is going to be fine."

Castor and Pollux lifted Pesto off the floor, holding him by the arms. His head was lolling from one side to the other. "I didn't eat the rice pudding. Honest."

"Hey, baby," I said, taking his face in my hands. "You going to be all right? Say something."

"Thanks for the pj's, Abuela. Pikachu's my favorite."

"Ain't that sweet." Tangle-eye mocked me. "Bug's gone freaky over—"

"Shut up."

E. Figg slid in between us and said into my ear, "Bug, listen. You're playing into their hands. You're still in the game. Don't blow it."

Across the floor, I saw Beals smiling and Old Scratch curling his moustache. He fanned his fingers at me, waving, and I noticed he'd changed outfits into a suit with a Panama hat, tinted glasses, and a black bow tie. All he needed was a mint julep and he'd look like something straight off the plantation.

"Double mocha latte with carob sprinkles," Pesto said, as the NADs carried him off. E. Figg followed them to courtside, where I saw her waving toward the bench.

The judge blew her whistle. "Here's the situation. Bug, you are one player down. Do you want to play this out or admit defeat now?"

"Ain't happening," I said. "I ain't admitting nothing."

"Just like old times, ain't it?" Tangle-eye clucked her tongue.

Beside her, Papa C had a funny look on his face. Not funny ha-ha, funny strange. Like he was embarrassed to be associated with her. Too bad. You made your bed, you lie in it.

The whistle blew again. "Black team's ball."

A yip cut across the gym. I spun around to see a young woman jogging toward us.

"Substitution," she hollered. She was dressed in a white sports bra and baggy shorts. Dang, she was cut. And short, about my weight and height, which meant we'd be giving up a bunch of inches to the other team.

"I'm in for Pesto," she said, her hair falling into her face. How could anybody play ball like that?

"Now listen here," Papa C gasped, and said, "Ain't nobody said nothing about no substitutions. Especially her."

"Mind your own business," the woman said. She stepped up, like she was waiting on him to start talking smack. "And do it better than you minded Bug's."

That shut him up. Scratch and Beals jumped from their seats, then fast-walked onto the floor, elbowing each other for position.

"Judge Hathorne, I protest this substitution," Scratch said.

Beals cut him off. "There is no proviso against substitutions, Your Honor. Ergo—"

"Do not start sentences with *ergo*," the judge said, "when you're talking to me." But I could tell she was thinking about it, stroking her chin and giving this new woman a long, hard look. Please, let her allow it. Please, please. No way could I win the game by myself.

Finally, she blew the whistle. "Substitution permitted!"

I gave my new teammate some dap. I owed her big-time for bailing my ass out. "Thanks for having my back. Didn't you play AAU ball a couple of years ago?"

With a wave, she blew off my question. "I'll take the big girl. You got the old man. Keep him on his feet. He's only dangerous when he jumps."

"How you know all this?" I said, trying not to be pissed that she'd disrespected me.

"I've been watching the game," she said. "Now *cierra la boca* and focus."

This girl didn't play. I liked that. The judge blew the whistle, and I checked the ball to Papa C. He tried to dribble down, and I was on him like white on rice. He tried this fancy crossover, and I was all over it. No way, no how was he driving the lane on me.

In the paint, Tangle-eye was trying to box out my teammate, who had thighs like braided steel cable. Tangle-eye got mad and threw an elbow. The new girl ducked it and laid Tangle-eye's ass out on the floor. Papa C lost focus for a second, and I swatted the ball loose.

Quick pass inside to my girl. Bank shot off the glass. Easy peasy.

"9–8!"

Papa C was supposed to check the ball to me. He held on to it, letting Tangle-eye get to her feet.

"Stalling ain't going to help your ass," I yelled at him.

"I'm proud of you, Jitterbug."

He was just trying to get into my head. I told him so.

"A man like me, he don't deserve a granddaughter like you," he said. "Don't you know, they ain't no way to get around Old Scratch? Once he got his hooks into me, it was all over but the shouting. It was my fate."

"Didn't nobody make you want that Cadillac. It wasn't your fate until you let it be. Now give up the damn ball, and let's play."

Looking like I'd stole his Twinkies, he flipped the ball to me, and I stutter-stepped past him. With my teammate taking Tangle-eye outside with a hip check, I had a straight shot at the net. I pulled up for a baby jumper and watched the ball float out of my hand, knowing I had barely missed the shot.

Damn. It was still in the cylinder when a dark blur flashed in front of me, and one of Papa C's long-ass hands pinned the ball against the glass. He yanked it down and then stood slinging elbows like Bill Russell was guarding him.

"Goaltending!" The judge gave us the point. "9–9!"

Now the crowd really went loco. So did Tangle-eye, who got up into Papa C's face—more like his chest—and started giving him hell about messing up. "She missed the shot, you stupid bastard! You blind or what? You trying to throw this game, ain't you? Huh? Huh?"

Papa C turned his back on her, walking back up to the top of the key. But Tangle-eye wasn't about to back down.

"Ain't nobody cheating me out of my soul, old man. I'd do anything, anything to get it back. Watch yourself. If I go down, you go down."

The new girl gave me a long look. Be careful, she mouthed.

Let Tangle-eye be careful, I thought. One more point, and I was free as a bird. I threw the ball to my teammate, and she stepped back for a jumper.

Go in, go in, I thought as she let the shot go. As soon as it left her hand, I could tell it was going to miss. I let Papa C slide past me to clog the lane, and I helped him get closer by pushing off against his back. I skied like I ain't never skied before and grabbed the ball as it bounced off the rim.

As I dropped down, Tangle-eye came out of nowhere and undercut me at the knees. I flipped over, and in the second before my head cracked the floor, I had two thoughts—

*Hang on to the ball.*

And:

*This is going to hurt.*

It hurt. And I didn't hang on to the ball.

All the air shot out of my lungs, and Tangle-eye snapped up the loose ball. She dribbled outside while the new girl hollered at the judge to make a call.

"No blood, no foul!" the judge said.

Tangle-eye started laughing. Her voice sounded all high-pitched, and there was a crackling light in her eyes. "Don't be worrying about calling that travel agent, Bug. You already got reservations for where you're going."

I caught my breath and got to my feet with a hand from my teammate.

I own this house, I thought. Come get some, hootchie mama.

Tangle-eye did a crossover, between-the-legs, behind-the-back dribble. My teammate stepped up to take her on, but Tang popped the ball between her legs, picked it up on the backside, and drove on me. I thought about trying to take the charge, then decided that it wasn't going to work and went for the hard foul.

It was like I was moving in sludge and Tangle-eye was a gerbil on a greased treadmill. She shot by me, took off, and air-walked her way to a two-handed jam.

The backboard exploded. The crowd exploded.

Air exploded out of the judge's whistle. "Foul! Illegal use of supernatural powers."

The crowd started booing, and Tangle-eye tried to chest bump Judge Hathorne. "Foul? That ain't no foul! You must be blind, you old cow!"

But the judge wasn't having any of it. "You want a technical? No? Then suck it up, princess. Free throw, white."

We lined up on the other end of the court, since there was glass all over the floor from the busted backboard.

The new girl slapped my butt. "You can do it."

Papa C winked at me. In the stands behind the scorer's table, Scratch leaned on the handle of his cane, watching. He lifted his hand and tapped his palm.

When college ballplayers talk about making pressure shots, they're thinking of being in somebody else's house. Standing on the line in front of a crowd of students screaming and jumping around, waving placards and colored balloons, trying to distract you.

Needing to make a free throw to save your soul, knowing you're going to send your granddaddy to eternal damnation even if you do hit it, that's pressure.

The heat pressed down like a huge iron on my chest. Me, I had about all the pressure I could take. Forget that. Forget it all. The bets. The head games. The contracts. The whole damned thing. I looked around my old gym. The walls, the hardwood, the banners hanging from the rafters. Then I stared at Beals and Scratch sitting next to each other in the bleachers, elbowing each other for shoulder room, acting like a game for world domination wasn't nothing but a pickup game.

Not this girl.

I set the ball on the free-throw line and started walking off. Bug Smoot wasn't going to play their games no more.

Boos rained down on the floor, and the djinn jumped up screaming and scratching the air. So what? Let them scream.

But then Papa C ran up behind me, catching me by the arm. "Jitterbug, you done lost your mind? You ain't going to walk out on this now. You're going to mess everything up."

I shook a finger in his face, an inch from his long nose. "Everything's been messed up, and you're the one's done it."

"When I made that deal with Beals to cheat Scratch, I didn't know nothing about what would happen to you."

"It was in the contract, Papa C. Don't tell me you didn't read that part."

"I didn't read none of the parts. I just signed where the man told me to." He looked down, ashamed. "All my life, I let folks take advantage of me. I ain't saying I didn't help them do it. But this thing is about more than me and you now. There's somebody else involved. Your mama."

"Liar."

"Jitterbug, are you blind?" He jabbed the air with a long,

bony finger. "Your mama is standing right there on the court. Your teammate."

"Mita?" How could this woman be my mother and me not see it? She didn't look nothing like what I remembered. Her hair, which still hung down in her face, was black. I remembered gold streaks. Her skin was light, but not as pale as I recalled. I touched my own arms as I was looking at hers.

I started toward her.

"Y'all got time for that later, Jitterbug," Papa C said, grabbing my arm again. "You make this one last shot, and it's all over. Don't be wasting my goaltending now."

I raised my eyebrows. "You did that on purpose?"

"Naw, that'd be dishonest, and if you cheat in this game, you lose." He winked and put the ball in my hand.

# CHAPTER 32

# The Shot Felt Round the Underworld

Tangle-eye and Mita toed the line on the foul lane, with Papa C standing closest to me. I stole glances at Mita as she jockeyed for position. She was a few feet away, but it didn't feel real. How could it be? I saw her burn to death, and there she stood, as young and healthy as me.

Maybe she could feel me looking at her. Maybe she just noticed I wasn't taking the shot. Whatever the reason, Mita tapped her temple, mouthing, Focus!

Yes, ma'am.

I bounced the ball twice. The sound of the bouncing ball echoed like a penny dropping into a wishing well, and I fixed my aim on the back of the rim the way I'd been coached to. Hundreds of times, I'd been in this same situation.

Me.

The ball.

The rim.

All you got to do is sink this, girl, and you go free.

I closed my eyes and visualized the shot going in. The swish of the ball through the net like string music. Me jumping into the air. My boy Pesto streaking out on the court, swinging me up in a hug. My crew high-fiving me. Beals having to take the scratch off my hand, leaving me to live a normal life.

I licked my lips in anticipation.

But what if I did hit the shot? Though I'd be free, Beals got control of Earth. My heart skipped a beat.

I kissed the ball, cocked my wrist, and lost my mind.

The gym was gone, fading like it was made out of mist, and I was on the sidewalk in front of Mrs. V's market. The street was empty. There was no sound of traffic, no folks standing on the corners sharing cigarettes and talking. No cars speeding down the street. No TVs blaring, no *niños* running through the flea market calling for their mamas for ice cream money. There wasn't nothing except me and the wind whipping sand around. It felt like my own body was an empty belly.

The center of the street began to bubble. The pavement melted away, and up through it came a pole made of glass. The pole got longer and wider, and after it came other poles, all of them thicker and wider until they formed a building. As I shielded my eyes from the sand, the whole block dissolved. The building grew taller and more massive, a palace of glass that jutted in all directions, like it'd been formed of salt crystals.

"This could have been your citadel to rule, Miss Smoot." Beals stepped through the swirling sand. "If you miss this shot, you will live there as a slave."

He grabbed my face with both hands and pushed his mouth hard against my lips. My mind filled with horrible visions: Napalm melting the flesh off soldiers. A cloud of chemical gas falling on a schoolyard of children, all of them falling, choking, clawing at their faces for breath. Thousands of naked people impaled alive on stakes, an army of djinn whipping and torturing them as they begged for death.

Then he let go of me and returned to the mist. I jerked like I'd been shocked awake.

The goal was in front of me again. A few seconds ago, I would've scored. But I couldn't now. If keeping my soul meant others suffered, then I didn't want it. Beals could banish me to hell, but I could screw up his plans first.

With the flick of my middle finger, I sent the ball to the edge of the rim, where it bounced against the boards, and then dropped to the floor. Mita took a step into the paint, and I lunged and caught her wrist. She tried to twist loose, yelling at me to grab the rebound. My grip was too tight, so she couldn't stop the ball from bouncing into Tangle-eye's lap, which is what I had in mind.

For a second, maybe two, Tangle-eye looked at the ball like it had fallen from heaven. She tilted her head at me, totally confused, and then dribbled to the top of the key. She gathered up all of her two hundred–plus pounds of muscle and fat and, maybe, happiness, and steamed down the lane and jammed that freaking rock home.

Papa C walked real slow toward the press box. He passed Tangle-eye, who was bouncing and dancing all by herself. She tried to do a chest bump with Papa C, but he wasn't having none of it.

"Ah, Charles, welcome back," Scratch called, and beckoned with a crook of his little finger. Papa C sleepwalked up the steps to him. "I will escort you to the afterlife personally. If you would be so kind as to wait one moment?"

Papa C gave me a sad little wave as he slumped up the risers. It about broke my heart knowing that he could've been the one who scored instead. The ball just didn't bounce his way. It surprised me that he'd given up so easy. It wasn't like him. I guess he was all out of deals to cut.

"Yo, Coyote." Tangle-eye grabbed my arm. "Beat your ass again, didn't I?"

I spun around. Brought up my fists. If she wanted to scrap, I was going to oblige her. "Go to hell," I said, my eyes starting to sting.

"That's the thing," she said, looking more awkward than arrogant. "I ain't got to. I made the winning goal, so I'm free." She held up her left hand. There was only a scar as thin as a spiderweb. "Back in the day, you would've made that shot. Guess your game's rusty, huh?"

"Yeah. Whatever." I turned away to look for Pesto. The djinn, who were standing up and waiting for orders from Beals, were blocking my view.

"No, wait. Wait." She stepped up in my face again. She pulled the ring off her finger. "This thing's been on my hand since I won it. We both know I got it by cheating. I tried to tell you that back at Pets' Palace, but you're one hardheaded coyote—I mean, sister, you know that?"

"Me? Never."

She popped me in the side of the head.

"Ow! Damn, Tangle-eye. That hurt."

"Don't be a smart mouth, then. Listen here." She slapped the ring in my hand just before she started jogging backward. "This belongs to you. Your nappy-headed ass earned it."

My fingers closed around the warm metal before I could holler for her to come back. There wasn't no point in it, anyway.

The girl was running so fast, she was down the court and out the door before anybody else noticed.

"Thanks, Tanya," I said, and let the ring drop with a dull clank onto the polished floor. It didn't belong to me, either. I hadn't earned it.

Across the gym, Beals and Scratch were walking up the bleachers to the press box. Instinct told me to follow Tanya out the door. Reality told me I wouldn't get far: Beals's mark was on my hand. He still owned me.

That left me and Mita alone in the paint. I kind of stood there, figuring out what to do or say. All I could think of was, "Mita?"

She pulled her hair back. A smile lit up her face, and in less time than a hummingbird's heartbeat, she grabbed me in a bear hug and swung me around like a rag doll. Dang, she was strong. And I was a little girl in a red velvet dress with white lace and patent leather shoes dancing the Cumbia. The gym spun around so fast, and I was in her arms again, full grown, having to face the consequences of my actions.

Which, I guess, we were.

"Mita, I had to miss the shot."

"Yes," she said, backing off. "I knew you would. It is who you are."

Not only was she backing off, she was fading, like an eraser

was rubbing her out of time and place. "Wait, where you—
Mita? Don't leave me now!"

"I'm only going, not going away." She blew me a kiss and
then started jogging toward the exit Tangle-eye had used. A few
yards from the double doors, she squatted down, then dropped
to all fours. And she was gone.

The doors swung closed. I thought seriously about following her until I felt something sting my palm.

"Damn, not again."

I was afraid to look. The scratch had opened up again.
Tendrils of black ink spread down my lifeline and up into my fingers. I flexed my hand. It was getting puffy, the skin stretching
tight. Whatever Scratch had done to heal me, it was wearing off.

Well, girl, you made your bed. Now, you've got to lie in it.

I strode across the hardwood toward the scorer's table,
where everybody had gathered around, as the djinn on a signal
from their boss marched single file out of the gym.

Beals and Old Scratch stood nose to nose jawing at each
other.

"She purposely lost the match!" Beals squealed.

"That's what you said about Waterloo," Scratch answered
back. He strolled up the bleacher steps in the direction of the
press box, with Beals hot on his heels. "Why not admit defeat?
The sooner you begin serving your sentence—"

"Defeat? Ha! Did you forget the roux line? You cannot banish me to the fiery pit. You have won this battle, but not the war!"

Scratch stifled a yawn. "That was a cliché before the Inquisition."

A few feet away, E. Figg folded her arms and leaned against the table, watching the demons and looking pleased. The NADs were fanning Pesto, who was laying down on the first row of bleachers, counting the number of fingers Mrs. V held up.

"Eleven," he said.

"No, *mi'jo*," Mrs. V said. "There can be only ten. How many now?"

"Fourteen."

"Hey, baby," I said, sitting down beside him. I cradled his head in my lap.

"How sweet," Pollux said sarcastically.

"I'll show you sweet, fool." I snatched the cap off his head and smacked him with it.

"Let's give them a moment," Mrs. V said, standing up.

"What about my toque?" Pollux protested.

I shook it at him. "What the hell is a toque? This is a stocking cap, and it's mine now."

Pollux tried to argue, but Mrs. V gave everybody the head nod, and the whole crew followed her over to the corner of the court. They whispered among themselves, stealing worried glances at me, while I brushed the hair out of Pesto's face.

He blinked at me. Then squinted. The light hurt his eyes, I could tell.

"You sure got game, dog." I kissed his forehead. "I'm proud of you."

"My head hurts," he said, then groaned quietly.

"I know, baby." I took his hand in mine and pressed it against my cheek. His skin was rough and cool on my skin. I kissed Pesto lightly on the lips, and he smelled so good. "I love you, remember that," I said, then carefully set his head down. He closed his eyes and was still.

Up in the press box, Beals stood next to Scratch, arms folded, defiant. He reminded me of a preschooler refusing to go to time-out. As for Scratch, the look on the devil's face was a mix of disappointment and amusement, like he'd had a great time but was sad to see it end.

"Yo, Beals!" I waved up at them. "I got a proposition for your ass."

"Silence, you impudent hag!" he screamed back at me.

Scratch smirked, and all of my crew jerked their heads around. They looked like they were about to charge in for the rescue. But I waved them off.

"I got this." I held up my scratched hand. "And I still got

this. Everybody knows I want to get rid of it. Just like everybody knows, you demons can't turn down a wager. So, Mr. Beals, I got a proposition for you."

Beals bounded halfway down the steps. He started rolling up his sleeves. "Enough of this, I let you linger too long in this world. It is time to send you to the fiery pit."

"Now, Beelzebub." Scratch laughed and stroked his chin. He leaned on the cane, and a light of mischief danced in his eyes. "What's the fun in that? At least listen to the *la belle*'s proposition. I'm sure it will be . . . entertaining."

Beals leapt past the last few steps. He landed inches from me with the grace of a ballet dancer. The look on his face was wild fire, and I could feel hatred radiating from his body. He snatched my hand and held it high, almost yanking my shoulder out of the socket. My flesh began to scald from his touch, but I sucked air between my teeth and pretended it didn't hurt.

"Behold my mark!" he called up to Scratch. "This! This is my definition of entertaining."

My head spun, and my knees turned wobbly. Hold on, girl. Hold on. I squeezed my eyes shut and made a fist with my hand. With my whole body.

"I propose a trade," I rasped. "Free me, and I'll give myself to you."

"Give yourself?" Beals spat out the words. "The time is past for that." His face twisted in absolute disgust. "Wretched creature, I would never lower myself to participate in such an abomination. Especially with a piece of half-bred, bastard vermin."

*Whap!* I smacked him across the face with Pollux's toque. "Asshole!"

"How dare you!" Beals bellowed. He crouched and covered the cheek like I'd smacked him with a baseball bat.

*"Touché!"* Scratch called. "Excellent *coup d'arrêt, ma chère*!"

Beals looked bewildered for a few seconds, then he shook it off. He snapped at Scratch, "I'll thank you to stay out of my affairs. As for you, Miss Smoot"—he twisted my arm behind my back—"walk this way."

He shoved me onto the court. I tried to fight back, but my wrist was jammed between my shoulder blades.

"Help!" I screamed. "E. Figg! Castor! Pollux! Help me!"

But they didn't move. They kept chatting like nothing was happening.

"Alas," Beals snarled, "they cannot hear you. Your voice is the sound of an insect buzzing in their ears, an annoyance, an irritant."

In the center circle, he shoved me hard to my knees. The pain in my hand! I could hardly breathe.

He threw his arms back, arching his head so that it faced the ceiling. His arms, his legs, his chest swelled out, popping his clothes at the seams, ripping the fabric into shreds.

"The Earth! Domination of mankind! It was in my grasp," he hissed, "and you, you gave it all away."

"It was n-never in your grasp." I said. Struggling for breath, I pulled the scratched hand, covered in thick blisters up to the elbow, against my stomach and wrapped Pollux's cap around it. "Scratch puh-played you like he plays everybody."

"You give me too much credit," Scratch's voice boomed from the press box. He came out to the bleachers, surveying the scene. "Tsk. This won't do. I need a better view."

My eyes followed Scratch as he kicked off his shoes and socks. He turned to the wall and ran straight up a steel beam to the ceiling. He didn't stop until he was perched right above us, his long toes clasping the lip of the beam as he hung upside down.

"Stay out of this!" Beals warned him. "She's mine. You renounced all claim!"

"I simply wanted a better sight line of the *phrases d'armes*," Scratch called, his hair and panama jacket dangling in the air. "*Ma chère*, pay close attention. This metamorphosis act of his is simply to die for."

A smell like vomit and cat pee filled the air, and Beals's clothes lay in rags on the floor. His legs grew spindly and wiry, and black hairs sprouted from his skin. His chest ballooned out, and a pair of bulbous, nasty eyes popped out through his beach ball–sized skull.

"Behold! Beelzebub, Lord of the Flies!" Beals's voice got higher and louder until it turned into a buzz. Wings sprouted from his back. Two legs erupted from his sides as he transformed into a massive fly covered in thick ooze the color of snot, and two ridged, scissored mandibles protruded from his mouth.

*Snick!* The mandibles snapped around my injured hand. A foot-long, hair-covered shaft shot out of Beals's mucus-coated mouth. It sank deep into the swollen, blistered flesh of my palm.

I swung at his underbelly with my free hand and screamed, "Let g-go of me!"

Then.

Beals pulled the shaft out of my palm. Buzzing louder than a swarm of bees, he convulsed like I'd sprayed him with poison. What the hell?

"*Touché* again, *ma chère!*" Scratch called down from the rafters.

The toque! As Beals scrambled for a foothold on the slick gym floor, I turned Pollux's cap inside out. On the brim was the ISIS emblem, the pentalpha. Which was, duh! the Seal of Solomon.

"Oh my," Scratch called. "She's puzzled it out, Beals. Perhaps it is time for a strategic retreat."

Clutching my hand to my side, I got to my feet. I swatted at Beals again, and he buzzed so loud, the lights dimmed. I staggered back and covered my ears against the noise.

"Shut up!" I screamed.

Then the glass in the windows shattered. Shards of glass fell into the top bleachers, and a desert wind swept through the building. The humidity dropped, the heat went away, and the dry, cool air made it easier to catch my breath.

As I got my strength back, Beals took the chance to spread his wings.

Literally.

Pushing with all six legs, he launched himself backward into the air. His membranous hind wings beat furiously, and I watched as he ripped from one side of the building to the other, zigzagging wildly through the rafters.

*"Très magnifique!"* Scratch called out.

*Bzzt!* Beals dive-bombed me. He slammed into my back, knocking me across the gym. I hit the hardwood hip first, caught my balance, and was up on my feet as he banked around for another pass.

Oh, hell no. I'd had enough of this mess.

"S-stop!" I yelled through the pain.

To my surprise, Beals's wings froze in mid-beat. He plummeted twenty feet to the ground and hit with a hollow thump. His fly body bounced twice like a flattened basketball before it came to rest. He lay on his side, buzzing like a rusted chainsaw.

"Damn," I said as I limped over to him. "That's some stocking cap." I held the pentalpha up to his compound eyes. "This whole buzzing thing ain't doing it for me. Shut it up."

The noise died, and the gym fell silent.

But I still had a problem. "Next, get rid of this mark."

"Pardon me for intruding," Scratch hollered. "The Seal of Solomon allows you to control Beals's movements, but tragically, the Old Law that allowed Beals to claim you also prevents you from forcing him to set you free."

"Damn." Think, girl. You can work this out. What did Castor say you needed to banish a demon? An object bearing the Seal of Solomon? Check. The Incantation of Solomon? Check. Love? I sure hoped so.

All right then, I thought, let's do this. "By the name of the one God whose true name is Yahweh and the Greeks call Emmanuel, I strip you of your wealth. By the number 644 which the Hebrew call *kaf mem dalet*, I strip you of your power. And by the name of the Spirit, who the Romans call Eleéth, I banish you to the pit."

Beals's fly body shook violently, but it didn't disappear.

"Oops, not quite the *coup de grâce* you were hoping for," Scratch interrupted as I scoured my memory for some detail of how to beat Beals. "Are you truly such an ignorant hussy after all?"

"Don't distract me," I said. "This is hard enough." Wait! Payne really had given us the way to defeat Beals. *You got to switch it around, you ignorant hussy.*

I looked up at Scratch still dangling from the rafters, munching on popcorn. "What's Greek for the number 664?"

Scratch shook his head. "Honor among thieves and all that, *ma belle dame sans merci.* It breaks my heart that I cannot tell you *chi mu delta* is the correct phrase."

"You could've said something before!"

"And miss this exquisite sparring match? Really, Miss Smoot. How could I deprive myself of such pleasure?"

I started to say something smart, but then thought better of it. Instead, I bent over Beals, whose fly body was pulsing with rage, and gave him a little kick.

"I got your ass now, demon. By the name of the one God whose true name is Yahweh and the Hebrew call Emmanuel, I strip you of your wealth. By the number 644 which the Greeks call *chi mu delta*, I strip you of your power. And by the name of the Spirit, who the Romans call Eleéth, I banish you to the pit.

"Go to hell, Beelzebub."

349

# CHAPTER 33

# Soul Survivor

Banishing a demon to the fiery pit for a thousand years is a lot like winning a basketball game on a last second shot. For a couple days, you're on a high, but then reality sets in. The rent has to be paid, clothes have to be washed, and the table's got to be set. Everybody says it, but no matter what happens, life really does go on.

I celebrated Thanksgiving and Christmas with Pesto, Mrs. V, and the rest of the *barrio*. E. Figg joined us to celebrate New Year's, and she helped give me a new start by hiring me at the law office as a clerk. The money was real good, and sitting behind an oak desk sure beat delivering pizzas. There was one catch—I had to go back to school.

So I enrolled in GED classes at the community college, which has a basketball program in the National Junior College Athletic Association. Next season, after I'm officially a college student, I'm trying out for the team.

Nobody's seen Mita since the ball game. For a few weeks, I watched out my window for stray coyotes and listened every night for that familiar howl. I even left scraps by the garbage cans, hoping the food would draw her in. But no coyotes ever came by, and I pretty much gave up the thought of ever seeing her again.

Me and Pesto? Still going strong. His bosses down at ISIS raised his pay grade after he captured Mr. Payne, and they put him in charge of three different flushing stations.

With the money I made at the law office, I could afford the apartment over the store. Mrs. V said she'd never seen anybody so happy to pay rent. Why wouldn't I be happy? The place was clean and well-lit, I was a flight of stairs away from a fully stocked grocery store, and my boy Pesto lived in the same building.

The only thing my life lacked was reliable transportation. For months, I'd been bumming rides or catching the bus, which was not the mark of a grown woman. So I saved every dime until I had enough to buy my own car.

Then I made Pesto take me shopping on the Boulevard. All morning, we drove from lot to lot, looking for the perfect ride.

It had to be in decent mechanical condition, which meant it had to at least start. The interior had to be in good shape, which meant it couldn't be covered in dog hair or stink like a back alley. And the price had to be right, which meant no more than I had in my bank account. No loans for this girl. It was straight cash from now on.

"What kind of cars are on your list?" Pesto asked after we parked the Gremlin next to a lot with a string of black triangle flags hanging overhead, flapping in the wind. "BMW, Lexus, Cadillac?"

All the cars had prices marked with white shoe polish on the windows. In the middle of the lot was a little metal building with a sign over it: CASH AND CARRY PRE-OWNED AUTOS.

"One Cadillac is enough to last me a lifetime," I said, laughing and taking Pesto's hand. "Let's find something with a lower profile, like a truck. But in my price range, and it has to run."

"Dude!" Pesto pointed at a red Ford truck. "It's perfect!"

"Hold up," I said. The car lot looked awful familiar. Black flags? Little metal building? "I can't be buying no car from here."

"Why not?" he said, with a funny look in his eye. "It's totally what you've been looking for."

"I know it's going to be perfect," I said, "which is exactly why I ain't buying, and why you're getting your ass off that property."

"Huh?"

"Just come on."

As I escorted my boy to the sidewalk, starting to explain which car lot this was, I saw a middle-aged brother step off the bus and head straight for a 1974 Corvette Stingray.

Out of the building came a beefy man wearing a silk shirt unbuttoned to the chest, which was covered in matted hair. I squeezed my eyes shut, not believing what I was seeing.

"Look who's pulled car salesman duty for old Scratch," I said, elbowing Pesto.

"Dude, no way!"

Yes, way. "Yo, Vinnie!" I yelled. The salesman caught my eye and flipped me a bird. "That's him, I'd recognize his stubby finger anywhere."

Vinnie swooped down on the man like he was fresh meat, extending his hand for a shake and patting him on the back.

Uh-uh. Not this time. "Yo, sir! Sir!" I hollered at the customer, whose eyes were full of Corvette lust. "Don't buy nothing from that fool! He's a crook. Don't fall for his easy-financing schemes, neither. You can't afford what he's selling!"

The customer looked back at me, and I swore I heard Vinnie hiss just like Beals used to do. "It ain't working, Vin. You got a long-ass way to go before you're as scary as the other demons."

"Shut your mouth, you frigging maniac!" Vinnie bellowed at me.

The man turned right around and went running after the city bus, which is when me and Pesto decided it was a good time to say *adios* to Vinnie and the Cash and Carry car lot.

But as we got back to the Gremlin, a coyote ran past us. She was small with white markings and ran with her tail down, stalking something. She trotted onto the lot and found the truck Pesto had admired.

The coyote sniffed the fenders of the truck, then raised her leg and sprayed a long stream of piss onto the front tire.

Across the lot, Vinnie screamed and charged like a raging pit bull. He chased the coyote to the edge of the property, where his feet flew up in the air, as if he'd reached the end of an invisible chain. He landed on his ass, then flopped to his side, groaning and holding his back.

The coyote cantered back to the lot. She sniffed Vinnie's leg and yipped. Then, she hiked her leg.

"Don't you even think about it!" Vinnie yelled as he struggled with the invisible chain.

She turned her head side to side like she was thinking just that. Then she snuffed, as if to say, Nah, he's not even worth it.

Then abruptly, with a quick, playful bark, she turned toward the highway. She pulled up to avoid a city bus in the right lane, ducked in front of a minivan, and then leapt over the hood of a MINI Cooper. She landed on the sand-filled median.

The drivers all laid on their horns, but she ignored them. She was running now, nose down, tail straight out behind, a blur of sand dust and brown fur roaring down the highway like a roadrunner. In the distance, the Franklin Mountains loomed, steel gray and black, with a cap of snow on the peaks.

"Wow," Pesto said as he leaned on the driver's door. "I've never seen a coyote run that fast."

"You probably ain't never going to see it again." But I hoped I would, someday.

"So back to business, right?" he said when she was out of sight. "Let's try some of the car lots across town."

As Pesto opened his door, I grabbed him by a belt loop. "Where you think you're going?"

He jangled the key ring. "I'm going to drive us to the next lot, dude."

"First, you're still too slow for me." I snatched the keys out of his hand. "Second, it's time for 'dude' to go because if you don't know I ain't a dude by now . . ." He started to argue, but I winked and gave him a shy smile as I slid into the front seat. "And third, you need to sit on the passenger's side, because Bug Smoot is taking the wheel."

He patted the hood of the Gremlin. "You think you can handle my *bonita*? She is very particular."

I turned on the ignition, then the radio. I switched the

station and lost myself for a moment in the deep bass thump of a song. "Dog, if I can handle a nephilim, a Gremlin ain't going to be no problem."

"Okay, du—I mean, Bug. If you say so." He got in on the other side and slammed the door. "But if I have to stop calling you 'dude,' you have to quit referring to me as 'dog.' Because if you haven't noticed by now . . ."

"A'ight." I started the engine. The Gremlin clattered to life. With the fan belt squealing like a javelina piglet and the pistons knocking like a pair of bony knees, I pulled out into traffic. "I'll call you something besides dog."

"*Gracias.*"

"How 'bout puppy?"

"No."

"Puppito?"

"No!"

"Puppicito?"

"Dude!"

"Dog!"

Up ahead on the highway, all of the traffic lights turned green. I hit the gas and swung into the fast lane, looking straight ahead at a wide-open highway, a road that could take me anywhere I wanted to go.

# Acknowledgments

A debut novel owes a lot of debts. To start with, to Joanne and Bob Smith for their support way back when. To the kids at Brainerd, who still inspire me. To James Maxey for the chocolate crucifix and to Codex for the community. My thanks to Marilyn Singer, who picked Bug out of a contest pile, and to Roxyanne Young and Kelly Milner Halls for being WINners.

Thanks, too, to my critique group—Julie M. Prince, Shannon Caster, Lauren Whitney, Lindsay Eland, Jan Lofton Lundquist, Linda Provence, and Jean Reidy—for reading early and often, checking spelling and weather, and sharing the taste of warm tamales.

To Debra Garfinkle for laughing in the right places. David Lubar for making me laugh in the right places. My cheerleader, Denise Ousley, for knowing no boundaries. My friends on LJ for cheering the highs and offering chocolate for the lows. Teri Lesesne, goddess of YA literature, for being a force of nature. And Clarke Whitehead, for the constant reminder that books save lives.

Many thanks to everyone at Greenwillow: Martha Mihalick, Sarah Cloots, Michelle Corpora, Barbara Trueson, Steve Geck, Tim Smith, Lois Adams, Paul Zakris, and the awesome Virginia Duncan, who knew I could do better. To my spectacular agent, Rosemary Stimola, for patience, wisdom, and calming e-mails.

Thanks to my teachers, Ted Hipple and Ken Smith, who left us before the book was done.

Finally, to Deb, Justin, Caroline, and Delaney, for not letting me get the big head.